Rockson [illegible] stol, sending f[illegible] He ducked do[illegible] took off from [illegible] of the boulder toward th[illegible]. It wasn't that far, but when fifteen crack shots are firing with everything they have at you, it seems like a million miles off. Bullets dug in everywhere around him, knifing into the dirt and rocks at his feet in little explosions of powder. He felt a sharp pain in his right calf, but was able to keep running.

"Get him!" Gunter screamed, rising from the ground and spraying his full magazine of 7.2mm slugs. "He is the leader. Kill him and you will be rich forever." The Wolfpack Squad rose as a man and let loose with a hurricane of firepower, the air whistling with trails of screaming white-hot bullets . . .

Also by Ryder Stacy and published by Futura

DOOMSDAY WARRIOR
DOOMSDAY WARRIOR 2: RED AMERICA
DOOMSDAY WARRIOR 3: THE LAST AMERICAN
DOOMSDAY WARRIOR 4: BLOODY AMERICA

RYDER STACY

Doomsday Warrior 5
America's Last Declaration

Futura

A Futura Book

First published in Great Britain in 1987 by
Futura Publications, a Division of
Macdonald & Co (Publishers) Ltd
London & Sydney

All characters in this publication are fictitious and any resemblance to real persons, living or dead, is purely coincidental.

ISBN 0 7088 3565 1

Printed and bound in Great Britain by
Cox & Wyman Ltd, Reading

Futura Publications
A Division of
Macdonald & Co (Publishers) Ltd
Greater London House
Hampstead Road
London NW1 7QX
A BPCC plc Company

Prologue

2089 A.D. Ted Rockson, alias "Rock," is the "Doomsday Warrior." He fights back against the Russian invaders who now control post-World War III America – a land decimated by nuclear missiles from Russia's first strike.

One hundred years after the Soviet surprise nuclear attack much of the United States is still radioactive and impassible. The world now has twenty percent less oxygen, strange and constantly shifting weather patterns, freezing nights and scorching days, purple clouds, and storms of black snow. In the USA are regions of land torn by chasms, landslides, and earthquakes. Mutated animals roam the plains and mountains. Killer dogs, weighing up to two hundred pounds, with dagger-sharp teeth, hunt in hungry packs. Blood-drinking rats, two to three feet long, move in masses of thousands across the terrain at night, devouring all that is in their path.

And there are the mysterious "Glowers," about whom the Russian occupying troops speak in frightened whispers – radioactive humans who live only in the hottest zones, who glow like a blue flame and whose touch kills instantly. These and even more terrible dangers await Rock as he makes his way across the new America.

Driving stolen Russian vehicles or riding his hybrid horse – smarter and stronger than horses of the past and more resistant to radiation – Rock, armed with his rapid-fire .12 gauge shotgun pistols and the "Liberator" automatic rifle with infrared scope, helps the "freefighters" of the free American towns and villages fight the Russian occupiers. Rock's only two goals – to throw the Soviet murderers out of the U.S., and to find and kill the squad of Russian KGB officers who murdered his family when he was a child. Hidden beneath a floorboard, he had memorized the faces of all ten of the elite Death Squad who had committed the blasphemies. One by one, he will hunt them down and kill them.

Ted Rockson's trail weaves swiftly across the land, the mountains, the hidden Free Cities, the vast hot zones, as he conquers all that gets in his way in the strange, terrifying world of America 2089 A.D.

* * *

TIME: It is one hundred years in the future. An all-out nuclear war has killed two-thirds of the world's population. The Russians, who were able to get off many more of their missiles in a first strike, were victorious over the United States. Now, in control of virtually the entire world, except for China, they ruthlessly rule the People's World Socialist Republic.

PLACE: Atomic bombs exploded all over the planet, but primarily in the United States. The U.S. lost one hundred million people within one hour of the attack. Another seventy-five million died within a year. The Russians immediately moved in with massive transports of troops and weapons and quickly took control of much of the country. They built forty fortresses in vital parts of the U.S., huge military complexes from which they sent out search and destroy units of tanks and helicopters, and radiation-suited troops to extinguish the still-burning embers of resistance.

The Russians use the American citizens as slave labor, forcing them to grow crops and work in factories. The Russian high command lives in luxury, the officers having taken the best housing in the remaining cities. The American workers must make do in shabby shanty towns around the fortress complexes. Thirty-five million Americans are directly under the Red rule. Sullen and docile, they carry out their Russian masters' orders, but underneath they hate them. They pray for the day when the legendary Ted Rockson, "The Ultimate American," will come with the freefighters of the hidden cities and release them from their bondage.

ENVIRONMENT: The great number of bombs set off altered the earth's axis. The polar caps began melting, and the forested regions turned to desert. The world is slowly warming, the higher amount of CO_2 in the air creating a greenhouse effect. Lakes, rivers, and streams have dried up in many places. The ecosystem has almost been dealt a deathblow from the war. Ninety percent of the earth's species of plants and animals are now extinct.

The East Coast of the United States is still extremely radioactive. Vast, bare plains stretch across hundreds of miles in New York, Connecticut, New Jersey, and Pennsylvania, upon which nothing grows. At the edges of these "hot" zones are forests of mutated bushes and trees covered with thorns and rock-hard bark. Parts of the Midwest were spared as the Russians had plans for eventually using the farmland to grow crops for their own clamoring masses back home. But the soil is now too radioactive to grow anything but weeds. American slave labor was taken out by the truckload to work, turning to the soil in the "medium hot" zones – meaning death within a year from handling the rocks and topsoil still hot enough to send a geiger counter needle off the edge.

The Far West has been hit hard. Colorado was spared, mostly because of some bad aiming, but, further on, in Utah, Nevada, California, there has been heavy damage. The area is now a misty, unknown land, inhabited by bizarre species of mutants and cannibals. Volcanoes and earthquakes have become common, and much of the Northwest has been turned into a nightmare of craters, some miles wide.

The South was hit in a haphazard fashion, as if

the Russians hadn't quite known what to strike. Some states, for instance, New Mexico and Georgia, were almost untouched, while others – Florida and Texas – were blasted to bits. Parts of Florida were gone. Where Orlando and Tampa once stood was now a great, jagged, hydrogen-bomb-created canal that stretched hundreds of miles across the interior, filled with a red, muddy water.

Slowly life tries to force its way back onto the surface of the ripped and savaged land. Many forests have expanded over the last century in areas that weren't hit. Great parts of the United States are now thick with brush and trees and resemble the country the way it looked in the 1800s. In other places the deserts cover the earth for four, five hundred miles in every direction – unrelenting, broiling, hot, snake-filled and cactus-dotted obstacles that stand between other living parts of the country.

THE HIDDEN FREE CITIES: Over seventy-five Free American hidden towns have sprung up over the last hundred years. Located at the edges of hot zones, which the Russian troops are reluctant to enter, these towns, hidden in caves, mountains, deep wooded valleys, are made up of armed resistance fighters. Each "Free City" consists of anywhere from one thousand to forty thousand people. They are fiercely democratic, using town meetings to discuss and vote on all issues.

The Free Americans, who have been bred out in the country, away from the Russian-dominated "clean" areas, have, through natural selection, become ten times more resistant to radiation than their ancestors. They are bred tough, with weak children placed out in the twenty-below-zero nights. If the child lives, it is allowed to develop. If not, then it is just as well to put it out of its misery now.

Ted Rockson fights out of Century City—one of the more advanced Free Cities and the manufacturer of the Liberator automatic rifle, used by freefighters everywhere. They harass Russian convoys, blow up bridges. . . . But they plan for the day when they can begin their all-out assault on the enslavers.

THE RUSSIANS: The United Socialist States of America is run by the red-faced, heavy-drinking General Zhabnov, headquartered in the White House, Washington, D.C., now called New Lenin. A bureaucrat, careful but not cunning, and a libertine, Zhabnov spends days eating and nights in bed with young American girls rounded up by his terror squads. Zhabnov has been appointed supreme president of the U.S. for a ten-year period, largely because he is the nephew of the Russian Premier Vassily. General Zhabnov rules America as his personal fiefdom. The only rules he must obey—1) no uprisings, and 2) seventy-five percent of the country's crops grown by the enslaved American workers must be sent to Russia. General Zhabnov no longers believes that the U.S. is stable. Now there are American resistance forces stronger than a few scattered groups that raid convoys from time to time. He no longer sees his stay here as a happy interlude away from the power struggles back in the Kremlin.

Colonel Killov is the head of the KGB in the U.S., headquartered in Denver, Colorado. He is a ruthlessly ambitious man whose goal it is to someday be premier of the world. Thin, almost gauntly skeletal looking, with a long face, sunken cheekbones and thin lips that spit words. Killov's operatives are everywhere in the country—in the fortresses and the Russian officer ranks, and, lately, he has even managed to infiltrate an American-born agent into the highest levels of the American resistance. Colonel Killov believes General Zhabnov to be a fool. Killov knows that the American forces are growing stronger daily and forming a nationwide alliance to fight together. The calm days of the last century are about to end.

From Moscow, Premier Vassily rules the world. Never has one man ruled so much territory. From the bottom of Africa to Siberia, from Paraguay to Canada, Russian armies are everywhere. A constant flow of supplies and medical goods is needed to keep the vast occupying armies alive. Russia herself did not do badly in the war. Only twenty-four American missiles reached the Soviet Union, and ten of these were pushed off course or exploded by ground-to-air missiles. The rest of the U.S. strike was knocked out of the skies by Russian killer satellites that shot down beams of pure energy and picked them off like clay pigeons.

Vassily is besieged on all sides by problems. His great empire is threatening to break up. Everywhere there are rebel attacks on Russian troops. In Europe, in Africa, in India, especially in America. The forces of the Resistance troops are growing larger and more sophisticated in their operations. Vassily is a highly intelligent and well-read man. He has devoured history books on other great leaders and the problems they faced. "Great men have problems that no one but another great man could understand," he lectures his underlings. Advisers tell him to send in more forces and quickly crush the insurgents. But Vassily believes that to be a tremendous waste of manpower. If it goes on like this he may use neutron bombs again. Not a big strike, but perhaps in a single night, yes, in one hour, they could target the fifty main trouble spots in the world and . . . order must be maintained. For Vassily knows his history. One thing that has been true since the dawn of time—wherever there has been a great empire, there has come a time when it began to crumble.

Chapter One

They fell from the sky like wounded birds, twisting, spinning out of control. Wingless, their arms and legs swung wildly in the cold air. The two men dangled from billowing black parachutes that ballooned out above them. They gripped the straps that led up from their shoulder harnesses for dear life as they watched the world below come shooting up at them like a bullet.

There were only seconds before impact and Ted Rockson and Archer, the giant near-mute member of the Rock team, dropped ever closer . . . to their doom. The MIG jet they had stolen and escaped from Moscow in (SEE BOOK #4) spun wildly past them, plummeting straight down. But it wasn't their quick descent that made their hearts beat faster and their eyes open wide—it was the immense iceberg-dotted lake that they were about to plunge into. Lake Superior, according to the maps in the MIG. It had seemed so welcoming, so comforting just minutes before as the two freefighters realized they were home—or nearly. But now as they prepared to splash into its frigid waters, having misjudged their drop angle and been blown by the North Wind, it changed every second into an enemy that was about to kill them.

All their attempts at altering the course of the falling chutes were in vain as the constant cold stream of air from the arctic wind slammed them down toward the dark blue water.

"Hold on, man, we're going in," Rock yelled to Archer who was about forty feet away and twenty feet above him. They hit the water hard, sending up great splashes of the frigid liquid around them. Parachutes slow descent, they don't stop it, and with the additional helping hand of the downdraft they were slammed into the lake like spears, going under nearly twenty feet into the murky depths. Rockson opened his eyes but could see nothing in the dark water, though the cold, near-freezing water burned his eyes as if it were alcohol. He knew he had only seconds before the parachute would fill and drag him down to the bone-littered bottom. Holding his breath tightly in his lungs he tried to unhitch the metal clasps around his chest. His mutant body had among other things given him the ability to hold his breath for nearly three minutes, so he knew he had time—if he didn't panic. Yards away in the near impenetrable gray water he could sense Archer struggling furiously to rip the harness off his body.

"Slow down—keep calm," Rock sent off in a telepathic burst to the giant of a man. His PSI abilities, developed by the Glowers, worked with them—but were not reliable on a human. He prayed that Archer would receive. The Doomsday Warrior at last got the chute clasp undone and eased out of the confining straps. He shot up toward the surface, lit with the flashing beacon of daylight, and broke the water, opening his mouth wide to take in the life-giving air. He waited a few seconds for Archer to appear, as he pulled the parachute into a tight bundle and wrapped his belt around the bottom of it, creating a six-foot balloon of air. Archer's chute still bobbed on the surface some twenty yards away, moving up and down furiously as if it had hooked some immense fish.

"Damn," Rock muttered, letting go of his make-shift life raft. He filled his lungs to their bursting point and dove back into the depths. He quickly found Archer, still tearing at the harness as if it were some jellyfish trying to swallow him. The bear of a freefighter was already sucking in water through his wide opened mouth. There was still time if . . .

The Doomsday Warrior swam straight down and over to the near-mute and motioned for him to relax and stop his frantic strugglings. But in his desperate panic Archer, who feared nothing on this earth except confinement, was panic-stricken to the point of hysteria. Rock knew there was only one thing to do. He made a spear hand with his fingers and drove the stiff tip into the edge of Archer's throat, just below the ear. The iron-hard punch hit into the thick flesh like a striking piranha, knocking the man out cold.

"Sorry about that, big fella," Rock thought as a pair of rainbow-colored fish nearly three-feet long with bands of red and purple streaming across their rippling scales swam by. "But I'm sure you'll forgive me later." He tread water just in front of the unconscious freefighter and quickly undid the parachute straps around the beer-barrel-sized chest. Rock grabbed hold of a big clump of the thick hair of the ex-mountain man and pulled with all his might, dragging Archer up from his watery imprisonment. Had Archer already sucked in too much water Rockson could never have done it. But there was obviously enough air left in the freefighter's lungs to make him buoyant.

The Doomsday Warrior broke the surface and sucked in the frigid air greedily. He yanked with all his strength and Archer's blue-tinged face came out of the water line. Rock swam the few yards to his parachute raft, which seemed to be holding the air he had sealed into it, and dragged the near-mute onto the edge of the floating black nylon. Seeing the big chest remain still, Rock, holding with one hand to the raft, swung down and over with his other arm, slamming into Archer's back like a baseball bat. The bear of a man sucked in a horribly raspy breath and then coughed violently, spitting up scummy water. He breathed in quickly about twenty times and then his heart and lungs seemed to get in gear as he opened his earth-brown eyes.

The last thing he remembered was Rockson punching him under the water. And as if the thought to strike back had been suspended between brain and hand, Archer's ham-sized fist rose to strike back. Rock blocked it with his free hand and yelled across to Archer as the parachute-raft bobbed more violently beneath them, stirred up by the changing tide of the nearly thirty-mile-wide lake. Waves four-feet high swept over them, heading toward the sandy shore some two miles off.

"You're up, man. Look around—you're safe," Rock yelled. Archer prepared to strike again, his animal responses too honed from years of living in the murderous wilds, the mountains and prairies of the West, to stop. But suddenly he looked around, his large, bearded face sweeping across the gray skies, the dark clouds like boulders dragging themselves across the silver sword of the horizon. His face went from primitive fury to a sweet joy in the space of a second. Rockson let out a laugh as he watched the transformation.

"Arrrrcher freeeee," the big man growled. Then he looked over at Rockson, realizing his hand was still suspended midway between them. He sheepishly let the fist open and dropped it to the parachute raft. "Roooccckkssonnn saaaaaaave," he moaned, looking down at the black nylon float with deep embarrassment in his eyes.

"Forget it, pal," the Doomsday Warrior said. "I probably would have done the same. You're too much of a warrior to ever stop fighting. Anyway, we ain't got time to make apologies," Rock said, pointing toward the shore. "We'll freeze to death if we're out here very long. And I don't know how long this parachute boat is going to hold up." As he spoke they could both see air bubbles slowly rising from the water at the far side of the chute from a small tear in the fabric.

The two freefighters pulled themselves halfway up onto the air-filled chute, and began kicking furiously, aiming the wobbly craft toward the near shore. It was a good two miles off but the combined force of their churning leg power, sending out a furrow of white foam behind them, and the tide which was headed in that direction made them move at a good clip. Still, they could feel their feet and thighs growing numb from the intense cold. Only the constant motion of their flesh and muscles, pumping blood through their systems, kept their bodies from freezing up solid like the small icebergs that floated around them.

The sky was growing increasingly dark with the far clouds growing ever closer. Storm clouds ready to release their storehouse of moisture as snow or ice. Rock had seen clouds like this before—filled with death, the Black Snow. Sometimes the coal-black flakes burned the skin, other times they just fell harmlessly, blackening the sky as if the sun had been extinguished but composed of normal water vapor. There was no way of telling until the flakes fell onto the flesh. And by then . . . They kicked their way nearly half the distance to the shore, tiring somewhat, the numbness creeping throughout their bodies. But the sheer willpower of the two freefighters kept them going, struggling to survive. Even when the body said enough, the mind said go on. Rockson could see by the increasingly blueish tinge of Archer's face that the big man wasn't going to last a hell of a lot longer. His own mutant body seemed able to withstand the rigors of the freezing temperatures more readily. But then his kind—the star-patterned mutants—had been bred by evolution to survive the new world, the world of 2089 A.D.

They were but half a mile from safety, the jagged shoreline peppered with bent-over black-barked pines within sight, giving both men a renewed burst of energy when Rockson noticed an object in the water some hundred yards ahead. It came straight toward them—against the tide. Suddenly a huge reptilian head broke the icy surface, lifting nearly thirty feet out above the lake.

"Jesus Christ," Rockson sputtered as they both let their legs stop dead in the water, the bubbling trail they had created stretching out behind them nearly a quarter mile. The lake reptile eyed them with burning red eyes as large as basketballs. Its razor-toothed jaws opened wide enough to swallow a buffalo, thick saliva pouring down into the rushing water. It was dark green, scaled from the neck on down, with foot-thick yellow bands circling its body every five feet. Much of the creature still lay submerged, but from the size of the head and the car-sized flippers that it splashed on each side to keep afloat, Rock guessed the thing was a good hundred feet long. And it didn't look on the friendly side. Archer reached behind him for his crossbow and swung it around, pulling out one of his two remaining arrows from his aluminum quiver. He quickly fitted one into the firing slot.

The monstrous lizard kept watching them as if savoring the meal it was about to partake of before actually taking the first bite. Archer let fly with the arrow which buried itself just above the creature's right flipper. The thing let out a roar of pain, throwing its head high in the air so that the neck stretched almost straight up like a thick green tree. Then it slammed down into the lake, disappearing within seconds beneath the surface, sending out waves in all directions from the explosive blast of its descent.

"Arrrcheeer killlllllll," the freefighter said with a grin, putting the metal crossbow back around his shoulder.

"I'm afraid it won't be as easy as — " But Rockson's words were cut off as the lake monster came up like a rocket from beneath them. Its green head slammed into the raft throwing it into the air, Rock and Archer flying off in opposite directions. They came to the surface spitting water, staring at one another from about ten yards apart. The parachute raft slowly sank some thirty feet away, ripped in half as big bubbles burped their way to the surface.

The reptile disappeared again beneath the rough surface of the lake but Rock knew it was only a matter of seconds before it made another entrance. It was playing cat and mouse with them, eager for some sport before the actual entree. Suddenly it reappeared some fifty yards out and came tearing at them, moving at lightning speed. It bore down on Archer, its steam-shovel jaws opened wide. The big man stared at the vision from hell, his body paralyzed. The freefighter glanced over at Rockson for a split second as if to say goodbye, then forward again to see his scaly fate bearing down on him. But the reptile had not finished having its fun. It veered to the side at the last second, slapping Archer with one of its fifteen-foot flippers. the force of the two-ton appendage knocked the near-mute twenty feet into the air, over three hundred pounds of struggling wild man. He landed just yards away from Rockson, dazed, and began to go under. Rock reached over and wrapped his arm around Archer's chest, keeping them both afloat.

The hell monster of Lake Superior surfaced again about one hundred yards away and again lifted its long, graceful neck. The red eyes in its head burned with hunger. It came at them, Rockson sensed this was going to be the last time. He searched frantically, looking for any kind of weapon. His pistol was empty but he suddenly noticed the small Emergency Pilot Pack strapped to the side of his stolen Russian uniform. He flipped the canvas pack open and, treading water furiously to keep them both afloat, glanced inside. There—at the bottom, beneath antibiotic syringes and a small stack of gold coins, was a gun of some kind. He pulled it out—a flare pistol with but one shell. He knew the charge wouldn't even make a dent in the creature's thick armor. He'd have to wait until the last possible second and then . . .

The thing bore down on them, opening its dripping jaws, seaweed hanging in slimy bunches from the foot-and-a-half-long triple rows of dagger teeth. It was going to swallow them both with a single bite—a mere snack. It built up speed, the head lowering down to the water line to swoop them into waiting jaws. The flaming red eyes made contact with Rock's blue and violet eyes and he could see the murderous primitive hunger in them. The curved teeth glistened from the thin rays of the diffused sun trying to burn through the thick cloud cover. The Doomsday Warrior waited and waited until the thing was just yards away, until he was able to see straight down the dark throat of the reptilian killer. Holding the flare gun straight out in front of him he fired into the monster's jaws. The flare tore into the moist innards of the thing and exploded with a roar, sending out a storm of sparks and burning white light. The creature threw its head back and let out a blood-curdling scream. It tried to bring its immense mouth down again but something was wrong. It seemed confused, its brain no longer functioning as the explosion had severed its spinal cord. The great neck swung back and forth wildly and then slammed down into the lake with a tumultuous splash. The immense body jerked violently, the fins and tail going into death spasms. It moved for about a minute and then was still, bizarrely motionless in the rough water. It glided slowly past them only feet away.

Archer suddenly came out of his stupor from the slap of the reptile's fin. He shook his head in confusion as if trying to shake brain cells into place. He looked up at Rockson, panic in his silver-dollar-sized brown eyes, and then saw the thing which floated dead in the water alongside them.

"Roooocksoon—thiiing killl," he growled, ready to dive back below the surface to escape.

"No, it's dead," Rock said softly. "The hunter got captured by the game." Archer looked skeptical as he began treading water. He could hardly believe that something so gargantuan, so fierce could have been killed. He kicked his feet out against the reptile's side to see if it was true. But it was dead, dead as cold stone, already stiffening in the freezing air as the pale slivers of the setting sun lit up the immense rounded side with a garish, merciless light.

Rockson glanced over to see the parachute-float disappear beneath the increasingly rough waters of the lake, twisting waves six-feet high snapping wildly in the wind with teeth of bubbling white foam. The Doomsday Warrior's body was starting to stiffen up from the bitter cold. They had been in the freezing waters for nearly forty-five minutes—there wasn't much time left. As tough as the two freefighters were, they were made of flesh and blood—flesh which would soon turn steel hard, blood which would freeze and coagulate in their stiff veins.

"Come on, pal, we're going to hitch a ride," Rock said, swimming the few yards over to the monster's corpse which slowly bobbed up and down in the dark lake. They grabbed hold of the slimy flippers and somehow pulled themselves up onto the outstretched green fins. Standing up on the green appendage, Rock grabbed hold of one of the reptile's row of spike like protruberances which ran along its back. Within seconds he had hoisted himself up onto the long curving top of the creature. He reached down a thickly muscled arm and helped the slipping and sliding Archer get atop. The slowly dissipating heat of the dead lake predator gave them a little warmth, making them more alert.

"Plesiosaurus," Rock muttered, remembering pictures he had seen of the thing back in the Century City archives. "Supposed to be extinct for a couple hundred million years. But I guess this one decided not to join its relatives—or else he was mutated from one of the native species in the lake." He remembered Dr. Shecter's theory that the heavy radiation of the war had caused many creatures that survived to undergo regressive evolution—the chromosomes reverting to a more simple configuration in attempts at survival.

From their position on the thing's back they could see the shore just ahead, not more than a quarter mile away. The tide was still pushing in that direction and—if God were favoring Americans today—it wouldn't change, at least for a while. Slowly, ever so slowly, drifting in slow curves, they rode the dead lake monster in toward the sands of the shore, the biggest horse that a man had ever ridden in the rodeo of eternal death.

Chapter Two

They stumbled ashore, wading through the freezing water which was sending up writhing sheets of steam as night came falling through the dense cover of storm clouds. The tide changed almost instantly and the huge lake reptile began drifting slowly back out toward the opposite bank, thirty miles off. Large, razor-beaked gulls came swooping in from all directions, landing on the thing's back and tearing out little morsels of the green meat with their powerful snapping jaws. Rock could see from the sudden quick jerk of the reptile that fish, beneath the waters, were also taking their due. The earth took back what it put forth in cruel harmony.

The freefighters made their way across the nearly quarter mile of fine white-sanded shore, at last reaching a forest of high firs. The temperature was dropping by the minute and Rockson knew they wouldn't stand a chance of surviving the night. Already their drenched clothes were forming a thin sheen of ice over them.

"If we're not going to make a career out of being snowmen," Rock said, "we'd better find some shelter soon." Archer grunted in agreement, not quite understanding the concept of a snowman, but getting the drift of the words. They walked for about a mile through the dense forest, blazing eyes sending out waves of hunger in the darkness. Archer loaded his crossbow and auto-set it, carrying the lethal weapon in front of him, ready for whatever hellish creature might burst forth. At last they came to a small clearing in the center of a grove of thick, blue-barked trees with five-feet-long red leaves, arranged in bulb like formations along the gnarled twisting branches.

"This will at least protect us from the wind," Rock said as the strong breeze continued sweeping down a painful flow of freezing air from the north. They sat down on the hard packed ground, a few desultory weeds growing here and there. It was the first time in hours the two men had stopped and they lay back on the earth to rest their weary bodies.

"Now if we only had a fire, things would be just wonderful," Rock said with a lopsided grin. Archer stood up suddenly and took the arrow from its slot. He reached behind him into a small pouch at the bottom of the now arrowless quiver and pulled out a coal-sized piece of flint. "Well, I'll be," Rock said, rising up and pulling up some dried weeds from the ground. "You do come prepared, don't you?" Archer beamed with pride.

"Aarccher fiiiiiiireee," the huge freefighter said. They built a small mound of kindling and pieces of dead branch from around the clearing. Archer held the flint next to the bottom of the pile and slammed the steel tipped arrow against it. Within seconds a spark shot out and flew into the paper-dry weeds. A thin flame caught hold and quickly set the pile of wood ablaze. The two freefighters sat on opposite sides of the flames, warming their frigid hands and drying their clothes.

"Now, that's better, isn't it, my friend?" Rock asked.

"Liiiike fiiireee," the grizzly-sized man said. "Feeeel gooooood." They were both ravenous but the woods were too dark and dangerous to start hunting. The cloudy night cast a deathly blackness like a shroud over the terrain. The fire's crackling flames sent out bizarre shadows over the thick trees that surrounded them. Hidden inside the woods Rockson could hear the low growls of hunting carnivores. He quickly gathered more broken branches from around the clearing and built a small pile alongside the fire.

"We've got to keep the damned thing going all night," Rock said, throwing a few more pieces into the lapping flames. "Or else . . ." He eyed the dark woods.

"Archer no liiike beee eaten," the big freefighter said, inching a little closer to the warmth and security of the blue and yellow tongues of flame.

"We'll have to take shifts. I'll stand guard for about three hours and wake you. OK—understand?"

"Nooo—Roocksonnn first. Archer noooo sleeep," the giant said firmly.

"If you insist." The Doomsday Warrior laughed, made a small cushion out of some moss and set his head down on it. His clothes were now dry from the warmth of the flames and he felt almost comfortable as he found himself quickly drifting into sleep.

Archer kept glancing nervously around as Rockson slipped off. He kept the crossbow on his legs, sitting cross-legged, leaning back against one of the immense blue-barked trees that filled the nearby forest. Like radar he turned his head from side to side, sweeping the darkness and the eyes—so many eyes, all glistening like orange and silver stars from the woods. All aimed at him. A sudden howl that went on for nearly five seconds, ending in a shrill scream of challenge, made him quickly throw more wood on the fire until it was sending up its protective flames nearly five feet into the sub-zero air. Sparks and streams of gray smoke lit up the sky, creating a fifty-foot funnel of light. There—let the damned eaters try something, he thought to himself and sat back down with a satisfied look.

But the warmth of the crackling wood and his lack of sleep for days made the big head slowly fall over to the side. Three times he jerked suddenly awake and rubbed his face, looking furtively around to see if anything had dared sneak up. But on the fourth demand of his tired body he fell into a deep sleep, toppling over onto the ground without waking.

Within minutes the trees around them began moving. Sensing that both of the flesh-creatures lying beside the fire were unconscious, the giant red-petaled flowers on the branches opened slowly, revealing rows of sharp spikes all aimed inward. Mutated Venus flytraps, they had grown to enormous size, trapping nearby creatures. The carniverous plants opened only in the dead of night, preferring to go into a defensive closed hibernation during the day.

But now they would eat again. The branches of the tree just behind Archer, which he lay asleep at the base of, moved around. Flexible as rubber, the dim mind of the tree sent out the command to kill through its chlorophyl nervous system.

The five-foot-long red petals, eight of them, closed in on the top of the sleeping creature, circling down toward him until the thick, green-veined leaves were open just above him. They dropped down onto Archer and closed around his head and shoulders, snapping tightly shut. The freefighter screamed out bloody murder as he pushed his arms up against the consuming petals trying to push them off. Rockson bolted out of his dark sleep and stared over at the attack incredulously. Suddenly he sensed movement all around them. All the branches, the blooms as big as a man with their red grabbing leaves, were moving toward him, zeroing in. The branches seemed to extend out, stretching, giving each of the meat-eating blooms thirty to forty feet of attack space. Rockson rolled over just as the nearest one plopped down onto the cold ground where his body had just been. The petals snapped instinctively shut but took in a mouthful of dirt. Rock reached into the roaring fire and took out a burning three-foot piece of branch, grabbing it at the charred but cold end. He jumped to his feet and rushed over to Archer, who by the looks of the furious struggle he was putting up was clearly still alive. How long he had before the digestive juices of the thing went to work was not something Rock dared wonder. He thrust the flames at the base of the man-trap, jamming into the fleshy outer layer of the thing, sizzling the vegetable flesh. The plant-thing shook wildly and then jerked back away from the flames, opening its spiked jaws and spitting out Archer. He rolled several feet and jumped up. Hundreds of small pinpricks had drawn blood from his body which oozed down over his big frame. But he seemed none the worse for wear.

"Quick, man, grab some fire," Rock yelled to Archer as more of the plant-things came swinging in from other trees to eat what their fellow Venus flytrap had been unable to hold onto. The two freefighters swung their flaming torches in quick circles around them, trying to keep the predatory flora at bay. The meat-eating plants moved slow, about five miles an hour, but there were nearly two dozen red-leaved jaws trying to get them and already the men were growing tired, as each darting red mouth came out of the darkness trying to reach them.

"This ain't going to work," Rock yelled. "We'll tire or we'll slip—and either way they'll get us." Archer glanced over at his mentor with blazing eyes, hoping he would come up with something. He always had—until now. "We've got to make a circle of fire—a defensive perimeter—around us." Rock rushed over to the huge freefighter. "All right, we'll stand back-to-back and edge over to that dead tree there. Grab as much wood as you can—big pieces. You got me?"

"Yeesss, Rooockson—get wooood," Archer growled back. The two men moved slowly so as not to slip on ice-covered low grass and weeds. The branches moved unerringly toward them from above, homing in like guided missiles. Rockson couldn't see any eyes on the things—they must use some sort of primitive radar. One of the veiny, six-foot flora made a swoop with its wide-opened petals but Rock thrust the flaming end of his stick right into its center and it shot backwards emitting an almost inaudible high-pitched scream. They grabbed as much wood as they could from the rotting tree, snapping off the dry branches until they were loaded down. Swirling the flames all around them, making streaks of fire in the dark night air, they headed back toward the fire. The entire clearing was now surrounded by the man-eaters, coming in from every angle, moving faster in some kind of feeding frenzy. Rock threw his entire load on the flames which caught ablaze within seconds. Archer dumped his and soon the fire was roaring, sending up a hurricane of white-hot embers far into the clouded heavens.

"Kick it around," Rock screamed above the snapping and crackling of the flames. "Make a circle of fire around us." He could see by the light in Archer's eyes that he understood. The two freefighters kicked the burning branches and logs out into the clearing until they had formed a loosely circular ring of lapping flames. They stood in the center of it, waiting.

The carniverous flytraps came forward from all sides but stopped just behind the fire. Even ten, twenty feet up, the heat was too intense for them. A few tried to dart forward and through the waves of murky heat, but jerked back as their green veins quickly heated up and began popping, spitting out a swampy green pus. It was a standoff as the flesh-traps whipped desperately around just outside the fiery perimeter. But in the war of predator and prey, the standoff goes to the victim—the winner in this battle of the endless, violent foodchain.

Other creatures were not so lucky. Sensing a small herd of mountain elk nearby the blooms pulled back and were still. Several of the leaders of the herd, three big males with two-yard-long staghorns capable of goring a sabre-toothed lion to death, edged forward about twenty yards from the fire. They sniffed cautiously, their black noses testing the air to see if the fire was moving, if it was a threat to them.

Like rattlers striking, three of the red things opened their spiked jaws wide and dropped down onto the elk. They fell onto the animals' back ends avoiding the horns which could even rip through their foot-thick outer red-fleshed leaves. The veined petals snapped shut and the elk were doomed. They tried to run, their front legs tearing at the earth like windmills. But it was all to no avail. Unable to use their back legs which were now held firmly in place by the closing red leaves, or their steel-hard horns, the creatures were pulled deeper into the meat-eating plants and slowly digested as the lips of the blooms moved up their prey inch by inch, at last engulfing them whole.

Rock and Archer watched in mesmerized horror, knowing how close they had been to a similar ghastly fate. The other elk, hearing the death cries of their leaders, stormed off through the forest, trampling small bushes beneath their strong brown-furred legs. The three flowers that had eaten pulled back up to their trees as if satisfied, for the moment. But the rest of the army of carniverous flytraps were hungry. They waited at the edge of the circle of fire, flailing around like whips, searching for some way through the wall of heat.

With a few more quick forays out into the clearing for wood, swinging torches in front of them for protection, the two freefighters managed to keep the perimeter burning through the night, frustrating the man-eating plants' every effort. At last the dawn sun crept into the gray sky on burning red legs. The heavens slowly brightened, the writhing shadows of night slipped back into their daytime hiding places. As if the very nurturing rays of the star that gave life to the earth was death to them, the carniverous blooms retreated, pulling back to their trees, as their flexible branches hauled them in. They closed their petals tight and seemed to shrink slightly, growing a darker, almost purplish color. Then they were still.

Rockson and Archer looked at one another, the few slivers of the pale sun cutting through the high-flying green strontium clouds lighting their faces with a corpselike hue.

"We made it—goddamn it," Rock half whispered to Archer who stood, bleary-eyed on trembling legs, still waving his burning torch in slow uneven circles around him. "Come on, let's get the hell out of here," Rock said, grabbing his emergency pack from the ground and strapping it back around his waist. "I don't want to be around when these vegetables wake up again." The two freefighters moved swiftly from the grove of predatory trees. Rock knew he would never look on the flora of the world the same way again. Nothing was what it appeared to be in the post-nuclear world. Every flower, every insect, every shimmering pool of water held incalculable danger and death.

They walked slowly through the barren rolling hills, dotted on the lower slopes by firs rising proudly toward the sky. They half stumbled as they walked, as they hadn't slept for days now. Rock knew there would be time for that later. Sleep was a luxury in the game of survival. Archer appeared much more exhausted than Rock, his eyes nearly closed, walking through sheer motor function, his body taking over on automatic control. The big freefighter lurched forward with just the hint of a smile on his bearded face. Rockson knew he must be dreaming of the old days—his mountain youth when he hunted the wild deer and pheasant of the lush countryside where the Doomsday Warrior had originally found him, saving the near-mute from a suffocation in a pool of quicksand.

The game was plentiful around them as they headed south through the low bushlands of the northern United States. Black-faced squirrels, horned field mice, an occasional porcupine with its quivering armor of icepick quills, all moved around them, scampering for cover as they heard the noisy humans approach. Rock knew they were somewhere in what had been Wisconsin with a good thousand miles to go before they reached Century City. Hardly a reassuring prospect, but then Rock had been through these long, perilous treks before, many times. In a strange way he relished them. No complexities of Century City social life, no political machinations with the city council and the military staff. Just he and Archer and the elements. For Rockson was a creation of the new world. He was defined, chipped into shape, by its constant attempts at taking back the life it had given him. His strength, his abilities all rose to their peak by the sheer opposition of a cruel Darwinian ecosystem. It is through opposition, even the squaring off against death itself, that men raise to their heights. "What doesn't kill me makes me stronger," as the adage of Nietzsche goes. Those who couldn't meet the challenge went under—fodder for teeth and claws. But the Doomsday Warrior welcomed the enemy—always. It made him feel fully alive. As a glowing ember sparks to life when blown upon, the stronger the wind the higher the flame, so Ted Rockson grew in strength, in power, according to the nature of his adversaries.

Rock walked sure-footedly across the increasingly lush terrain, his eyes swinging back and forth like search-and-destroy radar, waiting, searching for the next thing that would try to take him down. He was weaponless now except for the empty .45 that hung at his waist, and picked up a five-foot-long stick which he found on the ground, straight as a spear and green with the oozing sap of life recently gone. He tested the shaft as he walked—it would do. They had gone for about an hour, stopping just to drink some water from a running stream when Rock realized it was growing darker by the second. The big storm clouds galloping across the purple-hazed sky were dropping lower now. The air was thick with a cold moisture and the Doomsday Warrior knew it would be only minutes before they released their load of frozen water. He searched ahead for shelter—but there was none. The land was flat with but occasional banks of trees sheltering together against the harsh winds for survival. He silently prayed that it wasn't the acidic black snow he had experienced once before. Snow that killed, that ate all that it fell upon with wet teeth, dissolving flesh that shrieked in agony until all that remained of it was puddles of steaming bone.

He felt something wet on his face and looked up. Snowflakes—by the uncountable billions falling from the sky. But these were white. A gift of beauty not a murderous foe. Archer seemed to wake up from his semicomatose state as the flakes landed around his mouth and eyes. His expression brightened and he grunted approvingly at the descending sheets of white. The flakes were huge, nearly three inches wide, crystalline symetries of infinite complexity and perfection. Rockson remembered dimly something from his youth—that no two flakes were exactly the same. Each was a world unto itself, a sculpture by a god who seemed to revel in giving mankind glimpses of beauty amidst the constant devastation. Rock wondered if the beauty was sent to lead mankind on. To give him a vision beyond the destruction and the death. One could never lose sight of that beauty—it was a gift and a prophecy, that perhaps one day all of the earth could be that way: harmonious, shimmering and unalterably mysterious.

The two freefighters felt energized by the snowfall. As the earth became blanketed with a pure white, their hair and clothes were coated with the wet flakes. They could barely see more than ten yards ahead but Rock's sense of direction was unerring and they continued straight on. The wind had died down and the temperature was just at the freezing point so their constant motion kept them from getting too cold. They walked for about twenty minutes when Rock heard a low guttural growl through the thick flakes. He paused, motioning for Archer to stop too. They listened through the dampening pillars of snow. It was hard to discern anything but the soft whisper of the slow avalanche from the heavens. He had just started forward again when the sound came a second time. This time louder and the growl was now a roar. He knew instantly—it was a cat of some sort, from the sharp hissing sound. They suddenly heard another and then another of the heart-stopping sounds. They were surrounded.

The two freefighters backed off, each hefting his weapon. Rock lifted the branch in his hands, pointing it straight ahead ready to impale whatever appeared from out of the white haze. Archer swung his crossbow around and prepared to fire his last arrow. The two men stood side by side, ready to take on the world. Dim shapes became slowly discernible at the very edge of their vision. Low-slung, edging forward with the careless slinking grace of big cats. Their forms were suddenly visible—panthers—sleek and black as shining coal. They looked beautiful etched against the pure white of the ground . . . and deadly. The freefighters gulped as they saw that there were nearly a dozen of the predators surrounding them, moving ever closer, watching through flaring yellow eyes for any attempt at escape.

"I think this might be it, pal," Rock whispered over to Archer as they slowly backed away, one foot at a time, leaving deep prints in the already inch-thick covering. The largest of the panthers came forward;

opening its jaws to reveal curved ivory fangs that could rip a man's arm off with a single bite. It stared right at them and let loose with a blood-curdling roar, the scream of the hungry, of the king of the foodchain. A creature that had never known fear in all its days but instead created it in those that it stalked. The cats closed in from all sides moving in a perfect flanking attack formation with the instinctive strategy of any army of killers. The leader, a good six-feet long and a yard high at the shoulders, came straight for Rockson and tensed its front legs as it prepared to strike. The Doomsday Warrior relaxed his arms, ready to smash the thing the moment it leaped. One, he knew he could take. Two, maybe—but beyond that . . .

Suddenly a voice rang out from the impenetrable whiteness behind the black panthers. *"Eeeeyie kreega kara!"* The cats stopped dead in their tracks, moving neither forward nor backward. They kept the freefighters trapped in a cage of black furry hide. More shapes appeared from the blinding funnels of snow. Rockson could hardly believe his eyes. Seven women—pale skinned, beautiful and nearly naked but for loincloths made of the shining fur of their predatory pets. The women walked up to the two men, staying just behind the panthers. Their large firm breasts and their waist-long manes of jet-black hair were tinged with snow, but they neither shivered nor seemed in the slightest bit cold. Around their white throats were necklaces of gold and precious stones—and the curved fangs of the panthers that apparently did their bidding.

The cat closest to Rockson prepared to attack,

opening its salivating jaws wide, coiling low on its forward legs.

"Kreega, na kreega," one of the women screamed, jumping forward and slapping the cat on the side of the face. The panther let out a whimper and slunk back, crouching low, its tail dropping down in submission. The woman walked right up to Rockson, stopping a foot away from him, and stared at him with a strange lustful expression. She was one of the most beautiful women he had ever seen, with pale soft skin as smooth and white as alabaster. Her body was near perfection, muscled and lean with a slim waist and hemispheric breasts. Her flowing black hair adorned with claws and teeth dropped behind her, just covering her smooth buttocks. She looked the two men up and down as if appraising a slab of meat she was about to eat. Her mouth opened, revealing pearly white teeth.

"Donnez-moi votres weapones!" Rockson stared at her in incomprehension. *"Donnez! Donnez!"* she yelled out, pointing to Rock's staff and the crossbow held tightly in Archer's hands. Hesitant to turn over their only weapons, they stood there motionless until the female warrior motioned the cats to come forward again. The freefighters quickly handed the implements to the two women who stepped forward. The leader of the women whistled twice and the panthers backed off, sitting down at the sides of the female warriors. The women scratched their heads and spoke softly to them, making the big cats relax from their attack state.

Another woman stepped forward from out of the blinding snowstorm. Rockson hadn't noticed her, partially because she had blended in so well with her white surroundings. She was an albino. The palest, chalkiest white Rock had ever seen. If the other women were pale, this one was without any color, almost ghostlike with her translucent skin. Her hair was like bleached wheat and fell like a waterfall down her back to her waist. She looked at Rockson with pink eyes, taking him in—all of him. It was like looking into a vacuum, a vacuum of lust and rage.

"Les hommes sont moi," the albino spat out to the leader.

"Non, Ishtar, ne pas vous. Pour le tribe, le Kreega," the leader shot back, her face red with fury. The other female warriors looked on with concern, as the panthers grew restless. Rock could sense some sort of internal power struggle between the two women for leadership of the tribe—and possession of him and Archer. But the albino backed down, drifting back into the blowing storm with a single motion and disappearing among the flakes.

Their hands and ankles were quickly bound with thick leather thongs. The women smiled, glancing at one another with quick leering looks as they tied the knots. Rock realized the entire party was eyeing them both with a ravenous hunger. He wondered if they were about to be saved from the panthers only to meet the same fate from the tribe of Amazons. He had encountered cannibals several times over the years. But never ones as beautiful as these.

Chapter Three

"Me – Reina," the leader of the women warriors said as she led Rockson by a rope tether attached to his wrist bonds. "We – Kreega."

"Kreega," Rock stammered as she pulled him through the snow at a speed he could hardly keep pace with. She seemed to have the strength and agility of a cat. Her long lithe body in front of him though was all female, and abundantly so. Despite his tiredness and the throbbing pain in his lower back from a wound he had received in Moscow, he watched intently as her thin loincloth bounced around and occasionally blew aside in the wind.

Archer ran as fast as his large body could travel, pulled by three of the Kreega and surrounded on both sides by the panthers. He stumbled through the snow behind his female keepers grumbling loudly, casting half intelligible aspersions on their ancestry.

At last they came to a thick woods, with towering black-leaved trees creating a canopy of cover. Once inside, the snows were stopped far above by the myriad leaves and branches. It was also an instantaneous hothouse as a junglelike atmosphere was created by the rising moisture of the closely packed trees. Here, they moved more slowly as the dense undergrowth made movement difficult, catching hands and feet in vines and thornbushes. But Reina apparently knew her way. She followed almost invisible trails through the tangling growth. It quickly grew dark as they pushed further in, the light from far off and above only dimly trickling down through the maze of plant life. In almost utter blackness they headed on, Reina moving at a good pace, pulling Rock along right behind her. Every few seconds she would look back at him with wide eyes filled with undisguised desire.

They half ran through the leafy jungle for what seemed like hours until they at last came to a clearing, the camp of the Kreega. A space a good three hundred feet wide had been cleared of trees though those at the circumference of the space overhung it with their long leafy branches, protecting it from much of the snow and rain. Only a few flakes managed to squeeze through the outstretched branches and these were quickly evaporated by the heat of the surrounding jungle. But what instantly caught Rockson's eye were the structures that the Kreega lived in—teepees. They stood fifty feet apart, nearly a dozen of them, each about twenty feet tall, with animal hides wrapped tightly around their conical bodies. Thin streams of smoke rose from the opening at the top of each one.

Reina tugged tightly at Rock's bonds pulling him close in behind her as they walked into the center of the Amazon village. More of the white-skinned, black-haired women emerged from their teepees as a large muscular woman with gourd-sized breasts blew on a hollowed-out stag horn from her guard post at the edge of the encampment. The deep raspy note shivered through the air, sending a chill down Rockson's back. The women gathered around the returning hunters, reaching out to touch their male prisoners. Soft but strong hands grabbed at the two men as they walked through the gauntlet of female flesh.

Reina led them to the largest of the teepees, a good fifteen feet higher than the others. It sat in the center of the camp, emblazoned with bizarre geometric patterns. She opened the hide flap at the bottom of the teepee and pushed Rockson roughly inside. He flew forward, landing on a bed of black grizzly furs. Archer followed closely behind, kicked from the rear by two sets of female feet. He flew inside, landing on top of Rockson. The two men sat up as Reina walked in and stood looking down on them. Four of the women warriors stood just inside the flap, their hands resting on jewel-encrusted daggers at their waists.

Rockson tried working at the knotted leather binding clamping his hands behind his back. But the knots were tight as steel locks. Reina sat on a second fur bed several feet away from the two freefighters and began a discourse that Rock could barely understand. She spoke in a sort of pidgin French mixed with American slang and a smattering of local Indian dialect.

"*Desirez-vous prenez un bath*?" she asked first Rockson and then Archer who stared at one another in noncomprehension. Rock knew the language was primarily French. He had gone over basic language tapes back at Century City. But beyond his basic ability at faking Russian, useful to infiltrate Red posts, he was virtually in the dark about other dialects.

"*Un bath, un bath*," Reina said, irritated, raising her arms and making a washing motion, so that her large breasts swung from side to side like lush ripe fruits, waiting to be plucked.

"Oh—*un bath*," Rock said, getting the meaning of the charade. "Yes, uh, *oui*," he answered, remembering his one word of French. Reina snapped her fingers and two of the Kreega guards ran out. But the teepee flap had barely closed when the albino warrior walked in.

"Ishtar," Reina spat out as the albino's eyes met hers. There was obviously no love lost between the two. The albino must have made a quick change for she was now decked out in elaborate ceremonial costume, complete with warpaint on her face and a panther head, eerily lifelike with opened jaws and glowing eyes, atop her skull.

"*L'homme est moi*," she snarled, her fist wrapped around her dagger.

"*Quelle homme*?" Reina asked, her own hand drifting down to her razor-sharp blade.

"*Le plus belle monsieur avec le streak blanc dans les cheveux*."

"*Non*, Ishtar," Reina said, rising and walking several steps until she stood face to face with the albino. Ishtar reached for her blade but Reina froze her with a withering look that even Rock could see said: Are you ready to die. They were obviously continuing their argument about just who would get the right to kill—or maybe eat them. Rock suddenly realized how the black slaves of old must have felt—as their fates were decided by alien masters.

Ishtar's hand hovered at the knife handle for long seconds, but apparently not ready to take up the challenge she abruptly turned on her heels and headed through the flap. At the last second she turned and said with an ominous tone, "*Vous etes morte, Reina. Je suis destroyez-vous.*" Then she was gone. Reina let her own hand drop from the knife and then smiled at Rockson as if to show she wasn't afraid.

"Ishtar *est dangereuse. Guardez.*" Rock got the message. The flap suddenly opened again and a whole troupe of the women warriors came in pushing two immense wooden barrels filled with steaming hot water. "*Votre bath,*" Reina said with a sly look. The women pushed the hot tubs into the center of the teepee as Reina motioned for the two freefighters to rise. She cut their ankle binds with a single quick slice, but left their hands tied. The Kreega women rushed over to their two prisoners and began stripping off their clothes. Within seconds both Rock and Archer were standing stark naked surrounded by nearly a dozen of the Kreega who ran their eyes up and down the men's bodies as if taking in the eighth wonder of the world. Their desire was undisguised as their mouths opened slowly. Several of them rubbed their breasts, squeezing them tight between white hands. Rock and Archer gulped under the feminine scrutiny. Several of the women pointed at the lower portions of the men's bodies and made obscene remarks to one another punctuated by coarse laughter.

The freefighters were led over to the wooden tubs and helped inside. Rock hoped they weren't cooking pots. But the second he touched the hot, soothing water he knew that at least for the moment they weren't about to be made into soup. The two men sank deep into the four-foot-high barrels, scrunching their legs up so they could fit. The women surrounded them and, hefting big bars of animal fat soap in their hands, began scrubbing and massaging the male bodies. Reina stood beside Rock's tub, not touching Rockson's muscled flesh but watching, her eyes riveted to him like a precious stone. The women washed the two freefighters until all the dirt and grime had been cleaned from their bodies. They stepped out from the tubs and several of the Kreega wrapped them in thick homespun towels.

"*Un moment*," Reina said, suddenly stepping forward. She looked down at Rockson's back, noticing the inflamed red wound he had recieved from a Red bullet while stealing the MIG from the Moscow airport. "*Vous avez le wound*," she said, stepping behind him and touching the raw entry hole.

"*Oui*," Rock answered wincing. "And Archer also." He pointed over to the grizzly-sized freefighter who seemed to be enjoying the female attention immensely. On Archer's thigh as well was an infected wound, almost purple and filled with pus.

"*Le couchez, le couche*," Reina barked out, pointing to the two bearskin beds at the far side of the teepee. They were led by their still-bound wrists and deposited naked on the beds. Reina pulled a small deerskin pouch from the belt of her loincloth and opened it, taking out a handful of dried green powder. She wetted the powder down with some spit and slapped it over Rock's wound. Another Kreega did the same to Archer. When the wounds were completely covered with the green paste, they were wrapped with a crude white fabric. Rock was somewhat skeptical about the method of treatment, but powerless to do more than just turn his head and watch the proceedings.

When the wounds were covered, the two freefighters

were once again turned over. Four of the Kreega women jumped onto Rock's bearhide mattress, edging toward him, their hands reaching for his flesh.

"*Non, non*," Reina yelled, pulling the women off and heaving them halfway across the teepee floor. "*Le belle home est moi.*" The women snarled at their queen but none dared to challenge her. In a tribe of perhaps the toughest women who had ever lived on the face of the earth, Reina was the toughest.

Across the dirt floor Archer was covered by seven women, giggling and laughing as they squeezed out at the giant's flesh.

"*Je vous desire*," they whispered out to him, like a chorus of crooning sirens. Archer grabbed the closest one and hoisted her atop him as the others watched, their eyes wide with excitement.

Reina stood above Rockson, smiling down at him. She gazed upon him for several seconds and then slowly undid her fur loincloth. Naked, she lowered herself on top of him. Her smell, her warmth, her soft firm body was overwhelming to his senses. For a moment he saw the image of Kim's face in his mind. But then it disappeared. A man must do what a man must do. Besides he was a prisoner.

She leaned forward and kissed his lips, softly at first then with a desperate hunger. She rubbed her body on his with increasing vigor, her soft breasts pressing against his chest with a trembling urgency. He could feel her growing wet, her legs spreading apart, the scent of her moist sex hitting his nostrils like a powerful aphrodisiac.

"*Maintenant pour le sexe*," she said with a sly grin and began working her way down his body, kissing every square inch of his masculine firmness. She slid down until she reached his manhood, now stiff and engorged from the stimulation of the beautiful woman warrior and put her mouth over the spearlike shaft. She moved up and down it with her lips wide apart, moaning with her eyes tightly shut. When she had brought the rod to its full length she sat up on the Doomsday Warrior and, opening the lips of her now well-lubricated sex, placed the tip against her thick black triangle.

Reina groaned loudly as the steel-hard organ slid deep inside her, sinking down on it until she was penetrated to her core. She began moving up and down on the male shaft, all the while screaming aloud in French. Rock, his hands still bound, could only lie back and enjoy it. Within minutes she began building up to a frantic pumping motion, moving up and down on him like a jackhammer. At last she opened her soft mouth wide and let out a piercing scream. Her body jerked and shuddered wildly for almost a minute, making Rock join in the love-making culmination. When they had both relaxed she lay atop him again, stroking his arms and chest, and making little cooing noises. If this was what it was going to be like to be a prisoner of the Kreega, Rockson thought to himself, maybe he'd sign up for the long haul.

Across the teepee, Archer was virtually covered with female flesh. Four young and beautiful Kreega women lay draped over his immense physique. Rock could hear the thrashings and gigglings and Archer's occasional "Goooooodddddd," as he was taken on a love trip the likes of which he had never experienced in his life. As soon as one was done, riding atop the giant's immense organ, the next would take her place. They were working him like a stud horse, and he seemed equal to the task.

Reina became aroused again within minutes and she once again mounted Rock. When she had finished coming for a second time she at last got off of him and rose, putting her loincloth back on again. She leaned over and kissed him softly on the lips and then pulled a flask containing a dark blue liquid from a small gourd on the floor,

"*Bouvez, bouvez,*" she said insistently, handing him the liquid. They obviously weren't about to poison him and Archer, not if their lovemaking services were going to be needed, so Rockson opened his lips and she poured in a few slugs. The liquid burned like liquor but went down OK. Reina stood back, looking at him with a wistful expression and then snapped her fingers as she walked away. A bevy of ten women who had been standing near the teepee flap rushed over to the prone freefighter, scrambling quickly to be the first on line. A young, pear-breasted woman got astride him and took her fill. Then another and another . . .

Rock awoke early in the morning just as the sun was coming up. Outside the teepee he could hear the panthers growling at the dawn as if it were some prey they were about to attack. He could barely move; his body felt absolutely drained of every bit of energy. He couldn't even remember how many women he had had during the night—ten, twelve, fifteen. At a certain point he had lost count as breasts and thighs and moaning mouths grew into a blur of mad sexuality. It was obvious that the blue liquid they had given him and Archer to drink had highly potent ability to keep a man sexually excited—and the wherewithal to keep the action going. Rock wondered if he and Archer were scheduled to have sex with every damned woman in the tribe—just how many were there?

After about an hour of lying in the fur bed wondering if they were ever going to get any food, Reina came in with four Kreega guards and they led the Doomsday Warrior and Archer outside, after helping them on with their clothes. Rock wondered if they might try a break as the rest of the village was still asleep. But with four panthers following closely behind, their orange eyes fixated on the two freefighters, he decided to wait for a better opportunity. They were fed a gruellike porridge and pieces of sweet juice-filled fruit. Reina seemed in a good mood and kept looking over at Rock as they all sat around on logs arranged in a circle around a glowing fire that was constantly tended.

She began talking to him, a strange mixture of French and the few English words she had learned from captured trappers, and gradually Rock was able to learn the history of the tribe. They were the descendants of French Canadians. When the great "boom-boom" as Reina put it, came, their ancestors went as far into the primeval forest as possible—where the trees didn't wither like they had in all other places. There they had lived for the past century, fishing and hunting. Many babies died, but those that survived were taller and more agile than the ones before. But as time went on there were more and more female children than male—until eventually there were no males at all. The Kreega, after sixty years all women, began raiding the land to the south picking up stray males—scrawny pathetic survivors and traders—and took them prisoner to fertilize the eager and lonely women of the tribe. It was in one of these forays nearly twenty years earlier that they had discovered the remarkably fierce and intelligent cats and found that the virgins of their tribe had the ability to control them. As long as one of the younger virgin women of the Kreega was present the panthers would obey commands of any of the women. But without one around they reverted almost instantly to their savage state.

With the cats at their command, the tribe flourished, but to this day only female children were born to the women. Accepting and integrating this reality into their lives as some sort of divine will, they kept the men they seized only so long as their blue fluid of power permitted the men to fertilize as many Kreega as possible. Most men completely failed in their tasks, going limp after only days of super-studdom. But never, Reina told him in pidgin English, have we had men that lasted so long in just the first night.

"I'm proud to be an American," Rock said, grinning. He asked her just what happened to the men when they could no longer "function." Reina explained that they were fed to "Ogre", the Mother-Goddess who lived in the lake near where they had been captured. The Mother-Goddess who was the source of all good and strength, who lives in the deep blue wetness. Rock made a mental note to tell Archer not to mention the fact that they had done in the Kreega goddess. Somehow he didn't thing they'd appreciate the deed.

Chapter Four

Premier Vassily, ruler of all the world, was wheeled out onto the infrared heated balcony of the Hitler Pantheon in Berlingrad, the heart of New Germany. He stood on the tiled outcropping near the top of the immense marble-and-stone building, surrounded on all sides by the stern stone statues of the great Russian and German leaders of the past: Lenin, Stalin, Drubkin, Hitler and Goering. He addressed the multitudes below—over a quarter million olive-green uniformed soldiers in stiff straight lines reaching back as far as the eye could see. His frail voice boomed and echoed with authority, amplified and enhanced by the super-sensitive microphone on his throat. He sounded like Thor himself to the crowds, his voice rising over the strains of "The Ride of the Valkyries."

"Fellow socialists of the National Socialist Party, known here in the New Germany as the Nazi Party: I come in friendship and fellowship to celebrate the 160th anniversary of the pact between the beloved socialist leaders, Adolf Hitler and Joseph Stalin in 1943. Together they made war against the anti-socialist state of Poland. Today, I call again on that eternal bond between our two peoples to unite to defeat another anti-socialist enemy—the American rebels. The same Americans who brought about World War III, the same Americans who persecuted and forced into suicide your beloved Führer, Adolf Hitler, so many years ago. They must be crushed by our combined might."

The premier paused for a moment as the music rose to a crescendo, signaling the crowd to salute.

"*Sieg Heil! Seig Heil!*" they shouted by the hundreds of thousands, in waves that shook the ground. A thousand brown-shirted Nazi youth banged on huge typanies and crashed yard-wide cymbals together, creating a storm of noise and power worthy of Thor and Odin, the fierce gods of the Germanic people.

Vassily continued with his distorted history and his appeal to the masses of uniformed soldiers below him. "The spirit of our beloved Führer is here! I speak with his voice, his authority, with his love and racial purity." The voices screamed back a quarter-million *seig heils* with raised stiff arms. The premier surveyed the ranks and the vast Pantheon. On either side of the three hundred-yard-wide, half-mile-deep rows of assembled uniformed troops with their horseshoe-crab-style helmets stood immense Doric pillars. Atop each ten-foot-wide, two-hundred-foot-high pillar, a gas-fed fire roared and leaped into the air timed to the utterance of the premier to accentuate his immortal words. The orange flames glimmered in five hundred thousand blue eyes, reflecting their inner fire and mesmerized attention as the soldiers stood with their long bayonetted Goering rifles gripped tightly in their arms like long lost lovers.

Vassily knew he had them. He hadn't felt this way before a crowd since his inauguration as permanent premier of the Soviet empire some twenty years before. He felt younger, invigorated by the response of the fanatical crowd. Even *he* believed the power of his voice and its righteous tremulous words. Even *he* was swayed by the flaming pillars that cast flickering red shadows across the army of loyal troops before him.

Giant screens raised up on both sides of the elevated Hitler Pantheon on which he spoke as he reached the final page of his speech. Then from hidden holographic projectors the beloved face of *the Führer himself* beamed sternly out. By the miracle of modern science his face moved to the cadence of Vassily's words. It was as if Vassily *was* Hitler, the two of them merging, becoming a unity, a single fearsome. being.

"There is one Fatherland, one Socialist world community, one master Slavic-German race," Hitler shouted, his jaw jutting forward in pride, his head bobbing and waving in fanatical zeal. "There must be one world, one supreme goal for us all: the extermination of the radiation mutants. The destruction of the mongrel races of America. The Fourth Reich will stand ten thousand years, a million years, a billion years!"

Hitler himself now spoke Vassily's words, his face

shining with messianic fervor, his fists banging together with a violent rage. His lips spat out the demon's invective, jingoistic slogans appealing to the basest evil and lusts of mankind's savage underpinnings. "There is one world and it is Red. It is our destiny to spread the truth, the racial truth to all the world." Vassily was having a little trouble concentrating as he listened to the slight delay of his words become the booming strident voice of the hundred-foot-high projected image of Hitler. He took a quick sip of water and continued.

"We must strike hard at the mongrel Americans for the sake of the world gene pool. These mutant monkey men and women and their *Jewish* leaders—" he hissed out the word Jewish, so that it sounded slimy, serpentine— "they must feel the iron hand of the master race about their scrawny necks." He was reaching the climax of his speech but he felt himself growing tired, his lungs straining for air, his heart beating furiously in his heaving chest. He rushed on, his image as Hitler becoming more and more frenzied, the mouth twitching in ecstasy, the tuft of black hair hanging across Hitler's forehead swaying back and forth with the rapid jerks of his mustached face like a python hypnotizing its victim.

"*There is one master race and that is the Slavo-Germanic race. One world of power, and power is rightness. Power is truth. The Jewish conspiracy will be crushed, crushed, crushed!*"

The hypnotized throngs screamed back, over a quarter-million *Sieg heils* rocking the Pantheon as if it were in the jaws of an earthquake.

"*Was it not we Rusians who, when Germany and*

Russia were tricked by the capitalists into a brief fight with one another, still fed and clothed the cold German troops at Stalingrad like brothers, inviting them into the socialist fold once more?"

"Yes," thought row after row of wild-eyed soldiers. "It was so. These Russians and our Führer's Reich will be allies again—like it was at Stalingrad." Siegfried, one of the masses, standing near the very back of the vast Pantheon seats, screamed along with the rest of his Nazi comrades, yes . . . He remembered something as a child—a book his father had showed him. A book that said the Russians had been the bitter enemies of the Nazis. That they had murdered millions of German troops at Stalingrad and then invaded Berlin, forcing Hitler-the-Great to commit suicide. Siegfried frowned. He *had* seen that book—before his father disappeared, before the men in black leather had come with their long sleek car. The black car. They had never talked about his father after that. Denied he had ever lived there. And now the book was gone with his father. Ah, no matter. The crowd was cheering the Führer's final words and Siegfried joined in, screaming, his eyes wide and mad, spittle spraying from his lips.

"AND YOU WILL SUCCEED, YOU WILL DESTROY THE MONGREL RACES. FOR YOU ARE GERMANS—GOD'S CHOSEN WARRIORS." Hitler raised his arm high as the Nazi troops leaped to their feet en masse, eyes blazing in a frenzy of ecstatic hate.

The cheering lasted long into the night. Long after Vassily was rolled away in the waiting wheelchair to the jet that roared back toward Moscow. It was well that his black servant, Rahallah, had his ebony countenance hidden in the monk's cowl on the Pantheon platform, Vassily thought, as he half dozed in the seat of his luxury AB-131 Airlifter. What if the Nazi hordes had seen Rahallah's face? What would they think then of racial pride and purity? What if they knew that my most trusted aide, my second-in-command, is a full-blooded African? But deception is the word of the night—in politics.

Rahallah was awake five seats back, his heart pounding, as he looked out the window at the dark forests far below. The scene he had witnessed that evening filled his soul with disgust and repulsion. All these years he had faithfully stood by the Grandfather, thinking him to be the least of the monsters who ruled the world, hoping to affect the premier's plan through his unswerving loyalty and kindness, hoping to influence the premier with his constant pleas for peace and a free separate African nation.

But tonight, tonight he had seen the black man's ultimate nightmare—the monstrous Third Reich had been resurrected by Vassily to serve their world military needs, to invade the Rocky Mountains in America and find and destroy Ted Rockson and his famed Century City. But they had created something that Rahallah knew in his heart would not go away into a corner and die when it had served the Reds' purposes. No, the fiendish display of race hatred and anti-Semitism last night was a harbinger of an even worse dictatorship to come, one that would be so total and consumed with destruction that only one man—one megalomaniacal leader, *a Führer to come*—could rule it. And Rahallah in his heart of hearts, in his clairvoyant churning soul, knew that when Vassily died—when the others like President Zhabnov in Washington fell—it was the evil destiny of the world to have the horrors of a Führer named Killov, the Skull, ruling over all, like the Antichrist predicted in the ancient prophecies.

Rahallah, with the blood of African kings pumping through his veins, at last fell asleep, his hands tightly clenched like claws on his lap. He dreamed horrible things. He saw the death of Vassily, the placing of his frail old body in the Lenin-Drabkin tomb, the solemn looks on all the commissars gathered in the Kremlin. He saw the KGB Blackshirts sweep into the city in helicopter gunships, the mass arrest of all of Vassily's supporters, the execution by slow garroting and hot pokers of Zhabnov, the fat American president. Then he saw *himself* running, running bloody and wounded through the dark subway tunnels of Moscow. Then he heard the announcement on the radios, over the loudspeakers on trucks all over Moscow. "Killov is premier, Killov is the Führer, the world is united in his omnipotent leadership. All will obey his iron will—or die!"

Rahallah awoke, his white tuxedo stained with hot perspiration, his heart racing. What could he do? What could anyone do at this late stage? He had played the devil's game and lost—lost for Africa, lost for world peace, lost everything.

When Vassily awoke, his eyes touched by the dawn's icy fingers of green and orange splattering through the half drawn blinds on the window, Rahallah rushed to his side and poured him tea from the large silver samovar in the aisle and added the customary shot of brandy. He waited until the premier seemed fully awake and then said, "Your excellency, may I ask you one thing?"

"Yes, my faithful servant, what is it?" the premier asked, yawning. "You have been exceptionally quiet this whole trip. I think I know what it is—you heard me scream those racial insults last night. But, but, our forces are stretched too far. The brilliant Major Velikov has assembled this Nazi army for us by using all the old slogans and symbols of their past. But it is for *our* purposes that this propaganda must be made. Our armies are too drawn apart, too challenged worldwide. We need these German troops to destroy the evil of Rockson and the other so-called freefighters."

"Vengeance?" Rahallah asked, standing in the long aisle beside the aging premier.

The old man's age-spotted face grew red then purple. He clutched his bony hand against the chrome arm of the seat.

"Vengeance? Yes! You remember that man—that bastard coming to Moscow, drinking my vodka, eating my food. Him and that foul-smelling giant friend sitting with us, negotiating a fair and equitable treaty of friendship with most generous terms on my part." (SEE BOOK No. 4)

"Yes," Rahallah answered, remembering *the Rockson*, who had struck him as a decent man looking out for the interests of his own enslaved people.

"You remember what he did? Destroyed half of Moscow, crippling our defenses, casting our chances for world peace into a pit of blood."

"But you condemned him to the gladiator pits—

and certain death," the ebony-faced servant said firmly.

"Rahallah, you forget—and I forgive you for this—but he, this Rockson, escaped our hospitality and linked up with the ratlike dissidents in the old subway system. He killed many soldiers before I made that decision. Then he destroyed the people's beloved coliseum, blew up our missile and satellite command center, the bastard. And finally stole one of our most advanced fighter aircraft—and flew it to America. We know that from the radar reports."

"Perhaps he died—the plane's range was insufficient to—"

"No, Rahallah, I know Rockson lives! The mutant has uncanny luck. He must be clairvoyant, telepathic. Some of the mutants are rumored to be so. That would explain how he could outwit me—special powers. No ordinary man could." The premier seemed pleased at the face-saving explanation. "No, Rahallah, I need this Nazi army that so disturbs you to march against the so-called freedom fighters and their leader. *They* are the prime menace—even more than Colonel Killov. My stupid nephew, Zhabnov, has misjudged the whole battle—but I now know the danger these American rebels pose. But I promise you—once the rebels are exterminated, then we turn the Nazis loose on Killov."

Rahallah hesitated, then told the premier of his dream. When he had finished, Vassily was pale and shaken.

"I know of your great powers of medicine and prophecy," he stuttered out. "Can it be, Rahallah, son of the Plains Lion, that this will really happen?"

He grabbed his black servant by the collar of his tuxedo jacket. "When, *when* will I die—is it . . . soon?"

"I don't know, your excellency. I pray this fate can be averted. I will try to dream again—a solution. We must follow my dreams, must."

The entire White House and the surrounding grounds were now under the new plastisynth impenetrable dome—and President Zhabnov was pleased. This was more like it—winter outside, summer inside. He walked around his rose garden with white work gloves on, snipping the *Rosa Familiaris Cruxae* he had recently made by combining genetically spliced hybrid stocks. He glanced back past his aides towards the semicircular Ionic portico that held the Oval Office—the White House. The new paint, a glossy white, was shining in the dull sun that pierced through the towering three hundred-foot-high plastic dome above it. Clean, neat, that's the way he liked things. Gone were the huge concrete walls he had built for security around the presidential mansion. The clear foot-thick plastic was so much more unobtusive.

Zhabnov sighed. Turning back to his bushes he snipped a single blood-red rose off its dewy branch and held its fragrance to his fleshy nose. And sneezed. These hybrids didn't quite have the bouquet he had wished for. A nervous gardener handed him a handkerchief. He felt in such a good mood today that he said thank you. The aide was shocked. But why shouldn't he feel good? The sun was shining,

Premier Vassily was firmly on his side in the civil war against Killov—the Skull—and his rose garden was in full bloom.

Soon, Vassily's goose-stepping Nazi hordes would wipe out the American freefighters once and for all and then turn their might on Killov's Denver base. Then all would be right with the world once again. The ordinary affairs of state—not another disaster, not another convoy destroyed by rebel attack, or a bridge blown up—would awaken him each morning.

President Zhabnov snipped away at his American Beauty roses—Hybrid 5, Royal Russian stock—his prize-winner. There was a competition each year in Taskent, and each year his roses won. Over all the world's rose cultivators, he was number one. Zhabnov prided himself on that. There weren't many world leaders past or present who did more than rule. They didn't know a rose from an aster. But he was a first-rate horticulturist—a genius at creating new beauties for the White House gardens: hybrids of yellow-tipped, pink-tipped, red with green spots, a rainbow of soft-petaled flowers stretching out all around the mansion. He was a connoisseur of beauty—and that separated him from the rest of the power elite, all those generals and warlords who understood only cannon and blood.

He plucked the finest of each of the hybrids, the perfect specimens to send to the Taskent competition which was due to begin next month, handing each flower to aides rushing behind him who tremblingly took them, praying that they would not crush a single petal or . . . At last he reached the end of the garden and stared down at his newest creations—a bush filled with flesh-pink roses, their fleshy petals stretching out toward the sun like so many arms grabbing for the light. It reminded him of the little pink beauty his sex squads had found for him in Idaho and had flown to the White House for his pleasures tonight. He had seen the photos – a great catch – one of the little ones, a mere four-feet-ten-inches tall. And as innocent as the snowy land she was found wandering in. A real wild child that he could use to serve his whims.

He was eager to try her out. He snickered, wondering if she was big enough to take his ample member. Probably not. But he liked to hear the screams. It added to his pleasure. Pink – that was the color – just like the rose he now snipped and lifted from the bush. Pink-skinned little beauty, I will pluck your virginity tonight as easily as I pluck this rose.

"Ouch, damnit!" He sucked on his thumb as a single drop of blood squeezed out. "These goddamned thorns." Someday he would breed a rose without them.

Chapter Five

Rock's and Archer's lives were like a male dream of paradise for the next week. The big cats guarded the freefighters, always on alert outside the teepee, the women brought them food three times a day—roast succulent pigs, slabs of sizzling buffalo meat—and in the evening, their bodies. Reina was always the first to get Rockson. She would ride him two, three, even four times until she was so exhausted she could barely rise. Then the other women were allowed to partake of his manhood. But she would stand back and watch the goings-on with a jealous eye. Rockson could see that she wanted him all to herself. Several times Ishtar, the white-haired albino, who Rock had learned was the witch doctor of the tribe, tried to enter but each time Reina would reach for her knife and force the other woman out.

They were allowed to sleep seven hours each night to rest their weary bodies. In the early morning the stag horns were blown and they were awakened and "walked" through the leafy forest like pets at the end of a leash—for exercise. They were ordered to do calisthenics and climb vines to maintain their muscular builds. And like the cherished studs that they were, they were bathed and washed with gusto after their workouts.

On one of their forays into the woods they passed a small wooden temple, ornate and covered with depictions of naked women like wasp-waisted, watermelon-breasted Hindu goddesses in various complex poses carved in the hard wood. The temple was two stories high with an open space inside at the rear of which—Rock was permitted only to enter as far as the portal—amidst flickering animal-fat lamps, stood a giant stone-carved statue of the lake monster they had killed. Jewels gleamed from its body which stood nearly the full height of the temple, its flippers stretched out like a cross. Rock asked one of his Kreega guards, having picked up some of the lingo, what it was.

"This is for the two vestal virgins—the twin goddesses who live here and serve *L'Ogre*. They clean the temple and practice sexual abstinence." Rock saw the two women inside bowing to the monstrous statue. They were clothed in transparent gossamer robes, and unlike the other women who were black-haired these were blond with long flowing tresses and blue eyes. They were young—barely out of their teens.

"Why do they live here?" Rock asked. "Away from the tribe."

"So as not to be exposed to man-lust like we are. We keep the children pure—until they are twenty. They can talk to the animals; their purity allows *le tribe* to control the great cats." Inside, the two blond

Kreega were surrounded by a bevy of cats who glared out angrily at Rockson. He quickly moved on, but not before the virgins gave shy smiles.

I might have found the key to our survival today, Rockson realized, as he went through the proscribed exercises under the watchful eyes of eight Kreega armed with thick snakeskin whips. He glanced over at Archer who was in his two-hundredth pushup. The giant was red-faced. He hated this exercise period and was glad it was only for an hour each day. Paradise without exercise was what he wanted.

That evening Rock stirred Archer out of a deep sleep. "We've got to go," the Doomsday Warrior whispered. "We've got to get out of here. I've been analyzing their tribal structure—and the key is the virgins. If they are on our side the cats will not do anything to harm us."

Archer seemed dazed. "Goooo? We gooo? Rock-sssoon crazzy. Nooo gooo. This niiice. Meeat, wooman. Archeeer staaay." He turned his head and started to go back to sleep again.

Rock shook him awake. "You big fool. What do you think happens when they stop using us? When we get as many women pregnant as they wish? When we give out, even just a little bit? You've been given that blue liquid more and more. Mixed with your beer, haven't you?"

Archer nodded, bewildered. "It gooood. Make Archeer strong, make—"

"Have you seen the skeletons out past the garbage pit? All male skeletons—I know my anatomy. That's where they dump the men after they give out. The blue fluid robs you eventually of all your strength. It puts it into sex until you become weak as a kitten. What do you think they feed the panthers?"

"Meeeat," Archer answered hopefully.

"Man-meat. The cats never eat, do they? Not the whole time that we've been here. Have you seen the look in their eyes when they see us? How they drool? They don't drool when they look at the women, do they?" The immense freefighter suddenly looked very concerned.

"That's more like it, pal. I will try—and you can try too—to seduce the virgins. But don't do anything to actually deflower them. Control yourself for the first time in your life. We must tease and fondle and make them desire us—but don't enter them or we'll never get out of here alive. *Comprenez-vous?*" Rock was slipping into the French dialect from time to time as he heard it every minute around him. Archer nodded.

The next morning the Kreega women came to take them out for their exercise, first placing the collars on them under the watchful eyes of the cats. That afternoon, Rock winked at one of the virgins standing outside the temple. She blushed. Archer sent out a shit-eating grin at the other and she turned, red-faced, away. The flirting continued for several days until one night the two young blond women came to them, sneaking in through the back of the teepee. They dove on top of the two men with uncontrollable desire. Rock and Archer stroked their small pear-sized breasts, kissed their pink nipples. But they would not let the virgins push them down and mount them. They drove the girls to a frenzy, until they were nearly hysterical, and then sent them off in tears.

The plan was going to work. Sexual desire was the strongest instinct known to man—and woman. And Rockson was going to use it as a weapon to escape.

Trouble was brewing. Outside their jailhouse teepee, Rock and Archer could hear voices arguing loudly. They peeked through the flap on the front just as the dawn sun rose and saw Reina, the queen of the Kreega, and Ishtar, her hated challenger, standing face to face, their cheeks flushed with rage.

"Il est moi," Reina screamed. *"Le Rockson est moi."*

"Non, non," Ishtar yelled back just as loudly, her long chalk-white hair swinging behind her. *"Rockson ne vous pas. L'homme etes pour le tribe total."*

The disagreement over the use of Rockson's body grew louder and louder and though Rock couldn't understand half the words he got the drift. They both wanted him for themselves. The Doomsday Warrior felt a certain amused pride in being so desired. Ishtar suddenly reached forward and slapped Reina square in the face. There was sudden, complete silence from the other Kreega women who stood around the encampment watching, their mouths open, their faces frozen in shock. Reina stood back and smiled, a thin grim grin.

"Vous desirez la morte. Votre decision, bete." She turned on her heels and walked across the open area of the camp heading into her own tent, festooned with dayglow red and blue symbols of her power: running elk and deer, spears and knives. Ishtar stared after her for a few seconds and then rushed off to her

own tent at the far side of the village.

Rockson didn't know just what was about to happen—but obviously some sort of challenge had been thrown down . . . and accepted. This might be the moment they had been waiting for. They had already been in the Kreega's hands for nearly a week and though there was undeniably a certain amount of pleasurable activity involved in being their prisoners, Rock had more lofty plans in mind.

It was time to set the plan he had been formulating over the last few days in motion. The vestal virgins were working with the big cats in the center of the village—putting them through their paces, training them to perform increasingly complex tasks. The panthers were amazingly smart and seemed eager to learn. They were completely under the spell of the two blond-haired Kreega. Rock, his hands and feet bound as they always were when the Kreega were not using him for sexual service, crawled over to the teepee flap and motioned to the two beautiful young women. He couldn't yell or he would be noticed by others but after a few attempts he caught their eye. He smiled and gestured with his head for them to come to the teepee. The two virgins led the black carnivores back to their fenced-in pen and then with shy giggles, staring at one another nervously but filled with breathless anticipation, they headed over to the freefighters.

"Come in—*entrez*," Rock said with the most come-hither smile he could manage. Across the teepee prison, Archer heard the noise and with a groan opened his weary eyes. He had enjoyed all the sexual attention at first—but even paradise can become too much of a good thing. He had lost track of how many women he had had in the last seven days. When it rained, it hurricaned.

"Entrez, entrez," Rock said to the two virgins who seemed to hesitate slightly at the teepee entrance. But their desires were too powerful and overcame whatever reticence and fear they felt. They walked in and closed the flap behind them. Rock motioned for them to untie his hands and legs as he said, *"Je vous desire. Vous etes tres beaux."* The girls grew increasingly nervous, knowing that what they were doing was taboo. But desire is the strongest hunger of all and when it strikes, the rules fall by the wayside. Besides, it wasn't fair that all the other women of the tribe should get to experience the fruits of love and they should be left alone in their cold temple.

Rock wrapped his arms around the taller of the two and motioned for Archer to follow suit. The big freefighter blew out a deep breath, shook his head to wake himself up enough for the action and reached out for the young beautiful virgin who had untied him. Soon, the Kreega virgins were experiencing the highest pleasure of life on earth—but they were no longer virgins.

Outside, the Kreega warriors were stomping around, screaming as if all hell were about to break loose. The last Challenge had been years before and all knew that the future of their tribe would depend on who won the imminent battle between Reina and Ishtar. The women ritualistically drew the large fighting circle in the dirt about thirty feet in diameter. They put on their war makeup, jagged red and yellow stripes across their bodies, and sat at the edge of the circle waiting.

They didn't have to wait long. Within minutes the two challengers emerged from their tents and walked toward the circle, slowly, glaring at one another from across the open center of the camp. They looked fierce, terrifying with their full battle gear on. Each wore a fighting helmet made of a mountain stag's head. The fur covered the top of their skulls and from the stag skulls rose the dead creatures' horns, nearly five-feet long, thick and strong and capable of goring through flesh in a second. On their hands the two women wore the panther claws of dead cats. The cut-off paws were wrapped around their wrists coming nearly halfway up their forearms. The claws were extended, nearly six inches of razor-sharp, daggerlike weapons, able to slash open a stomach or a chest with a single swipe. Covering their chests were iron breastplates, one over each breast, covered with jewels and tied around their backs with leather straps. Each woman was unclothed beneath the waist but for their black fur loincloths and stripes painted down the sides of their legs—Reina, blue and Ishtar, green. The two warrior women reached the outer edge of the Challenge Circle as the Kreega women began beating on drums, pounding out a pulsating rhythm—the song of death. For two Kreega would enter the circle but only one would emerge alive. There was no mercy, no partial wounding. The Challenge would end when one of them lay dead in a pool of her own blood. The Kreega women looked excited, their pearly teeth flashing in cruel grimaces. This was their way. The strong ruled, the weak died and returned to the earth from which they had sprung.

Rock and Archer had completed their deflowering of the vestal virgins who lay back on the bearskin beds with dazed but happy looks on their flushed faces. They breathed deeply, amazed and delighted at their entrance into the world of women. The two freefighters on a signal from Rockson grabbed the love-swooning women and quickly tied them up, putting gags around their mouths so they couldn't scream.

"Sorry, girls," Rock said as he finished binding the females he had tenderly made love to just minutes before. "But we've got to get the hell out of here. And it's better that you're bound and gagged when the others find you. Tell them, *'Le Rockson make vous son prisoner.' Comprenez-vous?*" The two young Kreega women looked up at him with fear and betrayal in their sky-blue eyes. He felt rotten about it all. He had never hurt a woman in his life—and though these two certainly hadn't been hurt, still he knew they would face many problems from their adventures in the flesh. But then the freefighters hadn't asked to be made prisoner. He hoped they would survive.

He heard the drums outside suddenly stop and one of the Kreega women begin speaking. He peered cautiously through the teepee flap. A very tall and slender woman, herself with a stag helmet on her head but no other fighting apparel, was giving some sort of speech in the center of the circle. He could barely understand what she was saying but it was clear she was laying down the rules of the fight—and from what Rock could gather, there weren't any. Anything was allowed. Any dirty trick they could come up with was part of the Challenge. There was only one outcome and that was life for one and death for the other. The gods were looking down—they would decide who deserved to be the victor.

The speaker stepped back and the drums began again, louder, ever louder, as if the very bowels of the earth itself were pounding out the war beats. The Kreega starter of the Challenge lifted a torch in her hands and looked at both women, who had eyes only for one another as they shifted from toe to toe preparing their strong bodies for mortal combat. The starter let the torch fall to the ground and the moment it hit, Reina and Ishtar charged into the center of the circle, their clawed hands outstretched and flailing at the air.

They tore into one another like rams battling for supremacy. Reina let Ishtar think she was going to attack claws first and waited for her opponent to get within two yards. Then she suddenly lowered her immense stag horn helmet and charged into her adversary. Ishtar stopped dead in her tracks and tried to lower her own helmet to meet the attack. But her head was only halfway down when the sharp horns caught her full in the chest. The breastplates made of inch-thick steel prevented the horns from piercing her but she was knocked backwards, falling down in the hard-packed dirt of the combat arena. She rolled over twice as Reina slashed down with the razor claws but found only dirt.

Rock watched with fascination as the two female warriors battled it out about fifty yards away. The full attention of the tribe was on the fight. Every woman in the village stood around the outer edge of the circle, watching, wondering who their next leader, their queen would be. The two challengers circled one another more slowly now, riveted to the other's eyes, waiting for the flash of the pupil indicating an attack. Reina had hoped to take out the younger, less experienced Ishtar with the first thrust. But it hadn't worked. She knew the albino was tough—but not as tough as her. Reina had ruled for nearly ten years, since her mother had died. And she had killed many times. She would wait until Ishtar made her move—then she would strike.

Rock knew the time was as right as it would ever be. They had to make their move now. The fight could be over at any moment. Death, when it comes, moves fast, its skeletal fingers taking their due in a blur of blood.

"Come on, man," he whispered to Archer. "Time to head home." The big freefighter still seemed a trifle less than enthusiastic about leaving. After all, when would so many beautiful women crave his body in such a way again. With a deep sigh, he followed the Doomsday Warrior to the back end of the tent, taking a final look at the two non-virgins who struggled furiously to get out of their binds. He walked suddenly back and planted a soft kiss on their foreheads. In spite of his immense size and strength the near-mute was at heart a soft and tender man. He didn't want them to remember him with hate. Their eyes softened for a moment as they seemed to understand his message. Whatever happened to them now they had at least fulfilled their womanhood—and for this, even within their anger, they were grateful.

"Jesus Christ," Rock hissed from the far end of the

teepee. "Another kiss and you're going to end up panther chow. Come on." Archer turned and grabbed his crossbow which had been hung on the inner wall of the animal-hide tent. He rushed over to Rock who, using one of the long hunting knives from the belt of the Kreega he had deflowered, quickly sliced through the thick deerskin hide of the enclosure.

The two men slithered through the rip and crawled on their hands and knees through the dirt behind the teepee to some low bushes about fifty feet away. The moment they hit the other side of the shrubs they tore ass in a half crouch toward thick woods about a quarter mile off. Rockson prayed the fight would last long enough to give them a good start—and that the Kreega would be unable to control the panthers now that the virgins had been made impure. Because this time, he knew, the warrior women would not greet them with such open arms. Behind him he could hear the drums pounding fiercely in deep rhythmic patterns.

Reina and Ishtar continued to circle one another for nearly a minute before the albino made her charge. She thought she saw a weakness in Reina's foot movements—her legs crossing one another as she continued to circle. If she could just catch her when her legs were off balance, perhaps . . . Ishtar timed her charge just as Reina lifted her left leg and then rushed forward, her stag horn helmet lowered. But Reina caught the glint in the charging albino's eyes and pulled back, not completing her step. Ishtar charged past, the stag horns missing Reina by not more than an inch. But an inch was enough. Reina slammed down with both clawed hands into her opponent's back as she rushed by, bent over. The long curved claws dug deeply into the straight white back, gouging out ten slashes along the backbone. Torrents of blood gushed forth, drenching the woman warrior's flesh. Ishtar fell forward from the blow, slamming into the dirt on her chest plates. She tried to rise but was not quick enough. Reina, without a moment's hesitation, bent over and drove her horned helmet into the struggling enemy's back. The horns sank in nearly a foot, driving Ishtar to the ground, severing her backbone in four places. She flopped wildly for a few seconds and then was still, her eyes staring down at the bloody dirt—eyes that could no longer see.

The queen of the Kreega stood up straight, her face flushed with victory as the lifeblood from her dead challenger spurted out in thick gushes from the gaping wounds in her back. The heart still pumped although its body was already turning cold. Reina turned around and around in the center of the circle raising her arms to the sky.

"Merci, mère L'Ogre," she screamed triumphantly. *"Je suis le queen de la Kreega."* When she had finished her thanks to the gods she fixed her eyes on the women of the tribe. *"Desirez-vous, challenge moi?"* she asked them. But none would take up the challenge. Reina was the queen. For now. The strongest, the toughest. The vision of Ishtar's blood-soaked body would stay with them all for a long time—until some other aggressive warrior, dreaming secretly of the queenship, raised the courage to strike her down. But for today her position was built in stone and blood. The Kreega all bowed to her as she continued

to turn.

Suddenly they heard shouts from the prisoners' tent. *"Les hommes sont disappearez,"* one of the Kreega who had rushed from the audience in sexual excitement for a brief fling yelled out. The tribe jumped to their feet and ran to the teepee. They found the two virgins tied up. Reina ran to the panther pen and opened the doors.

"Destroyez!" she screamed out in rage, pointing to where she could just see the two men disappearing into the thick forests to the south of camp. The panthers looked confused. The mental control that the virgins had exerted over them was gone. Yet still they were the creatures of the Kreega. They ran frantically around the camp not sure what to do, growling and snapping at one another—primitive beasts once again without the firm guidance of the telepathic commands they had always obeyed.

The leader of the carnivores, nearly seven-feet long, understood the commands and tore off in the direction that Reina was pointing. But only one of the other cats took up pursuit; the rest were confused, frantic. For the first time in their lives, without the commands coming to them, they reverted to a more primitive state, clawing and snarling at the women who edged away, reaching for their weapons.

Rockson and Archer hit the edge of the forest and rushed into the covering canopy of thick brown trees. They had to slow down a little to avoid the twisted gnarled branches which jutted out from everywhere but still managed to keep up a fairly fast pace. They had gone perhaps a quarter mile when Rock heard twigs snapping behind him.

"Look out," he screamed to Archer, turning and reaching for the knife he had stolen. But the immense panther was upon him before he could defend himself. It knocked him flat over and instinctively snapped out for Rockson's jugular. Rock prepared to die, steeling himself for the fanged clamp of the predator's jaws. But it never came. The weight of the four hundred-pound cat on his back suddenly went limp and the Doomsday Warrior quickly rolled out from underneath. Archer's last remaining arrow lay imbedded in its throat. Rock flashed a quick smile of thanks and the thumbs-up sign to Archer who began to smile back. But the expression suddenly changed to horror as his eyes took in the second black shape hurtling through the woods. This time Rock had a second of warning. He jumped to the side as the smaller panther leaped with fully extended claws. Rock plunged the knife into the creature's side and instantly pulled it out again. The panther turned, showing its fangs and letting out a thunderous roar of anger and pain. It jumped again, this time landing full on Rockson's chest, knocking both of them to the ground. Rock stabbed up with the blade again and again, into the thing's chest and stomach as its jaws locked onto his arm. He could feel the teeth sinking into his flesh but didn't have time to feel the pain. After the fifth deep thrust the cat relaxed its hold and then, as if surprised that anything so puny could hurt it, fell over onto its side, its guts spewing out through the shiny black fur onto the black and brown leaf-covered ground. Rock thrust the knife a final time—deep into the carnivore's throat. At last it was still, a scarlet puddle of blood spreading out from beneath its motionless form.

Archer rushed over and reached down for Rock, a terrified look in his huge brown eyes as he saw the Doomsday Warrior coated with blood. Rockson took hold of the baseball-mitt-sized hand and rose from the ground. He winced as he touched his bleeding arm and peeled back the shirt. The teeth had sunk into his upper muscle, but the bites were clean. It didn't feel like anything had been torn and the slow leak of blood indicated that no arteries had been severed. He ripped a nearby vine and tied a tourniquet around his upper arm. It would have to do.

The Doomsday Warrior walked back to Archer and both of them stared down at the dead cats, their power and grace now smeared with pungent blood. Rock felt a certain twinge of sorrow at their destruction. They were nature's creatures, carrying out their own unthinking commands. But death didn't see beauty or ugliness. When it came time to go—all things were equal in the grim specter's dark eyes.

Chapter Six

Rock knew they were somewhere in what had been central Iowa—but just where he had no idea. The two freefighters had traveled for nearly two days before stopping. The prospect of being taken captive again by the Kreega was strong motivation to keep going even when their feet painfully told them to stop. The land was fertile in this part of the country. The big bombs had only fallen in a few spots, and though their craters were still as devoid of life as the dark side of the moon, within miles of them dense almost tropical thick forests had sprung up, complete with hundred-foot ferns and dark red vines that snaked around their trunks, disappearing high in the air. They found wild fruit and berries and were able to bag an occasional rabbit, throwing the knife Rock had taken. Archer was now without arrows; his last shot into the panther's neck had snapped the shaft in two. He was unable to make the machine-crafted steel arrows out here in the woods and grumbled from time to time, feeling naked without his customary armaments. He hoped that nothing bigger than a fox would start sniffing at them.

They moved during the day and slept when the sun fell from the purple skies, building fires shielded by groves of trees just in case red spy-drones were planning a surprise visit. Out here in the middle of nowhere, without weapons, Rockson didn't feel like having to take on a parachute commando force of Red army goons.

On the third day after their escape from the Kreega they came to a vast plains which swept off in all directions as far as the horizon. The land was dark, almost metallic looking and didn't appear to have a single tree or bush in sight. They headed down a long rocky slope onto the flatlands and gingerly edged out onto the smooth terrain. Rockson remembered once before going out onto smooth ground—which had turned out to be composed of glasslike crystal that had opened up beneath him and his party taking two lives. This time he would be more careful. He motioned for Archer to hold back for a moment as he walked several feet out onto the nearly smooth, steel-hard ground. It was firm at least. In fact it seemed to be made of metal, without the slightest resiliency or give. He stomped his foot hard and it hurt. But it would hold them up.

"All right, pal, let's get going. I don't know what the hell's out there but we gotta get across. Just keep your eyes open." The two freefighters headed out across the hard ground, gingerly at first, and then as they gained confidence in not being sucked down into its innards, hitting a good pace. As the noon sun beat down through a clear sky, tinged only with a few lazily drifting wisps of strontium-green poison high in the atmosphere, Rock could see that the iron-hard surface was grooved and ridged like the sides of a piece of machined metal. At certain angles it gave off an almost rainbowlike coloration, as oil does, shifting, translucent, reds and greens and aqua blues all melting together. But the color was within the surface itself, not just on the top as there was no trace of slipperiness as they walked. After they had gone for about an hour Rock began noticing small inch-high formations popping up here and there on the surface. He stopped and looked closer and saw what looked like shavings of metal piled atop one another. He reached out to touch one but the shape pulled back suddenly.

"Jesus Christ," Rock muttered, jumping back from the thing. "It's alive." He examined it carefully, circling the shiny metallic lifeform and took out his knife. When he held it toward the thing, the shavings leaped toward the metal, the structure exploding out in a puff of dust. It was magnetic – held together by its own magnetic energy system. The particles began banding together on the long blade, surrounding it. Within seconds they had formed a pythonlike grip and began tightening around the steel blade. Did the things eat metal? Rock wondered in amazement. He took a piece of the bandana he had been wearing around his neck to absorb his sweat and wiped it along the edge of the knife. The living filings came off easily. He didn't know if they had a taste for human flesh or not and threw the handkerchief to the ground. Within seconds, the filings had moved back onto the surface and reformed into their original knoblike shape.

"All right, let's go," Rock said, motioning toward Archer who had been watching in consternation, wondering just what in blazes Rockson was so interested in – and if his brain was starting to evaporate from the heat.

But it was just another bizarre lifeform that seemed to be the rule rather than the exception in modern America. Archer had seen enough mutations and monstrosities to not even pay them any mind—unless they tried to eat him. But Rockson was always on the lookout for new information, new life. He stockpiled everything he came across in his mind for future reference. The earth was now a madhouse of living things but if man was ever to retake his rightful dominance over the planet, he damned well better know what was out there. This would be the first case of living metal Rockson had ever seen. Dr. Shecter would be fascinated back in Century City. If they ever got there.

They went on for miles, the flat terrain unchanging, other than the subtle shading of the steel surface which turned from black to a slightly browner color, almost of rust. More and more of the metallic scrap structures appeared as they went on, growing larger, some nearly a foot high. They leaned toward the two freefighters as if sensing them in some unknown way—but seemed to have little real interest in anything that wasn't made of metal, and quickly pulled back again. Their free-floating iron particle formations held in an energy configuration took on the rough appearance of cactuses made of scraps, twirls and razor-sharp slivers of glistening steel. The ultra-hard ground seemed to go on endlessly as the two freefighters trudged on, searching for some sort of change ahead. But not a blade of grass dared take root in such hostile soil.

Suddenly the air seemed to grow an eerie blue, luminescent, pulsing. They both felt a shift in air pressure as their flesh crawled with static electricity, the hair on their arms and head standing up straight.

Something was building—some energy overload was occurring and Rock didn't like it at all. But there was nothing to do except move straight ahead. "Come on, let's double-time it," Rock shouted to Archer and they started running at a medium pace side by side. The sky overhead began growing darker, filled with swirling thick masses of clouds, tinged with the same ominous blue core as the air, as if it were almost on fire, sending out a glow like that of a throbbing heart of the purest dark energy. The two men ran now at full speed, not wanting to get caught in the imminent storm.

Suddenly the pent-up electricity of the cloud mass released explosive bolts of jagged lightning, piercing the sky everywhere above the freefighters. It was as if an army of gods were hurling their spears from the clouds as the yellow slashing swords of electricity slammed into the metal ground all around them. A jolt snapped down with a shrieking whistle just feet ahead of them, sending out a thunderous roar as it exploded into the ground, releasing its ten-million-volt charge in a single burst. Rock and Archer felt the electricity travel through the metal surface of the ground and literally lift them up like a giant hand. It threw them flying into the air. They both fell unconscious for a second or two as the exquisite pain of the bolt—a sensation beyond sensation—coursed through their bodies. Then they hit the steel surface of the mutated land around them hard. Rock rubbed his head as another cracking bolt slashed into the earth. He began to rise when his eye caught a dim glow far ahead in the cloudy darkness. And it was coming straight at them.

"Down, down!" the Doomsday Warrior yelled to Archer who was just beginning to rise. The big freefighter looked confused but had been through too much with

Rock not to instantly heed his warnings. He slammed down onto the hard terrain, throwing his hands over his head. The dim light suddenly grew brighter and then turned into a screaming ball of electricity which tore just over their heads and went burning off into the darkening air, flying just a foot above the ground.

"Ball lightning," Rock whistled between his teeth. He had read about it in Shecter's science video library. It had never been positively proven to exist—but it did. It sure as hell did, Rock thought, as another one of the energy balls, this one shining as brightly as a white star, rushed forward and straight at them. Nearly three feet in length, the lightning ball seemed to be shooting out rays from every side, strands of million-volt tendrils, pulsating and reaching down toward the metal ground to release their charge.

Suddenly they were whizzing over the freefighters, coming from everywhere. They seemed to drop down from the black and purple twisting snakepit of clouds that were now just several hundred feet above the ground and then took off like so many billiard balls of blue and white and yellow, searching for opposite polarity—for discharge. Rock knew they weren't really *after* him in the sense of hunting, but were carrying out the laws of physics blindly and obediently—all things reach toward their equalization, their neutralizing. Still, he knew that if any of the pulsing lightning balls, too bright to even look directly at, should open up its storehouse of energy on one of them, it would be the fastest barbecue in history—well-done and on the burnt side.

"Stay down, don't move!" Rock yelled over to Archer who didn't seem able to hear him with the explosions of the bolts and the balls of lightning that surrounded them in a maelstrom of electric death. The Doomsday Warrior motioned with his hand, lifting it up and realizing as he did that he was creating a ground for the ball lightning. One of them came toward the upraised hand flying at nearly two hundred mph. But Rock saw it off in the distance shooting at him like a meteorite and slammed down into the stone-hard ground whipping his hand to his side. He breathed out and made himself as small as possible, stretching his body flat trying to become part of the earth. The buzzing ball of death shot past him, just inches over his back and tore in a straight line toward the far mountains behind them.

Rockson knew the better part of valor sometimes is to do absolutely nothing. Not even move one inch. So he didn't. Archer, as well, had gotten the message and was trying to make himself as flat as a pancake. The storm clouds undulated overhead like a sea of black piranha. At last the energy dissipation seemed to release enough of the stored megawatts in the storm's innards—and the clouds lifted up from the ground and quickly evaporated high above. The sun came out and it was clear, cobalt blue, the sun pure and perfect like a shimmering pearl.

The freefighters rose, shook themselves off and looked at each other. Archer tilted his head to the side and whistled. Rock laughed. "Yeah, that was as close as they come—and you still get to talk about it. I think I must have gotten a flat-top haircut from one of those electric balls." He ran his palm across the white streak that cut down the center of his midnight black, unkempt hair. But it was all still there.

They started forward again and walked for hours, not daring to rest in the event that the storm returned. At last, as the sun began sinking a putrid brown in the far sky, they saw a low range of hills ahead. They walked toward them, the hills growing ever so slowly until suddenly they were upon them. They hit the first foothills at midnight as a brilliant moon cut its scythe across the dark slopes. They started up the first rise, eventually stepping on earth that gave a little, rather than the steel terrain they had left behind. Something with weeds and flowers and grass instead of metal filings. As they reached the peak and started down the other side they could scarcely believe their eyes. There, below them, was a series of dirt roads coming together and meeting at the foot of a neon-lit twenty-four-hour diner.

The diner stood in the center of a blacktop parking lot as if it were still 1989, as if the war had never occurred, as if it were still the old America now seen only on crumbling picture postcards. It was all chrome and glass with black and white stripes running down the sides, giving it an almost zebralike appearance. Above it a huge red neon sign flashed out JOE'S DINER, blinking on and off every two seconds. Huge picture windows ran around the entire structure and the two freefighters could see, even from several hundred yards away, that the place was packed. They descended the gravelly slope and made their way through the parking lot filled with a bizarre collection of vehicles—VW bugs, schoolbuses, trucks and tractor-trailers, and huge tail-finned cars, all standing side by side like some sort of twentieth century automotive museum. They were rusted halfway through and many had missing doors, hoods, even roofs—but they obviously worked. Somehow the damned things had been kept in running condition. Both men had seen many strange things in their travels, but this was unquestionably a new peak of madness in the myriad twists and turns that American culture had taken in the postwar world.

They hesitated at the entrance, looking at one another with raised eyebrows.

"Hungry?" Rock asked Archer.

"Fooood," the mountain-sized man replied, licking his lips as the odors of sizzling meat and thick rich stews wafted through the walls.

"Well, let's sample the chow," the Doomsday Warrior said, pushing open the glass door.

Inside it was like a time warp as Rock in his Russian military khakis and Archer with his cavemanlike fur vest and deerskin pants walked into the crowded diner. Bobby-soxed teenage girls were dancing near a jukebox with their young men in jeans and turtleneck sweaters, twirling them around. They rocked to the tune of "Beat It," their bodies soaked with sweat. The clock on the wall said 12:30—but incredibly the calendar with a yellowed pinup of Raquel Welch said July 1, 1989. Rock, with Archer trailing nervously behind him, sauntered up to the pink formica counter and sat down on one of a row of red stools that ran along the front. No one seemed to give them more than a brief glance which was hardly surprising as the dinner crowd were all dressed in full-fledged regalia from the last century. It was like a fashion show circa the late 1980's, with men in full suits and ties sitting with their families at booths, happily chewing away. Their wives wore white, pink or green sweaters, their hair tied back in little bows, while the children were attired in miniature versions of Mom's and Dad's outfits. Each booth seemed to be a microcosm of a particular subculture from the old world. One table was crowded with men in cowboy hats and gold-buttoned embroidered shirts, another group wore baseball uniforms complete with team caps. Along the counter sat everything from Indians with feathered headdress to Wall Street executive types, attache cases at their sides. Rock wondered if they'd walked into a madhouse.

A blond waitress on the other side of the counter wiped a greasy hand on a stained white apron. She wore a white paper hat and was chewing gum as she held a griddlecake flipper in the other hand. A glass-encased menu hung on the pink wall behind her with a list of everything from Snar-lizard Stew to Buffalo Burgers to apple pie to choose from.

"What'll you have, bub?" she asked with a sexy smile that revealed poorly capped rows of teeth in a heavily lipsticked mouth that chewed furiously on a piece of gum.

"Well, er, what do you got?" Rock asked.

"Can't you read? Menu's right on the wall," the waitress snapped back. "Wait a second, I got a customer down the counter. Be right back." She eyed Archer as the giant gingerly settled down on the stool next to Rock's, which creaked with a loud groan.

The two freefighters craned their necks as they went down the list. "I think I'm going to have some of those burgers," Rock said to his compatriot, having read about them but never having experienced their culinary delights.

"Archeer want steeeak. Loootts steeaks." The waitress walked back over to them and smiled.

"Ready to order fellas?" she asked. "You get french fries and salad with any entree." She licked a well-worn pencil with the tip of her tongue. Rock noticed she had the word Shirley sewn in red over the right side of her cream-colored waitress jacket and the words JOE'S DINER, ROUTE 6, over the other breast. And breasts they were, straining in propped-up glory under her tight jacket. She smiled at Rock's attention.

"Like what you see? Well, buster, it *ain't* on the menu! Now what'll the big fella have?"

"Nooo salaad—meeat, meeat!" Archer grumbled.

"Gotcha, bud," Shirley said, scribbling with a quick twist of the pencil into a little tear-off pad. "Now you, handsome, what'll you have?"

"Two buffalo burgers, rare and some hot apple pie with vanilla ice cream on top." He looked at her curiously, wondering if they were really going to get these archaic treats.

"Hey, George," she yelled into the kitchen. "Two buffalo T-bones with the works and a pair of B-burgers—rare—lots of fries." She smiled at the two of them as if taking them in for the first time. She tapped Archer on the chest and asked slyly, "You one of them rich trappers that blow by here now and then? You got dough?" Archer just stared at her, mystified. "What's the matter with your friend here? He don't talk much except about meat."

"He's shy," Rock said with a grin.

"He got a lady friend?"

"Unfortunately he does," Rock answered, sensing the direction the conversation was taking.

"Well, just my luck," Shirley said, chewing her gum faster. "The rich ones are always taken. How about you, handsome, you're a cute guy. But this trapper pal of yours has all the expensive, *and smelly*," she added in a whisper, "furs. You must be the poor one of the pair, wearing those filthy khakis. People usually dress up when they come to Joe's."

"We've got enough to pay for the meal here." Rock smiled. "Thanks to my trapper friend here."

"I didn't say you looked that poor, stranger. We trust people here. Lots of folks swear by our food. We're just one big happy family at Joe's. Ain't we?" she half-yelled over to some of the customers seated on the stools.

"Yeah sure," a couple of truckdrivers nursing their cups of steaming black coffee muttered back from a few feet away. Rock wanted to ask the big semi-drivers just what the hell they were hauling out here in the middle of nowhere and where it was going. But he didn't feel like getting into a barroom brawl. Asking too many questions in a strange place when you're outnumbered twenty-to-one by a bunch of anachronisms wasn't a good idea. They'd just eat without questioning where the food came from and get out.

The waitress returned several minutes later with their steaming plates of food. She slammed them down on the counter and then handed them each a glass full of a dark liquid. Archer's meal disappeared in six quick bites washed down by the bubbling beverage.

"Here's your orders, mister," Shirley said, looking askance at Archer. "The Coke's on the house—comes with the dinner. Say, you guys got something to trade of course for your meals. We deal in barter here—tobacco, pelts, ammo, stuff like that's OK. What do you got—before I order another round of T-bone for your hungry friend?"

"Well, we've got some gold coins," Rock answered, taking a bite of the juicy burger and a sip of the legendary Coca-Cola which he had never tasted before. "Will that do?" Rock rolled a twenty-ruble gold coin from his Russian Emergency Pack across the table. The waitress's face twitched.

"Put that away mister. Guys around here get plenty jumpy when they see loot like that. I don't know if I have enough change for something that big."

"We'll be ordering some food to go—you have things to go, don't you?" the Doomsday Warrior asked, taking a big mouthful of the deliciously greasy fries.

"Mister, for a double-eagle gold piece, you can have all the food in the place. Where the hell did you blow in from anyway?"

"From up north," Rock mumbled between bites.

"North—incredible," Shirley said, her eyes widening. "How far, Pritchyard Junction?"

"No, Lake Superior." Rock said it a little too loud. The chatter stopped around the diner. A tree-sized man rose from his nearby booth and came walking over.

"You shitting liar, mister," the tree said angrily. "There ain't no north—not since the big tornados of 1989."

"Tornados?" Rock asked incredulously. "You mean the all-out *nuclear war*?" Shirley gasped, dropping a plate on the countertop.

"Mister," the tree said slowly between clenched teeth. "You start rumors like that—that there was some damned nuke war back then—and I'll have your hide. Stories like that cause trouble around here. We call '89 the year of the big tornados." He squinted his eyes at both of the freefighters. "Get me?"

Rock was mad for a split second, but then thought better of it. "Yeah—we get you." The big man smiled.

"Well now, that's better—ain't it, folks? The fella made a little mistake. Now it's all right. Hey, folks, get back to eating. Anyone got a nickel for the juke?"

Rock remembered the anthropology lectures by Dean Keppel back in Century City. "Never buck a local superstition, Rock, it could mean your life. People like to be affirmed in their beliefs—no matter how bizarre it may appear to you." So the folks around here didn't even believe there had been a war. So be it. He slapped Archer on the back to relax him. The big freefighter was still glaring over at the table of the tree ready to have a go at it. But the second helping of steak appeared in the nick of time and Archer dug in.

"Eat hearty, my friend—we have lots of credit here." Archer did—and then ordered again.

Chapter Seven

When they'd finished eating as much as they could possibly stuff into their stomachs, both men felt exhausted. Rock wished he could get a bath and just sack out for the night—without half-naked panther women tying him up, or flaming balls of lightning on his tail. The waitress noticed Rock's weariness and suggested the Three Little Bears Motel just down the road about a hundred yards.

"You have to watch carefully," she said. "The neon sign's been out for years. But they got good clean rooms and—" she leaned forward so as not to be heard by the other diners—, "back behind the office is a little room where a gambling man and his friend could find some high-stakes players. If there's more where that twenty piece came from." She winked. "Just tell 'em, Shirley sent you. After you check in and all."

"I'm afraid," Rock said, "we're dog-tired. We'll probably just get some sleep and—"

"Game goes on twenty four hours a day," Shirley

continued, wiping the counter with a peculiar white towel made of bubbly white paper that seemed to absorb any spills quickly. "You can go in anytime. Someone will be there to take your money—or give you his. The game's fair. The motel owner, Morrie Maliber, won't have it any other way. It's good for biz."

Rockson thanked her kindly and the two freefighters slogged back out to the road. Archer had been given some pink liquid from a tablespoon by Shirley that seemed to have cured his indigestion after all those steaks and fries and donuts. Now all he complained about was, "Sleeeep, sleeeep."

"Yeah, me too, pal. You and I will rent a nice soft bed for ourselves. Maybe three—two for you and one for me." They walked down the dark road and easily found the motel deep set in a grove of pine trees with its paint peeling off and its sign—three bears sleeping in feather beds—half hanging from its hinges. The filthy khaki-clad Rockson and the pungent beaver-fur-jacketed Archer made quite a pair as they rang the bell to the office.

"Door's open," a voice yelled out from inside as a table lamp was switched on. The motel manager, dressed in a red lumberjack jacket, his head as devoid of hair as an egg, was yawning loudly. He eyed them suspiciously. "Can you pay?" he asked. "Up front."

"Shirley sent us," Rock said, rolling a shiny gold piece across the wood counter. The motel keep snagged it and quickly bit into the coin.

"Damned if it ain't real." He smiled broadly. "The name's Maliber, Morrie Maliber, hospitality chief of the Three Little Bears. I got a nice double—big beds, shower and everything. And you probably know about our . . . parlor." He pointed to a door which was open to the back room just a crack. Cigarette and cigar smoke drifted out amidst the sounds of cards slapping down on a table.

"Yeah, thanks," Rock said. "But we have to clean up and get some shut-eye. Maybe later."

"Well, sure, any friend of Shirley's a friend of mine," the manager said. "I'll ring for the bellboy." Maliber pounded a little bell on the counter, put a small round red hat on and came around the front. "If you'll follow me this way, sir." He led them outside and down a few yards to one of a row of small bungalos. The room inside was big and comfortable—wood panelled with pictures of seagulls hanging on the walls. It even had an ancient television set inside. "Sheets, towels, everything's all ready," Maliber said, waiting by the door with an expectant look on his face.

"Oh yeah," Rock muttered, remembering the etiquette of old. He took out the smallest coin he could find, a five-ruble silver piece and handed it to the man. Maliber's eyes lit up like pinball bumpers.

"Thank you, thank you very much, sir, and I hope you have a pleasant night." He gently closed the door but they could hear him laughing out loud as he walked back to the office.

Rock tested the bed—soft as cotton and then walked over to the TV set. He knew it had to be dead but couldn't resist turning the knob. It lit up—with a picture of John Wayne, lit from behind by a light bulb, staring out at him. A voice on some kind of record spoke out from the speaker. "Reach for it, pardner, or I'll blast you to the sky. Reach for it, pardner, or I'll blast you to sky." The recording played over and over, skipping slightly on a scratch. Rock turned it off. Somehow he doubted that ancient TV had been quite like that.

He heard noises from the other room. Archer was already in the shower, humming his version of "Home on the Range."

"Save some soap—and water—for me," Rock yelled, flopping down onto one of the two massive beds made out of tree logs. The images of the diner kept sweeping through his mind like a mad dream. Just when he thought he'd seen it all, something would pop up to challenge any ideas he had about becoming jaded.

The water stopped and Archer came out wrapped in a towel that barely covered his midsection—with the three bears printed on it.

"You must be Poppa Bear," Rock joked, rising and heading for the shower himself. He took a long one, washing off the grease and dirt of their last few days' ordeal. When he came out he heard elephantlike noises from one of the beds. Archer was snoring like a buzzsaw. But Rock was so tired that the second he hit the cool white sheets he fell into a deep sleep—snores or no snores.

The doorbell to their cabin rang when it was already bright and sunny outside. It was Maliber, holding a tray of scrambled eggs and bacon. "Breakfast in bed. You might want to tip the bellboy, gentlemen," he said, the absurd little hat perched on his head like a red bird's nest. Rock found another small silver coin and pressed it into the motel manager's meaty hand. "Thanks, mister. Checkout's at 11:00—unless you want to pay for another night."

"What's the daily rate?" Rock asked. Maliber took his bellboy cap off again.

"Ten dollars each per night—plus five for the water."

"Sounds steep," Rock said, aware of his dwindling supply of gold.

"Mister, this here's the only operating motel north of the Mason-Dixon line. You're lucky as hell to find us."

"Well, maybe I can win some of it back in the game room," Rock said, grinning.

"That's the spirit," Maliber said. "You might. Then again . . . "

Rockson grabbed his plate off the tray just as Archer was about to consume it, having long since finished his. "Not so fast, pal," the Doomsday Warrior said. "I may be smaller than you but I got to eat too." Their clothes had been cleaned and pressed overnight and lay folded over an armchair by the window. "Never knew these leggings were brown, not soot black," Rock remarked to Archer. "And that white shirt offsets your beard very nicely. Come on—we have to win some of that money back."

They entered the back room where a card game was in progress. Five stone-faced men looked up as the two freefighters came in and sat down around the green felt-top table.

"We're playing poker—five card draw," the dealer said. "You know the game?"

"I've played a few hands," Rock answered, putting his elbows up on the table. The men introduced themselves. The dealer was Handsome Jack, with black Stetson hat and bow tie, who looked as smooth as the red silk vest he wore. Next, Bart the Bastard with his thin mustache and dark leather jacket. "Watch out for him," Maliber, who had come into the room, whispered in Rock's ear. "He might have an ace up his sleeve—or a gun." Then there was One-Eyed Swamprat, a goofily grinning toothless old man with lots of what looked like gold staples in his ears and almost pink colored hair, who seemed friendly enough despite his weird appearance. At the far end of the table were two beefy lumberjacks in blue jack shirts, who looked Rockson up and down coldly.

Handsome Jack took a drag of a rhubarb cigarette and dealt the cards like a pro, snapping them out at lightning speed around the table. The stakes were small at first but quickly grew as they downed coffee after coffee and the room filled with acrid smoke. Rock tried one of the cigs offered by Handsome Jack. "A mixture of rhubarb and swamp-grown tobacco," giggled One-Eyed Swamprat, as Rock choked and blew out the wretched-tasting smoke. "Grewed it myself on pig manure," Swamprat said, taking a deep drag.

"Great." Rock frowned, guzzling a cup of the good hot brew. That at least was real.

With Rock's PSI ability he could sense if the person who was raising had anything or was just bluffing. It paid off. A pile of gold pieces, watches, jewels and rings filled his side of the table. Handsome Jack looked more and more disturbed and at last took out a big silver-handled revolver, placing it on the table in from of him. "To keep it honest." He smiled.

"Suits me," Rock said. "I never cheat."

"Mighty lucky fellow," Maliber said. "But I've been watching him. He ain't cheatin', Handsome. Relax." But the gun wasn't removed.

Handsome Jack won a few rounds but Rockson thought he saw something flick down his sleeve several times. He placed his long-bladed Kreega knife on the table next to his cards. "To keep it honest," he said between tight lips.

"Sure," Handsome snapped. But there were no more movements down the sleeve. Soon the crew—except for Rock and Handsome—were out of cash and madly scribbling IOUs. Maliber's lumberjack friend, who was apparently a cousin of his named Surefoot, was down on his luck that day and finally opened a greasy wallet from which he extracted a key. "Keys to my '83 Buick Roadmaster, specially equipped for long hauls in hostile territory. Guess that keeps me in the pot—must be worth one thousand rubles at least."

"I'd like a look at it," Rock said as it was his twenty-ruble gold pieces that were being met.

"Just take a look out the window there," Surefoot said, pointing to the back of the room. Rockson rose and pulled back the yellow curtains and looked out behind the motel. It was a beautiful-looking machine. Red, with hardly any rust and huge thick-treaded tires. Some sort of chimney had been punched right through the roof and it appeared to have a square sheet of steel welded to the back. Rock closed the curtain and turned, sitting back down at the table.

"Does it go?" he asked.

"Go? Man, that thing will beat hell out of anything on the goddamned roads," Surefoot said proudly. "Runs on alcohol, got the engine in the back seat and a two hundred-gallon storage tank. Got a machine gun—a .55—mounted in the front and that there inch-thick steel sheet on the back. Fuckin' thing will stop a cannon. Also got an instant fuel-dump, which shoots all the alcohol out in case of an accident or something. Also got—"

"OK, OK," Rock said, holding his hand up. "I believe you. All right, I'll accept the car as equal to the stakes on the table. Deal," he said to Handsome Jack. Rock watched him carefully. He noticed eye signals between Surefoot and Handsome during the game. They were working together to get Rock.

Sure enough, Surefoot threw a full house on the table—kings and queens. He reached out to rake in the fortune in jewelry and gold as the stakes had been raised and raised.

"Hold it," Rock said. He threw down a royal straight, higher than a full house, and pulled the enormous pot, with the keys to the Buick along with it.

"Well, I'll be a shit-eating rattler," Surefoot said, jumping up and pulling a small pistol from his pocket. He stared over at Handsome Jack. "You pretend to be my partner and suck me into this. All the time you been working with this newcomer here, settin' me up." He cocked the gun, swinging it around at Rockson but suddenly felt the presence of Archer standing behind him with a raised fist, ready to slam the man's head into splinters.

"Wouldn't fire that gun if I were you," Rock said. "My friend here can get pretty mean." The rest of the players beat a hasty retreat out the door. Surefoot lowered his pistol and put it back in his waistband. He stared long and hard at Rockson, then exited. Rock pushed enough gold coins over to Maliber, who stood there frozen, to pay for their rent and water. Then he and Archer rose and headed outside. He suspected that Surefoot had something in mind—like shooting them both in the back, before they could get the car out of the lot. The two freefighters lugged their winnings—some skunkskin pelts, a bag of wrist and pocket watches, a half dozen leather-bound books, several bear traps and two pistols, along with the loot over to the car. Rock walked around the freshly painted red vehicle. It had a chrome grill through which the muzzle of the .55mm machine gun poked. He stuck his head in the driver's window and saw bucket seats made out of Fiberglas and a surprisingly sophisticated dashboard with dials and computerized systems checks. A joystick at the other side of the seat apparently controlled the machine gun with a red button on top for firing. But there wasn't time for a complete investigation. He wanted to get out of there before they were attacked by the whole damned community. He wasn't in the mood for taking on truckers, lumberjacks, cowboys, bobby-socked teens and god knew what else.

He and Archer climbed in as Maliber walked over to them, his hands at his sides to show he had no weapons.

"Just want you to know that I think you won every bit of this here car fair and square," the motel-keep said, putting his hand out. Rock shook it and smiled.

"Thanks for the hospitality. I appreciate it. I'll tell all my friends to stop by here if they're ever up in this neck of the woods."

"You do that, now," Maliber smiled. "And come back yourself. You got to give us all a chance to win back some of this stuff."

"Sure," Rock shouted as he turned on the engine. The alcohol drive sputtered to life as a puff of black smoke shot out the chimney on top. The car shook with power. He put the roadster in gear and pressed the accelerator. The tires trailed rubber for fifty yards as they shot down the blacktop like a bat out of hell. Archer turned pale and groaned, "Slooow, Roocksoon, slooow, pleeeassse." But Rock wanted to get out of there fast. He had a feeling . . .

Sure enough, as they hit the end of the lot and reached the dirt road heading south, two shots rang out from behind a tree, narrowly missing them as two holes appeared in the center of the windshield. They turned a bend in the road and were quickly lost behind trees. Archer kept growling and as soon as they were out of sight of the motel Rock slowed the car a little. It handled fine, but the going was bumpy and he wanted to get the feel of the wheel before he really opened her up.

He reached over and turned a dial marked Tape Cassette. The strains of a rock song from the late 1980s blasted through the car's four-speaker stereo:

Cruising at fifty thousand feet
Moving three thousand five hundred miles an

hour
We're flying the super jet
The one they call the phantom FIVE
Crew of eight, carry twenty two warheads
All aimed at the Soviet Union . . .
We're proud to be the men of the
U.S. Nuclear Strike Force.

Oh, we're gonna die listening to rock and roll
Rock and roll
Rock and roll
Yeah, we're gonna die listening to rock and roll

They headed down the dusty one-lane road that had once been Route 66, quickly hitting eighty miles an hour. Archer tried to hum along with the bizarre lyrics as the air rushed in the opened windows, splashing them with cool, refreshing air. Rock drove with one hand on the wheel and the other resting on the window as animals darted for cover as they heard the roar of the roadster approaching. Suddenly Rock felt happy to be alive. With the sun beating down and the breeze on his face, his heart welled up with an inexplicable joy. It was a hell of a world in America 2089 A.D. Yet he wouldn't choose to have been born in any other time or place.

Chapter Eight

Hands with fingers as thin as bone pressed against the dark blue glass of the eightieth floor of the Monolith, the headquarters of the KGB in America, making damp impressions on the cool surface. Colonel Killov stared through the tinted picture window that surrounded his top floor suite of living quarters and private offices. Killov, the "Skull," the "Colonel" or just plain "death" to those who knew him or had the unfortunate fate of feeling his wrath. His official title was Colonel Killov, commander of all U.S.S.R. KGB forces. Every blackshirt in America was under his iron-fisted rule. The blackshirts with their death's head emblems on their lapels who went out into the night and killed and tortured and mutilated America's slave population. But not just the natives had cause to worry, for Killov was also the Political Doctrine Upholder of the troops of the regular Red Army. Meaning soldiers up to the rank of general could be "disappeared" if the KGB warranted.

Killov ground his teeth together in slow circles making a crunching, gritty sound as if the very edges of his jaws were sanding each other to dust. His thin lips were squeezed tight as the greedy mouth of a small wood's rodent, his drug-crazed eyes burned like incandescent blue bulbs. He reached for another Alevil and a capsule of Transcendal. His drug use had reached insane proportions. Even he knew that. His doctors—those who dared speak up—told him he had only a few years to live if he didn't change his habits. He barely slept anymore, his life was more of a walking dream—a nightmare in which death slept under every door, crawled beneath every log, glistened in every eye. His body had shrunk to hanging leather flaps of skin that sagged down from his arms and legs. His face was concave, the cheeks sunken as if shovels had dug out whole chunks of flesh. A protruding red scar ran along his cheek from just below the eye to his jawline A present from Ted Rockson. Rockson who was always somehow just out of reach.

Killov pressed closer to the glass as if trying to push his way through. In the dark purple of the early dawn he could see the Colorado Rockies just miles away, towering peaks of purest white. And there—somewhere in the midst of these granite mammoths—was Century City and the Doomsday Warrior. But where, where, where? He would give half his wealth, half the Red kingdom that the KGB ruled, to get Rockson. The white-haired streak down the center of his black scalp, those aquamarine and violet eyes staring at him without a trace of fear. He would make them feel fear. Someday Rockson would be before him, begging, bloody and screaming for his life.

Yet now Premier Vassily wanted the Doomsday

Warrier even more. Wanted him dead. Killov, the death's-head emblems perched high on his leather field jacket, turned and walked to his long curved black marble and plastic table—seamless, almost translucent, it seemed to throb with a dark energy as if it contained the souls of all those Killov had killed. He reached for the three reports that he had received that afternoon. All three confirmed the same fact. Premier Vassily was on the move with an army composed of German neo-Nazis. And the reports gathered from his agents in Europe, Moscow and Washington related that the troops were to be used in a strike against Rockson to avenge the humiliation that the premier had endured when the Doomsday Warrior had signed the peace treaty with the Soviet high command and then proceeded to escape, blow up half of Moscow including the main ICBM control center and escape in a commandeered MIG.

"But how do I know?" Killov wondered for the hundredth time in the last twelve hours, popping another morphine tab to calm himself down. "How do I know for sure that it's not directed against me?" He knew that the premier had considered *him* the foremost threat to the empire and had vowed to destroy Killov before his own death. Yet now it was Rockson who incurred his wrath. Killov could believe that the Grandfather would be angry enough. It almost made him smile, or as close as the steel-lipped mouth could come to curving itself out of its eternal grim line. The colonel pictured Moscow burning, the Coliseum reduced to rubble, gladiators strewn like pieces of butchered beef. Fuck them all. Moscow was just filled with a bunch of fat army bureaucrats. *He* would rule over them all someday. Would bring his brand of order to the planet Earth. The rule of the death's-head, the rule of blood.

He had to be cleverer than them. Had to prepare himself. If it was a strike against Rockson—so be it. But if they suddenly veered toward him and the Monolith . . . He laughed suddenly, a mad shrill noise, through vocal cords unaccustomed to such a sound. He was ready—far more ready than Vassily or his fat nephew, Zhabnov, could imagine. He picked up his phone suddenly and tapped a button on the computer auto-dial. It was 5:30 a.m. but all of the colonel's staff knew he didn't relate to the nine-to-five routine.

"Yes," a sleepy voice at the other end said, sounding somewhat annoyed.

"Wake up, fool, this is Colonel Killov."

"Yes, sir," the voice fairly screamed in panic.

"Wake up Eighth Wing Commander Petronin. I want the entire squadron on twenty four-hour alert. You understand, idiot? This is a mode blue status."

"Yes, sir, immediately, sir," the voice stuttered back.

"Have Petronin call me within fifteen minutes." Killov slammed the phone down with a bang and had begun dialing another number when he heard the dimmest of knocks on his door.

"Come in, come in," he screamed, letting the receiver fall back in its cradle. The door opened a crack and a hesitant, terrified elderly servant, pale as a ghost with but a single clump of hair in the center of his white scalp, peeked in. He had drawn the unlucky lot among the servants to wait on the colonel tonight. The slightest misstep, the dropping of an egg, the spilling of a glass of water, had in the past meant death when Killov had been in a nasty mood. The servant started in, moving as slowly as a turtle, so as not to drop his tray or disturb anything in the room.

"Y-your v-vegetable juice," he said softly. "Your doctors told you—"

"Yes, yes, bring it here," Killov barked. "Quick, don't move like a mutant—move like a man." The servant rushed forward, nearly slipping and spilling the entire contents of a pitcher of twenty five vegetable and fruit juices fortified with massive doses of vitamins B and C. This liquid meal was all that the colonel had consumed for months now. Even he knew he had to drink the stuff—or he would die. But so filled with drugs was he that the idea of consuming anything healthy, wet and wholesome filled him with a terrified repulsion. He grabbed the jug from the servant, tilted his head back and drank down as much as he could without vomiting. The thick greenish liquid trickled down over his face and chest, splattering the black leather jacket and pants and boots that came up nearly to his knees. At last when he could stand no more he flung the plastic jug halfway across the room. The servant ran and picked it up.

"Out, out, leave me alone," the colonel yelled, trying to burp and keep the vitamin essence down. The nearly bald servant rushed from the room and quickly closed the door. Killov sat alone staring straight ahead. He could see his reflection in the glass window about eight feet away.

God, I look mad, he thought. He could feel the maniacal energy flowing, blazing from every pore of his face. Yes, but madness was a kind of genius. And he was a genius of death, terror and betrayal. He stared deeply at the blue-hazed reflection of his glowing skull-shaped face until he could bear it no longer—the fused ugliness, the darkness of hell itself rippling in dark purple circles that spread out from beneath his eyes like radar blips. He turned back to the reports, twisting his hands together, wondering whether he was somehow being outsmarted. He would have his neutron bombs ready—five of them, his entire system of antimissiles, and ground-to-air defenses which were brimming with nearly two hundred projectiles surrounding Denver and his Monolith headquarters. His spies were planted in the German army and even among Vassily's top military staff. Oh yes—he had his finger in every pie, and when it was time to take his slice, he would get *all* of it. He stared at the reports over and over, searching for the one vital fact he might be overlooking—the difference between ultimate success and total destruction.

Ten stories below the musings and rantings of the KGB commander, a black-cloaked figure moved steadily up the smooth glass-sided outer surface of the Monolith. On each of his hands and knees were attached large rubber "suckers" that stuck firmly to the wall when he planted them there. Then he carefully lifted the next—but slowly, always have three planted—two were not enough. There was all the time in the world to kill Colonel Killov. The assassin stopped and looked down for a moment. He was already seventy stories up. The grounds, the gates far below that surrounded the immense circular building, the guards making their regular rounds—all looked as small as bugs, mere insects incapable of even seeing him up here in the darkness. He loved it like this—the harsh ninja training had all been worth it. The years of strict and esoteric regimen in Russian camps on the Chinese border where ninjas had been taken prisoner and forced to teach all the tricks of their trade. Thus, had Illyich Durzevsky been transformed from a regular army commando into the "Hard Faced One," as he had come to be known. For he had chosen as his attack suit, a many-pocketed multi-weaponed black nylon ninja suit and cape—and the black opaque face mask, shaped like a Kabuki demon through which only his bottomless brown eyes showed. He had been one of the best and had killed many men already. But now, President Zhabnov himself had commanded him to destroy "The Skull." He was one of a group of five assassins sent out on the mission. Two had failed already. But the Hard Faced One would not.

He edged up the side of the building seeing the roof just above. He was at the eightieth floor. Careful—Killov was almost certainly in there. He would be alone, any sound would jar him in his drugged-out nervous paranoia. He must be fast and instantaneous in his attack. Killov was far tougher than he appeared. The Hard Faced One's masked eyes rose slowly up to window level and peeked in. There—he could see the KGB commander sitting at his table just a few yards away. His back was turned toward the window as he bent over, looking feverishly at some papers. The ninja edged along sideways keeping the colonel's back just in eye range. He moved a good fifty feet along the side of the building until he was past a wall and facing another section of the top floor suite. The clouds rolled by just over his head, a few hundred feet up. The night was black and harsh, streaked only with lines of even darker mists spiraling down from the poisoned lungs of the Earth's atmosphere.

The Hard Faced One reached up with his hands and a diamond-edged blade snapped out into his right hand from a wrist-spring beneath his wide-sleeved silk jacket. He began cutting a circle in the glass, moving slowly, so as not to make a sound. The cutter was powered by supersonic waves along the blade edge, enabling the diamond teeth to cut quickly and deeply into even inch-thick glass without a sound. Within minutes the ninja removed the oval piece of cut glass with a sucker and rested it against the six-inch-deep metal ledge that ringed the building. He hoisted himself up and through the hole moving one joint at a time, making no sound. He had trained in all the martial arts, in yogas, in meditations so esoteric that no normal man could even comprehend them. And now he was able to move like a gymnast, a spider, a warrior—all in one black-garbed body.

He stepped down on the floor of the room. Killov was within reach, just on the other side of the wall. From underneath his robe the ninja pulled it out—the weapon with which he would destroy "The Skull." It was a simple device, a piece of wire with a two inch blade at the end, attached to a motorized metal handle. The ninja grinned beneath his black demonic mask and pressed a button on the side of the handle. The steel blade began spinning at the end of the steel whip which shot around in a circle in front of the ninja's chest. He pressed another button and the wire fed out another two feet. A whip of blood and death.

The Hard Faced One walked through the door and toward the colonel, stepping light as an ant, moving as he had been trained to walk across rice paper without tearing it. The cutting wire swung around and around reaching toward the colonel's neck, reaching to slice through bone and sinew like blades of grass. One more second and . . .

Killov felt a tingle run up his curved spine. He didn't move a muscle. Something, something. Yes, a breeze, but all the windows in the Monolith were closed, locked, incapable of being opened—all the air was filtered and fed through a duct system. The colonel leaped to the side suddenly, knocking his chair over. He felt something whiz just by his head and slice into the table. Killov struggled to his feet, scrambling on the Persian rug that filled the center of his office floor. He turned and stared wide-eyed at the black-cloaked figure that suddenly jumped atop his desk, whirling the bizarre weapon in front of him.

"Very good, Colonel Killov," the voice said in a hoarse whisper from beneath the mask. "They said you were fast. But not fast enough." The ninja leaped forward with a powerful spring of his muscular legs, landing nearly alongside Killov. The spinning razor wire ripped toward the KGB commander who fell back, receiving a deep slice in his upper arm. He slammed his hand over the wound and looked at it for the barest second. He could see the flesh opened up in a bloody V and in to the wet white bone below. He stepped back as the assassin slowed down, taunting Killov, wanting to enjoy the hunt.

"Colonel—don't you want to die?" the assassin goaded him. "Come now, you are the master of death, aren't you?"

"Whoever you are—I don't care—let me live. I'll pay you ten times whatever they're giving you."

"Colonel, I have enough money, women, food to last me ten lifetimes." The ninja laughed contemptuously. "You see, I've trained my entire life to kill you. This is my fate—the completion of my ninja destiny. Once your death is mine—I will not even care whether I live or die."

As Killov listened to the assassin's words, he slowly walked to the front of his desk. If he could just lure the killer onto the section of carpet in front of the center of the desk. For there he had a little surprise. The ninja was talking too much, Killov thought to himself. Forgetting the truth of murder: when you can kill—kill. Don't fuck around.

"And now, Colonel, that you have felt the sharp tongue of my spinning friend here, perhaps a few more cuts and then your head." The ninja jumped into the air, slicing down at the colonel's thigh. But Killov, in his desperate drug-crazed state, was hypersensitive and jumped, half screaming as the spinning blade tore down the side of his leg, slicing a deep piece of the outer thigh as if it were a cut of roast beef. The skin flapped down, hanging only by bloody veins, as red gushed down the trembling leg. Killov lurched back, wincing in pain. Yes, yes—come forward just a little more my stupid friend, he thought behind his dark blue eyes. The ninja advanced, sensing the end. He raised the whirling strip of death to cut the KGB leader for the final time.

Killov timed himself. Just as the arm moved he fell forward and pushed a hidden button just below the inch-thick edge of the table. A metal plate covered by the rug on which the ninja was standing suddenly whirled to life as a million volts of electricity shot through it. The metal plate secreted in the ceiling above took the charge and huge snapping bolts of white electric spears shot back and forth between the floor and ceiling. The body of the assassin jerked wildly as the cracking streaks shot through him. He was now a human conductor. The bolts ripped through his feet and legs, through his groin and his skull—a thousands ripping knives of burning infinite pain. The Hard Faced One screamed and screamed again as his body began smoking, his eyes and brain bubbling in a streaming pink porridge made out of sockets and earholes.

Killov, his hand wrapped over his leg wound, walked back behind his desk and sat in his chair watching the burning, spasming creature before him. It was already dead, the colonel was sure of that. Its outer skin was already turning black and charring as the head burst into flames from the inside. Tongues of fire shot from the dead thing's mouth, licking out nearly a foot. Still, it jerked back and forth caught between the electric fires. Amazing, the colonel thought as the corpse smoked, how much flesh and parts there are in a human body to make fuel. Perhaps someday . . .

He watched until the ninja was just smoldering bones and lumps of fused charcoal on the singed rug. Then he pressed the red button on a control panel just inside his drawer. The current stopped, leaving a mist of bloody flesh and charred tissue floating thickly in the air like the leftovers of a hurricane spewing red rain. The colonel pressed his Emergency button and within seconds two of his bodyguards ran from a side room, where he usually kept them, out of sight, not being able to stand the presence of another human being for very long. The guards looked at the smoking thing with horror as they began stammering out apologies for not having stopped the would-be killer.

"Shut up," Killov barked. "Call my doctors. Tell them to meet me in operating room three." He felt his mind beginning to spin, growing weak from the loss of blood. But he would live, he knew that. His surgeons would sew him up again and fill him with the blood of others. He was too tough to die. None of them understood his duty here on earth—or who he served. For nothing could defeat his Master—nothing.

"Sergo," he ordered one of the bodyguards who was already on the phone frantically getting the operating team assembled. "Sweep up the ashes."

Chapter Nine

The two freefighters made good time in the Roadmaster they had won in the poker game. Once Rock got the hang of it he was steering down the plains and hills of Iowa like he was going through an obstacle course. The only drawback was the constant booming and chugging of the alcohol engine that took up the entire rear of the car, the small tin chimney poking through the roof and spitting out a constant stream of thin gray smoke. The weather remained fairly cloudy which was just as well as far as Rockson was concerned. There would be Red spy drones in this part of the country and he didn't feel like walking anymore. If a drone dropped down close enough it would pick up the engine and metal parts of their vehicle and close in for closer examination and then . . . But they'd just have to chance it. Through the thick cloud cover they could occasionally hear the far-off whine of one of the unmanned video-equipped spy rockets—but they would never see it.

Over the next three days they covered a good six hundred miles along the fairly flat salt seas and pebble-strewn dead lands that stood between them and Century City. On the third afternoon they came upon a herd of black furred buffalo, immense and mangy, chewing the thin cover of grass and staring uninterestedly at the approaching car. Rock slowed to a stop and let loose with a few rounds from the front grill machine gun. A buffalo toppled to the dusty ground like a felled tree, nearly three-quarters of a ton of muscled meat. Archer jumped out and with the deft expertise of a tried and true mountain man, skinned off some of the best and most tender meat from the shoulders and upper thighs. He cut the meat into twenty inch-thick steaks and headed back to the car, which stood waiting, puffing out a funnel of smoke as the roadster shivered in neutral.

"Maybe the top of that alcohol engine back there is hot enough to fry up these steaks here," Rockson suggested to Archer who immediately took two of the bloody slabs and slapped them down on top of the sizzling hot metal of the engine cover. Instantly the blood sizzled and sent out the mouth-watering odor of tender meat being charred. After they ate, Rockson kept on at a dead-ahead course, keeping the sun in view as he tracked it across the hazy sky, a dim beacon behind the curtains of writhing clouds.

The terrain became bumpier and the Doomsday Warrior glanced out the side window. They were low enough down in the bucket seats that it was like riding just inches above the earth. He felt as if he were actually floating just inches from the ground. He could see little bumps everywhere on the ground as if the soil had erupted with sores, pimples of radioactive disease. Far off to the right and left of the speeding car stood two immense A-bomb craters like dead volcanos. But their legacy of radioactive poisonous death still lived on. The car shuddered as it rode over the mottled ground and Rockson could feel his muscles and bones vibrating inside his body as if he were being shaken in a blender.

Suddenly he saw a blurry shape off to the right coming in fast. It looked bizarre, some sort of trucklike top built on a small-framed car body. The high truck looked absurd bouncing from side to side as if it were about to fall off, obviously too big for the frame that supported it. On the top, three men began firing at the Roadmaster, shooting from big-muzzled shotguns that spat out loud puffs of steel shot. The Doomsday Warrior floored the accelerator and took off, angling away from the attacking antique, metal strips ripped from its side, faded green paint with the words "Alfie's Supermarket" still barely visible on its side, and bulging tires that looked as if they were centuries old. Still, the thing moved and moved fast as it charged toward them, trying to cut off their escape. The men shooting from the truck's top looked quite barbaric with scars covering their faces and brightly colored mohawk haircuts. Dangling from the sides of the lumbering vehicle was what looked to Rock like human skulls slapping against the metal.

He was slowly gaining distance on the pursuing bandits when the Doomsday Warrior saw another vehicle coming at them from straight ahead—a trap. There was more than one—possibly many more.

"Archer, man the guns." Archer sat bolt upright in the bucket seat as he saw the Volkswagen Minibus ahead, armed with a giant ramming spear on the front bearing down on them like a warship on a whale. "The gun, man—just aim it forward and fire." Rockson was too busy with the controls of the roadster to handle the .55 too, as he had to continually feed more alcohol through the flow lever to increase the speed of the car. Archer took hold of the joystick controls of the .55mm poking through the grill of the Roadmaster and pushed the Fire button on top. Seventy-five feet away the approaching van took a swarm of shots dead center in its engine block. The front end erupted into flames as the bus veered sharply to the side. From the back the tattooed attackers jumped out, hitting the ground and firing up at the fleeing Roadmaster with an assortment of ancient weapons.

But the truck was still after them and Rockson had a growing feeling that there was more to come. He saw them—a line of four advancing cars, each over a century old, their very bodies cracking apart, their windshields held in place by ropes, their wheels ground down so that there was just inches of rubber between the ground and the spinning steel axles. Yet they moved, lurching and weaving, they came forward.

Rockson bore down on them. "Shoot, man, shoot," he yelled to Archer as puffs of smoke began spitting out from the windows of the approaching vehicles. Men leaned out of them, with pistols, rifles, shotguns, firing, their faces contorted in rage and hate . . . and hunger. "Spray 'em," Rock screamed as he floored the car and pulled the wheel sharply to the left, seeing a space between two cars on that side. Archer pressed the firing mechanism and slowly turned the machine gun across the row of enemy cars. The bullets sliced across grills, doors and tires like a scythe of death, slamming into metal and twisting it apart as if it were being gouged by a giant can opener. Two of the cars caught fire, their fuel lines severed. Rock tore past the blazing vehicles, squeezing between them at fifty mph. The side of the Roadmaster slammed into one of the flaming attacker cars and sent it flying over sideways, coming to a rest on its crushed roof.

But they had barely gone a few hundred yards when the Doomsday Warrior's heart skipped a beat. There—ahead of them lined up like an armada of steel was a whole army of archaic vehicles. Nearly a dozen of the half-rusted cars and trucks from prewar America, each filled to the brim with barbarians screaming out their death challenge. Four of the trucks had wooden platforms built on their backs, rickety structures that rose a good fifteen feet into the air, atop which small cannon had been erected. The fleet advanced toward Rock, their wooden platforms shaking and leaning back and forth as if they would fall over. Rock could see the men behind the metal cannon loading them by hand with fist-sized shells.

"Jesus Christ, it's a fucking army out there," Rockson muttered. "There's no way in hell we're going to get through that bunch," he said, shifting the wheel to the right. "I'm going to tear ass to the right. The second you feel the car move, fire—and keep firing with that .55. You got me?"

Archer grunted, his hands tightening on the firing controls.

"And aim for those tower things—the cannon. You see them?"

"Killll cannoooon, Rocksooon," the freefighter snorted contemptuously.

"OK, hang onto your balls, man," the Doomsday Warrior said and spun the wheel as far as it would go to the right, slamming the accelerator to the floor. He opened the manual alcohol feed to full. The damned car might explode for all he knew—but when it came to choosing between death and possible death he didn't ponder the philosophical implications. The roadster shot forward like a rocket sending up a cloud of parched yellow dust from the ground. For a second they were lost to the view of the attackers who screamed out to one another. They didn't want to lose this one. He had challenged them, had killed some of their army—the Car Ones—as they called themselves. None had ever done so before. They ruled this part of the world, undisputed. And all those who entered this plain of death were theirs for the taking—and the eating.

As the Roadmaster sped across the front line of the approaching attackers, Rock hear a loud roar and saw an explosion of dirt just ahead. He swerved to the left and began zigzagging. The Roadmaster was handling amazingly well for such an antique—Surefoot had really put his heart into it. The death fleet was closing in fast, changing their angle of attack to try and head Rockson off. But though the army of ragtag vehicles was equipped with an arsenal of weaponry and could move, not one could keep up with the super-souped-up Buick. He made it past the truck at the very edge of the fleet and headed out toward the miles of flatland ahead. But the Car Ones turned and took up the pursuit.

"Man the back gun," Rockson screamed. Archer looked at him in confusion. "There—there," the Doomsday Warrior yelled, straightening out their escape path, and moving the car to the max. "That lever, see—it changes the controls from forward to rear machine gun." Archer reached tentatively forward, looking at Rockson to make sure he wasn't doing the wrong thing and then pushed the switching lever down. He grimaced as it clicked into place, and then smiled, happy that he had dealt successfully with modern technology—his nemesis with its hidden gears and wires. Unable to see through the steel plate that covered the back window, Archer, keeping one hand on the firing button, leaned out the window to get a better view. The pursuers were right behind them, neither catching up nor falling behind. They had broken their straight line formation and were moving in groups of three or four vehicles in three separate packs. The trucks with the tower cannon were in the second pack and were just getting a fix on their would-be victims. Archer suddenly saw a puff of black smoke erupt from one, knocking the wooden tower a foot back with its recoil. The shell whistled toward the Roadmaster, hitting the dirt just to the front and side of the car. The shock lifted the entire vehicle up for a second. But it kept going.

Not knowing quite what he was aiming at, Archer decided to just push the Fire button and hope for the best. He could see the trail of hot slugs tear out behind them and slam into the windshield of one of the lead cars. The glass blasted apart sending a hailstorm of razor-sharp shrapnel into the driver's face. The car skidded sharply to the left and slammed into another, the two of them erupting into a single ball of flame. Archer burst out in a guttural laugh and swiveled the machine gun slightly to the side. He fired again but quickly saw that the stream of bullets was going between the next two trucks. Slowly, firing all the time, he swiveled the death dealer inch by inch, until the trail of slugs bit into a truck just preparing to fire its cannon. The thing went off just as the .55s bit into the bottom of the wooden platform below it and the entire structure collapsed down onto the truck. The cannon flipped down at the instant it fired and the big shell tore into the hood of the vehicle sending the entire truck up in a roar of fire and smoke and burning flesh.

Some of the other cars were starting to fall back, unable to keep up the pace, as thick streams of smoking oil streamed up from their exhausts. They were not used to having to pursue their victims more than a few hundred yards before a bloody capture was made. Archer turned back toward Rock and held up four fingers.

"Four," the Doomsday Warrior said, smirking. "Well, I guess that's lowering the odds a bit. Keep firing. As some famous baseball player of old used to say 'It ain't over 'til it's over.' And it ain't over yet." Rock swerved to the side again, making the car lift up onto two wheels for a few seconds as he heard another cannon shell scream in toward them. The blast went off just yards away from Rock's opened window and the hard dirt rained over his face and body. He kept the car going straight, clamping one hand to the wheel, but had to slow down as his eyes filled with dust. He wiped at them frantically, not wanting to lose the precious lead they had gained. But his eyes teared through a veil of pain.

"Give me the water," Rockson said to Archer, who continued to lean out the window, occasionally ducking back inside as a hail of shotgun pellets flew by, as he fired back with the .55. "Water, water," Rockson fairly bellowed out and Archer at last heard him and turned around.

"Weee slooow, Roooocksoon."

"I know, I know – give me the canteen." Confused but quick to obey even the most outlandish of Rock's requests, Archer reached down in the back space behind the seats and lifted the canteen, handing it to the Doomsday Warrior. Rock unscrewed the lid and poured the precious liquid over his eyes as Archer stared in bewilderment.

He could see again. His eyes hurt but he didn't think he'd suffered any permanent damage. In the time that he had slowed from over sixty to about thirty mph, the remaining two trucks and two station wagons, guns poking out of every opening, had come to within a few hundred feet of the roadster. Shots pinged off the back of the Roadmaster, but bounced harmlessly away from the one inch steel plating that covered the entire rear end of the car. Two more cannon shots rang out from the wildly swaying towers. One landed just behind them, the other almost under the car.

Rock accelerated full blast but the roadster kept veering to the right. He could hear the flapping sound of the rubber from one of the tires. They'd been hit. He might be able to keep going but there was no way he could outrun what was left of the armada who were closing by the second. Suddenly he remembered what Surefoot had said about the emergency fuel dump ability of the car. That in case of a crash or attack it was possible to release the entire two hundred-gallon capacity of the alcohol tank in one mighty burst. It was time to find out if the damned thing really worked.

"Close the windows, pal." Rock grinned. "We're in for a little firestorm." Archer grudgingly complied, not wanting to give up the machine gun as he had been getting increasingly accurate at controlling it. Rockson let the approaching attack cars pull even closer. Just as he heard the roar of another shell he pulled the Evacuate lever at the right of the steering wheel. The alcohol shot out from the bottom of the car in a loud whooshing burst instantly rushing out for about thirty feet in all directions, creating a mini-sea of pure distilled alcohol. Rock floored the Roadmaster just as he heard the shell coming down upon them, the lead tower gunner having at last gotten them in his primitive sights. The shell hit the ground just behind the accelerating Buick and exploded in a dirt-heaving blast. The pool of alcohol instantly ignited, sending a sheet of flame into the air just as the attackers raced over it. The flames shot up nearly ten feet, the alcohol burning with a quick but violent fury, and caught two of the attack vehicles directly underneath. Their fuel lines burst into flame and both joined the conflagration. The smell of melting metal and human flesh filled the air. There was but one truck left and it continued the charge forward, the tower gunner feeding another apple-sized shell into his makeshift mortar.

Rock spun the wheel as far as it could go and the car spun instantly around, making a full 180-degree skid. The two vehicles—the hunter and the prey that was not dying so easily—came toward one another. A hundred yards, seventy-five yards . . .

"Shoot, man, shoot," Rock yelled and Archer, staring through the thick windshield, began pumping the firing button. Shots sprayed out the back of the Roadmaster flying into the no-man's-land behind them.

"The lever, the lever," Rock croaked as Archer continued firing in confusion. The Doomsday Warrior reached forward and pulled lever back up into its forward firing mode. The .55 on the grill shook as it sent out a tornado of white-hot lead.

It was a game of Chicken—post-nuke style—as neither vehicle shied away from the final confrontation. Only one of them would come out alive—and the gods would decide. The mortarman had his shell in and was reaching for the firing mechanism, a pistol trigger fitted onto the side. They could see his face, scarred and pitted, with eyes blazing like the fires of hell itself. Archer swiveled the .55 back and forth, slowly raising up toward the truck's tower. The bullets slammed into one of the support beams—a long branch with twigs still sprouting from the side. The two vehicles were now just thirty yards apart and Rock could see the mortar trigger pull back. He veered to the side so sharply that the entire car went over onto its back. At the exact instant that the shell tore from the muzzle of its mini-cannon, Archer's final burst of slugs found their mark, hitting one of a pile of shells stacked next to the gunner. The top of the truck erupted into a fireball, sending the man and his death tower into instant oblivion. The mortar shell beelined for the Roadmaster and slammed into the dirt just feet ahead of the downed Buick, sitting like a turtle on its back. Rock and Archer could feel the entire car shake as pieces of jagged metal flew into the doors. But the fuel was gone—there was nothing to catch fire.

The two freefighters squeezed out through their opened windows. Rock pulled out his Kreega hunting knife and Archer swung his crossbow around to use as a club. But there was no one left to fight. They were all dead. A pile of burning cars and trucks extended back toward the horizon, each sending up its own swirling funnel of thick oily smoke. The men inside the last truck that had come bearing down on them were all dead—hanging over their seats, their bodies ripped and twisted apart, sliced like badly butchered meat, ripped into bloody corpses by the proximity of the munitions explosion.

The freefighters walked back to their Roadmaster and examined it. The thing was gone. It had served them well, but now after more than a hundred years of service it had met its maker. The front tire had been completely ripped from its axle by the force of the explosion; the engine seemed to have numerous holes in it. It leaked oil like dark blood onto the yellow ground.

"We're switching horses," Rock said to Archer, who was trying to extricate the last of his few belongings still stowed inside and the remaining steaks. They took their supplies and the winnings from the poker game and carried the load over to the truck. They kicked the still-smoking timbers from its back and then hauled out the dead men from their seats. The thing smelled like a charnel house, but when Rock flipped the ignition switch, the engine roared into life. Roofless, doorless, peppered with little holes from the roadster's .55—the damned thing still ran.

"It goes," the Doomsday Warrior said with a sardonic grin as Archer jumped up through the opposite door onto the seat beside him. They shot forward into the unknown, leaving a graveyard of smoking steel behind them.

Chapter Ten

Hundreds of planes filled the skies—huge K-121 Airlifter four-engine jet troop carriers that had set out six hours earlier from Munich, Berlin and Stuttgart. They soared down from out of the clouds over the Red fortress city of Dzersch in southern Colorado, setting down one by one. Hundreds of thousands of Nazi troops, tanks, armored vehicles and heavy artillery were ensconced in their steel bodies. The German invasion force was arriving in America. The second time in history that foreign troops had set foot on American soil. One landed every minute on the two-mile-long desert runway, unpaved hand-pounded dirt at the outskirts of the newly built invasion camp.

Exhausted American slave workers looked up with fear in their narrow eyes as the giant transports dropped from the brown skies, their jet engines roaring out a symphony of impending doom. The ragged, beaten and sullen men—there were no women, they had been sent to breeding farms in

Russia—had been up for days and nights, smoothing down the hard-packed runway with shovels and hand-pulled rollers. The wretched half-men had never seen such a concentration of power, as everywhere now in the pre-fabricated alumisynth Quonset huts that they had also assembled over the last month, officers and troops were stowing their gear—preparing for the slaughter of Century City. Trucks and armored vehicles roared by everywhere—Red army flags on their front fenders but swastikas on their doors—all converging at the Soviet Army Command Center, a five-story building in the center of the concentric circles of huts that spread out around it for nearly a mile. High cheekboned officers emerged from the vehicles and rushed into the headquarters, thick satchels of orders and maps under their arms. At the side of the ominous windowless building a wooden platform stood, still splattered with blood from the night before. The scaffold of death—for recalcitrant American workers who were brought there and slowly, over hours, strangled and tortured to death while their screams rang through the hovels at the northern end of the camp that served as the slave barracks.

Ralph 66, one of the unfortunate American "no men" who had been shipped here months ago along with nearly twenty thousand other slave laborers from Red Fortress Cities around the country, was barely able to walk. He had been up for eighty hours without sleep. But those who fell did not rise again without being pierced by a Red soldier's bayonet. So the bearded, pale worker staggered along for yet another day of backbreaking toil.

"I am less than nothing," he mumbled to himself as he stumbled out to the landing field along with a hundred other bent slaves who gasped for air with each faltering step. Nothing—no mind, no food, no sleep. Since they had taken his one possession—a cracked glass with a decal of President Kennedy on it—he had nothing at all. He mustn't think of it, just step, step—his life was to step, step. . . .

There was so much noise now from the jets that it hurt his ears. The huge skylifters stacked like angels of doom in the pulsating green radioactive sky above Colorado dropped down like steel hawks, their tails of fire passing just over his head.

"Vat haf ve here?" a Nazi officer asked him, noticing that Ralph 66 had been looking up instead of down at the ground as was the law for all slaves. "Do you zee something interesting?" the German asked, his thin lips grinning like stretched steel.

"Nothing, nothing, I'm sorry," Ralph 66 muttered, bowing his head low and trying to move on. The Nazi major slapped Ralph 66 on the side of the face with his swagger stick.

"You like troop planes, do you?"

"No, no, I only want to work, only work."

"That is good." The steel-gray eyes bore into him. "Hmmm, let me see your profile." He pressed the end of the leather-bound stick against the stubbly face. "I see upon looking at your upraised face that you are of partly Aryan stock. I have a different chore for you, mongrel. Come with me."

"Please I only want to—"

"Shut up, cur. You don't realize how lucky you are today. You will serve to replace a dead boot lackey in my commandant's quarters. You will be fed, shaved, bathed, clothed." The Nazi officer smirked. "Now do you wish to go to work?"

"Thank you, sir," Ralph 66 replied without raising his head.

He was taken to the servants' quarters in tents behind the general's building. Other American slaves took off his filthy clothes sending them to the garbage dump. He was cleaned, scrubbed for the first time in his miserable life, salved over his festering sores, dried and then clothed in a magnificent dark green Nazi servant's tunic. He felt like a new man—he was now a boot servant, a high post indeed for a no man. In just a few hours he had to accomplish the task of learning the deferential way to approach the general and help him on and off with his boots. He practiced on the other servant's feet until he was sore. His muscular though wasted arms gave him the strength to put on the boots—with pressure—all the time lining it up and pushing or pulling. No twisting, for the general had a sore leg. The last boot lackey had been executed for twisting the general's ankle.

"Do not make the same error," the head servant told him again and again.

He was taught well and felt fully competent by the the time the evening boot removal was to take place. Still, it was with some trepidation that he approached such a powerful German. And with hate. The Reds must be weak, he thought. Why do they need the Nazis to fight for them? Had the legendary Rockson killed President Zhabnov and the rest of the Red rulers in America? He came to the two guards at the door of the general's quarters who looked at his ID papers and allowed him to pass through. Inside, he hesitated just outside the commandant's office suite, listening to a phone conversation through the half opened door. They spoke almost always in Russian, these high Germans, as a sort of acknowledgment, a courtesy. And Ralph 66 knew Russian well. Those who didn't follow hasty Red orders were dead men. There were no excuses.

The Command barracks were a giant, heated affair, three stories high with immense double swastikas on the outer walls, sitting on the southern edge of the vast encampment. In the main first-floor room, the commander of the American theater of operation sat on thick furs, drinking hot tea from a steaming samovar. Herr Ubenfuhrer Marshal Von Reisling, a tall squarish man with a patch crossing his left eye where he had been stabbed by an enemy years before. Moist pinkish lips sipped almost daintily from the china cup as the impeccably dressed general with purple resplendent uniform, gold swastikas on each lapel, sat back, resting for the first time in days. There had been so much to do, so many preparations as the largest invasion force since the first days after the nuke war a hundred years before entered America. But all had gone well. The transports had all landed. The camp had been ready to receive them, having been hastily assembled in just a month. Nearly ten thousand of the original thirty thousand-man American slave force had died in the process of building the Nazi city of Dzersch—but no matter, there were many more where they came from.

The general was preparing to meet with Gunter Klaus and Helmut Heinz, the commanders of Wolfpack 201, the winner of the German all-army games the year before. For the presentation of the Lead flag, for the 201st would spearhead the invasion, he would wear his full uniform with gold brocaid, and his knee-high black boots. His new servant knocked nervously at the door and came in bowing effusively.

"Yes, yes," Von Reisling said with distaste, "put them on." Ralph 66, sweating from every pore of his terrified body, carefully slid them up the wide calves an inch at a time.

Outside the commandant's barracks, Gunter and Helmut stood at rigid attention, waiting, at the honor guard's command, to enter the forbidding quarters. Gunter was the regimental leader of the 201st, a tall angular-faced man with perfect Aryan features. His icy blue eyes seemed to ooze death of which they had seen much. Beside him stood Helmut, shorter, plumper, but just as tough. He had worked his way up in the Nazi ranks and had fought his way at every inch. Brown-eyed, his features were much coarser, almost swarthy. It had been rumored by several under his command that his hooked nose betrayed Jewish blood in his heritage. But none dared breathe a word of such thoughts—for it would be their last. The two men stood like frozen statues, just feet outside the general's quarters. Only their slightly breathing chests betrayed the fact that they were alive. They visualized the beaming yet stern face of Von Reisling as he would present the glorious flag to them. They did not shiver in their thin parade uniforms though the midnight temperature hovered at five degrees.

At last they were escorted in by the goose-stepping

honor guards and proceeded down the red carpet in the front hall to the general, who sat on a green silk chair mounted atop a marbled platform with foot-high gold swastikas surrounding it. The general rose, and as the two men stood at rigid attention, he walked around them.

"So you are Gunter," Von Reisling asked with a stone face.

"Javohl, mein general." Von Reisling placed the Order-of-Hitler medal on his chest.

"Your 201st Wolfpack will be the spearhead of the operation. Congratulations—you are no longer lieutenant but a major."

"Thank you, *mein ubenfuhrer,*" Gunter said, clicking his heels together with a sharp crack.

"Und you, Helmut," he said, placing a medal on his already decorated chest, "will be promoted to major as well, effective immediately. You will be second-in-command of the Wolfpack. *Sieg heil,*" he barked, holding his arm up in stiff arm salute.

"Sieg heil," both men yelled, raising their arms to the ceiling.

"You are dismissed," Von Reisling said. "And may the brave blood of the undefeatable German soldier flow through your veins."

When they left, Von Reisling sat back on his military throne and yawned. Such displays were necessary for morale but he had much to do. The Grandfather himself was to call him from Moscow exactly at midnight. He called in the boot lackey again to remove the tight-fitting knee-highs which were beginning to pinch his throbbing leg. The lackey seemed to tremble as he removed Von Reisling's boots, slightly twisting the right leg. The general winced in pain.

"Get out, fool," the commandant screamed, kicking Ralph 66 in the face, knocking him backwards. The boot servant ran from the room, tears in his eyes. Von Reisling got on the phone immediately. "Stein, this is Reisling. This new servant you sent me today—he is inadequate. Please, get me a new one and one with the intelligence to put on a pair of boots."

The voice on the line asked him a question. "No, don't execute him. We've lost too many workers lately. Put him back on the airport detail."

"Jah, mein general," the voice replied, clicking the phone down.

Standing just on the other side of the doorway, overhearing the conversation, was the man who was clean for the first time in years, rested, well-fed. Ralph 66 was going to be replaced. No, no, he screamed silently. He had just had a taste of the good life. He would rather die than be returned. He lifted a glass ash tray from a small table in the hall and cracked it against the table edge, breaking it into three razor-sharp fragments. He slipped one of the glass blades into his uniform pocket.

General Reisling picked up the ringing phone next to his tiger-skin bed.

"This is Premier Vassily," the quavering voice at the other end said.

"Yes, sir," Von Reisling said, tightening his voice.

"Good you are there, Reisling." Vassily left out the

Von, a treasured family name aborted by the Red master. The general reddened but tried not to let it affect his voice.

"I'm checking to make sure that all necessary preparations are proceeding according to schedule. There can be no slip-ups."

"German efficiency has put us *ahead* of schedule," Von Reisling said proudly. "The planes all landed with but a single malfunction. The men are in their barracks, armed and ready. I am meeting with my officers tonight to give them final instructions. Morale is high, sir, very high."

"Excellent," Vassily said, his white lips smiling at the other end, nearly twelve thousand miles away. "You know what the capture or death of this Ted Rockson means to me. When you have successfully completed this mission—there will be a position of power waiting for you here in the Kremlin. You understand me?"

"Fully, sir," Von Reisling said, reaching over and lighting a cigarette at the end of his ivory holder. "We will capture this Rockson, of that you can rest assured. A quarter million German soldiers will make sure of that. There is no way that he will escape." The general snickered at the thought.

From the servants' area, a door was being slowly opened. Ralph 66 stepped through, moving just an inch at a time so as not to alert the general whose back was facing him. Reisling was alone and on the phone. Good, his death would come easily. He moved toward the general. None would ever be so close to this all-powerful overlord, Ralph 66 thought. I will die for sure, but I must take this chance.

Perhaps American slaves will say my name tomorrow with awe. Perhaps my name will be banned from even being uttered—like Ted Rockson's. I must be careful. . . .

The general lifted his Tokarev Service Revolver from its holster, turned and placed a single bullet through the advancing servant's forehead, dead center between the man's eyes. The body was dead before it hit the plushly carpeted floor.

"What was that noise?" the premier asked.

"A difficult servant has been replaced, Grandfather," the general said, reholstering the gun. He smirked—the eye patch was in fact a sophisticated radar device with a 360-degree field of scan. Von Reisling had had too many enemies over the years, too many assassins trying to take his life, to have not learned a few tricks or two. And this measly mongrel slave thought *he* could kill the leader of the German army. Fool—he had seen the man coming from the moment he stepped through the door.

The lifeless eyes of Ralph 66 scanned the thick purple curtains that ringed the general's living quarters. The good life.

Gunter's 201st Wolfpack commando detachment were the first to advance to the invasion site, some thirty miles from the comforts of the sprawling base of Dzersch. The 201st's orders were to scout the terrain and send back intelligence reports for the rest of the 250-thousand-man army of this unknown and treacherous land in the midst of the Rocky Mountains. And if the freefighters were waiting, they would be the first to engage in combat. Gunter was ready, proud to hold the banner of the bravest, the best of the German army.

The men lined up at the open door of their K-121 Airlifter, their parakites strapped to their bodies, as the icy air rushed in, blasting them with a frigid introduction to the American Rockies.

Gunter, who always led his men into battle in the front ranks, rather than the rear as many officers preferred, was the first to hit the silk, leaping from the wide bay door. His parakite snapped open and he caught one of the high currents, heading into a slow curving glide. But he didn't like what he saw below: swirling clouds, snapping around the atmosphere like serpent's teeth, ready to strike out with all of nature's omnipotent fury. Fierce winds whipped his parakite, stretched out to its full eight-foot wing span, the nylon foils catching the full force of the blasting wind, buffeting it back and forth like a leaf in a hurricane.

It was hard to keep the damned thing homed in on the radar signal that had been dropped the day before by parachute, marking their drop site. The rest of the Wolfpack were hanging onto their parakites for dear life. They filled the skies around him, over two hundred of Germany's toughest fighters—men he had known since they had marched together in the Hitler Youth. Men who would die for the purity of the Aryan Race. In their hearts burned the flame of the Reich. He skillfully steered his parakite through the increasingly stronger blasts of hail and snow until at last he saw the outlines of a three hundred-foot wide outcropping on the mid-slope of a towering ice-capped mountain. That would be Pike's Peak, 14,100 feet above sea level. His lungs burned trying to breathe in the thin air as he dropped like a hunting hawk in ever lower circles, edging toward the plateau.

But the landing site was coming up too fast, a blurred vision of trees and rock. He veered up at the last second, pulling the tail control of the kite, and managed to stop the parakite almost in midair just inches above the ground. He touched down with his feet, holding the kite around him at waist-level, and stepped out of the support bars. He had made it. Gunter quickly turned to see the rest of his Wolfpack soaring this way and that, like a flock of birds gone mad. They were all having trouble in the stiff winds and the now-blinding snow blowing horizontally. He saw a man high above smash into the edge of the mountain and fall from his parakite, quickly dropping thousands of feet to the rocky floor below. But the rest of the squad somehow made it, slamming into the plateau in crash dives, jumping from them, even landing upside down. Within five minutes all but three of the pack were on the outcropping and gathering around their leader who shouted out instructions. They broke into their preordained groups and began heading up the mountain, Gunter, taking the lead, and his right-hand man, Helmut, bringing up the rear. Heavy snowflakes blanketed them, cutting their visual range to less than three yards.

It was the kind of storm that didn't even exist before the nuke war. The all-out atomic holocaust had set the earth wobbling on its axis, reversing the magnetic poles and beginning a "nuclear winter" which lasted for years over much of the Northern hemisphere. Nearly eighty percent of the earth's population was dead in three years. Then a miraculous cleansing action began to take place—the cosmic rays, the unfiltered solar rays, began to change the radioactive molecules, reducing their half-lives—the time it took for the deadly rads to become half as virulent. Slowly, ever so slowly, the forces of nature began to reassert themselves. But there would never be an earth that the people of the 1980s would recognize as home. Now it was a world where non-mutant men, except in the lowest elevations, were forced to don oxygen masks when walking or exerting the slightest effort. It was a world with a flashing aurora-filled purple sky at night and green strontium clouds floating like omnipresent symbols of death high in the daytime sky. And the mega-storms—with their winds of hundreds of miles per hour, hurling rocks the size of baseballs through the air, twisters spawned by the hundreds, ripping up all that stood in their path, rains of putrescent skin-dissolving acids, and spiral-shaped black snowflakes of super-hard ice that could tear and rip an unprotected person to shreds.

Or a storm like the one Gunter and his Wolfpack were trying to fight their way through now, crawling along bent over as if they were savage no-men instead of proud soldiers of the master race. Nature humbles even the mightiest, turning them, when it wishes, into mere ants, blown like so much dust in the wind. Gunter was covered head to toe, as were all the Wolfpack in form-fitting plastisynth armored suits with an oxygen mask and radiation filtration system shaped somewhat like the astronaut helmets of old. He had just the slightest opening between his gloves and the snow-resistant suit when one of the black spiral snowflakes whipped into his wrist at 150 mph. Blood poured out, soaking the bottom of the glove. He could hear the agonized groans and screams of his men who had not secured their face shield properly. They had all been warned and briefed over and over about the necessity for complete cover—but men will be men, and their laziness in America 2089 A.D. meant death. A sudden gust of super-wind, over 200 mph, tore off the unsecured helmets, ripping them from nearly a dozen of the Wolfpack's heads. The razor-sharp spikes of black flakes slammed into their faces like knives, cutting, slicing through cheeks, eyeballs and throats. Men threw their hands over their faces, as blood and flesh poured out like mush and was caught by the screaming winds, sending out sprays of red that quickly dissipated in the blizzard.

Gunter looked around him in horror. They hadn't even encountered the enemy and already they were losing men every few yards, bodies falling to the black-covered ground, twitching as the ebbing heat of their dying bodies melted little ready-made graves for them. Nature was more than happy to oblige. "Your masks," he screamed out over the throat mike in his helmet, capable of sending out a signal up to a half mile. "Make sure your masks are properly sealed." They were barely gaining ground now, the men clutching arms in long lines to avoid being blown away, right off the plateau to the rocks below. Surely the gods—Freya and Thor—must do something to stop this storm, Gunter thought. Or they would all perish. The undefeatable powers of the super race reduced to pitiful midgets against the raw forces of the American hinterlands. Was this their fate? To die here without ever sighting a single rebel?

He pressed the telecommunications button on the side of his mask and radioed a report back to the launching camp at Dzersch. "What are the weather reports? We are being destroyed out here."

"Clearing expected in two hours," came the succinct reply. They would have to hold out. As they made their way up the treacherous slope, Gunter bumped into an ancient, nearly faded road marker—still standing long after the road that it demarcated had disappeared beneath trees and bushes. He scraped the black ice from it: MURCHISON PASS, elevation 13,200 feet. He stumbled on, trying to keep the lead, trying to make an example for his men. They must not stop, not for a second, or they would be buried under a shroud of the black death. He placed one foot after another, moving somehow through sheer will power.

He tried to think of other things, force his mind from the storm. He remembered back to his home, to Germany. The beautiful motherland with its history of conquering armies, of imperial wars, of uniforms and whipping flags and great Nazi banners awesome in their splendor and history. And he remembered the breeding farms—the factories for the creation of the master race. Gunter had never known his true mother. The woman he had come to call "mother" was in fact assigned to rear him after he had been created from carefully selected sperm and egg cells with the required Ayran genes—strength, intelligence, fearlessness and obedience—all the things that would ensure that another perfect Nazi soldier had been produced. Embryos were grown in long tanks of fluids; pink fluid, he seemed to remember. There was the haziest image of him staring up at curious doctors who manned the birth tanks, of being manipulated by machines, sent down chutes, sanitized when dirty, lifted by mechanical hands that fed and exercised his young body. He remembered the tapes, played over and over, twenty-four hours a day, that told him Hitler was the father of the German people, of all the test-tube babies—his glorious creator.

Later, he had been placed with a flesh-and-blood mother and father who had been just as cold and uncaring and mechanically systematic in his feeding and caring as the coldest steel. Only sometimes—sometimes at night, as a child, he would awaken from nightmares, the vision of a void so deep and black that he would tremble violently and cry. His foster father would hear the cries and come in enraged, screaming, "What is this crying? The master race of children do not cry, do not fear." And with that he would tear off his thick black leather belt and beat Gunter into silence. Only once had this human father touched him, held him, caressed his head. Once, but never again.

No! Not to think of that, Gunter thought, suddenly coming back to the here and now—the black storm which continued with unassailing fury as if it wished to wipe every man of his Wolfpack off the face of the earth. The cold—it is the cold and being pinned down by this fierce storm, that and the thin bastard air of America, that is making me hallucinate. Be strong, do not allow emotions to enter. They are weakness itself. Cowards. The race—think only of the master race. His allegiances to the fuhrer, to the fatherland. If Hitler could see him now. He pulled back the tears that had been welling in his eyes, back and down into the darkest pits of his soul. Emotions are for weaklings, tears for women. His father had been right to beat him when he cried. This was the way of strength. His father had failed when he had succumbed to a child's snivelings and held him.

The storm winds at last died down, gone as suddenly as they had come. The rad-snows faltered and stopped. Gunter took stock of their losses—the fools who had allowed their face masks to come off were all dead, lying strewn around the slope waiting only to be consumed by the scavengers that would soon emerge from their dank holes and hiding places beneath rocks and logs.

Chapter Eleven

The Glowers danced. They heard the music, the harmonies of the stars streaming down like the choruses of the gods. They danced to the music of the heavens, of the clouds, of the writhing molten lava and gravity waves deep within the earth. They moved in concentric circles, their blue bodies crackling with pulsating electricity. Without touching they moved just inches apart, their outstretched violet fingers sending out flames of pure energy to the next of their kind in the spinning circle, cutting through the air like swords of lightning. They danced out the rhythm of existence, the movement of the energy spectrums, the meshing of rays and bands of energy beyond human comprehension, moving with the eternal flow and ebb of the universe.

With their star-blue eyes they could see the waves of gravity of the earth rising up to grab all things, the mega pulses of the quasars shot a billion light years through black space. Through their phantom flesh they could feel the roaring, sucking multidimensional forces of the black holes strewn throughout the galaxies like endless black pits—from which nothing returned. They saw the stars, each distinct, different from the next—blue, yellow, white, gold, brown, green—burning with the atomic fires that fueled existence. They touched the meteors with their minds, flashing through the purple skies above, felt the comets winging their vast migration routes through the universe, cold balls of fire, in a never-ending trek through infinity.

They felt the magnetic waves of Mother Earth beneath their glowing feet, reaching up with her billion billion arms of electro-magnetism, pulling everything to her bosom. They felt the tidal ripplings of the planet, the great surges of a trillion tons of water, arching, moving forward and backward in great walls of blue. They felt the dance of all things and they moved with it. Their bodies were impossible, grotesque, mad things, that were surely put together by a god who had gone insane. All of their internal organs had been placed on the outside of their blue flesh, pulsing, heart beating like a glistening ultraviolet living creature. Internal organs writhing, sending out their currents and electric blood to one another. Their brains moving slowly like slugs, twisting this way and that within the transparent brain cavities, sending out and receiving the telepathic multi-spectrum messages of their fellow beings.

The Glowers—human beings transformed and mutated into their present terrifying appearance a century before. Descendants of astronauts trapped aboard an orbiting space station who returned to earth after the great war. But the massive amounts of radiation they had absorbed in space from the detonation of twenty thousand nuclear warheads and the fact that they had to return through the highly radioactive parts of the upper atmosphere in their space shuttle made them give birth to children, creatures the likes of which the world had never seen. And their touch could kill. Unwittingly, the first of the new species had destroyed their own parents as they reached out for love.

But now they were together, all seventy nine of their kind. Creatures linked mentally and emotionally in a single telepathic consciousness. But ironically, though they were closer than any living thing had ever been, they could not even touch one another. For that touch meant instant death to anything with a cellular structure. Of all creatures, they were the closest and farthest apart from their own species—their blessing and their curse.

They danced for hours through the long black night, creating a rainbow of throbbing color in the center of their wasteland home in the Far West of the U.S. An energy bond was built between them that seemed to rise in intensity as their bodies grew ever brighter, until the very air was snapping in thunderous explosions from the sheer power of the electric streams whipping between them.

At last they stopped and stood motionless, their hands still extended. Their bodies' internal organs pumped violently, sending blue blood coursing through their transparent flesh. They no longer ate human food. Anything they touched burned up and evaporated in puffs of radioactive smoke. They ab-

sorbed the energy around them, shooting down from the sun, the cosmic rays, the earth's electromagnetic charge, these were their lifeblood fueling them, filling them with megawatts of power. In the total stillness their minds met, meshing firmly together like a vast mosaic that when assembled reveals but a single total picture.

"The battle is here. The test of the Armageddon has arrived." They spoke as one—putting forth their thoughts into the single mind. "The Rockson has returned. He has survived his ordeal in Moscow and now he is back. The warrior yet lives. But even his strength is not equal to the evil that is about to descend. He is but a man. We must act."

"But we have never acted," a single voice spoke out from the many. "We have always watched, observed. We have been part of the harmony. We have never entered or affected the world of the humans."

"But now is a new time," one of the many answered. "The moment of megadeath is upon us. There may be no more humans. No more Glowers. No more Planet Earth. This cannot be."

"Cannot be, cannot be," Their mental voices whizzed in the air between their rock-still electric blue fleshed physicalities, their arms outstretched, almost touching, like a circle of nightmarish Christs.

"We must affect time/space," one of the many spoke. "We must join the humans."

"Join, join." There were some voices that spoke no. But the unity was more powerful—was perfect. All was as one. They joined together in a mounting chorus of mental connection, until all were linked in perfect waves of agreement, their minds and emo-

tions in absolute harmony.

"We've never destroyed before, except those who came to destroy us. But now—we must stop those who would send our planet into the black ether of frozen space. We must use our power—all of it, to turn the tide of history." They pulsed together, brighter and brighter until their bodies seemed to fuse and there was but one blue ball of fire, spinning around them so that they appeared to be one solid entity of brilliant flame. Just as suddenly the glow died out and they bowed to one another.

They headed out to their three vehicles—sand ships—with towering energy collecting metallic sails atop the sand ships headed toward the east, soaring just inches above the shifting earth. They quickly reached their cruising speed of fifty miles an hour as they sped past immense black cactuses and wasteland animals that ran off at their approach. The Glowers stood on the bows of their craft staring straight ahead at the dark horizon. The sun began setting as they rushed forward, glowing like blue jewels in the night—to try to alter the destiny of mankind.

Nearly three hundred miles south and east of the Glowers' advancing fleet of sand ships, a team of hybrid pack horses, their backs weighted down with heavy equipment, marched stubbornly across the rocky terrain. Small bald men, thin as rails and hardly bigger than children, coaxed the 'brids on.

"Stubborness equals will power times the desire to avoid work," Ullman the Equator said, whipping at the backside of the hybrid in front of him. Nearly thirty of the humanoid creatures, not one over three feet high, worked and yelled at the pack animals. These were the Technicians (SEE BOOK No. 1)—a race of super scientists, the descendants of the original missile crew that had manned the complex of silos in the Far West where the radiation had evolved their children into their present spindly form. The Doomsday Warrior had made contact with them nearly six months before and had brought back weapons, the black-beam-particle pistols that the race had created. Weapons possessed of extraordinary power, the silent black beams could destroy trucks, tanks, even planes from miles away with awesome results. A second team had been sent out from Century City to obtain more weapons and try and persuade some of the Technicians to return with them so that Dr. Shecter, Century City's science chief, could learn how to produce the mysterious weapons himself. Erickson, the tall Swede, and Lang, a star-patterned mutant like Rockson himself, had been chosen to lead the second expeditionary force. After much hardship and struggle they had reached the underground silo home of the scientifically ingenious mini-men and the entire race had elected to return and help the American freefighters.

"We are tired of this stasis anyway," Ullman had told them, returning with the vote. Now, they moved slowly across the vast no-man's-land on the way back to Century City. Erickson and Lang, tough as nails with the same blue and violet eyes as the Doomsday Warrior, helped the Techs move the hybrids along. The thirty pack animals were piled high with black beam rifles and pistols—enough to arm nearly half the fighting force of Century City. And at the rear of the force, pulled by two teams of ten hybrids each, were two immense black beam cannons, almost ten feet long, black and smooth as glass, mounted on crude wood-wheeled wagons. Weapons capable of reaching to the moon, though thus far the enemies of mankind had not managed to gain that as a military base.

Lang rushed forward to Ullman who along with Qatar the Algebraic and Stryx the Quantum were leading the head of the hybrid team, pulling at the foul creatures' reins, coaxing them, yelling at them, doing everything they could imagine to make the beasts of burden speed up.

"How's it going?" Lang asked Ullman, who had a black beam pistol perched precariously in the waist band of the plastisynth gray jumpsuit that he wore. The Technicians' leader's bald head shone like a light bulb in the shimmering heat of the noonday sun.

"It is progressively linear," Ullman replied in the strange mathematical jargon that all the Techs spoke. "According to calculations we should reach your habitation within five or six time intervals."

"You mean days," Lang said, grinning as he always did when he spoke with the race of mini-scientists.

"Time periods of twenty four hour gestation, affirmative," Ullman answered, licking his dry lips. "But this physicality needs more liquid sustenance as do all the beings." He swept his hand over the huffing and puffing hybrids, short stocky creatures bred specifically for carrying heavy loads on their thick, wide backs.

"Yeah, they're looking a little pooped," Lang said,

slapping one of the 'brids on the thigh, which snorted angrily and snapped its head around in a halfhearted attempt to bite him with its wide cavity-mottled molars.

"Water necessity equals weight of being times metabolism times the square root of temperature times .1222981," Ullman said matter-of-factly. "My calculations lead to the conclusion that cessation of physicality will occur within 3.2 days, unless liquid sustenance is obtained."

"We passed a water hole, an underground spring on the way here," Lang said, trying to reassure the somewhat nervous Ullman. This was the first time that the race of Technicians had gone more than a few miles from their subterranean missile complex, with its machine shops and storehouses of particle beam weapons. They had believed, until Rockson had shown up, that they were the last beings left alive on earth and that the entire planet was as black and charred as the terrain around their base, which had taken nearly a direct hit from a twenty-megaton kiss, courtesy of the Soviet empire, a century earlier. Everything had been killed for miles around them, and even after a hundred years not a blade of grass had shown its green face through the hardened lava-like surface. Now they were out in the wilds of America, excited, brave and terrified.

"Water supplies will reach zero equation in precisely 17.6 hours at present rate of consumption," Ullman said, looking up at Lang, who towered over him, with his glistening wide brown eyes. And as if the mere thought of being without the precious liquid filled him with trepidation, Ullman hefted his gourdlike canteen from his waist band and took a deep slug. Several of the 'brids eyed the fluid, licking their huge tongues out in the air.

"It's there, I promise you," Lang said. "I've got no interest in disrupting my physicality, as you say." Ullman smiled for the first time in days at the human's attempt at Technician talk.

"You are like the Rockson," Ullman said, remembering the man who had taught him and his race about survival, feeding them from their own supplies, then taking Ullman and several of his people out into the wastelands where he had showed them how to survive, how to hunt and how to kill. "You are an equation of strength."

Suddenly there was a wild commotion at the back end of the weapons train of hybrids. Ullman and Lang swung their heads around as they heard the frantic brayings of the pack animals. One of the black beam cannons, weighting nearly three fourths of a ton, had begun sliding to the side of the crude wooden wagon, made of branches thatched together with wire, that it rode on. As it tilted to the side, the front left wheel of the wagon cracked in two and the entire primitive vehicle began tipping over to the ground.

"The cannon must not make ground impact," Ullman yelled out, "or its molecular structure will implode." Lang tore back to the slowly sliding cannon as the team of 'brids in front of the wagon stopped in their tracks and jumped around in noisy terror. Lang saw that he would never reach it in time when he suddenly saw Erickson coming up from the back, running at full speed. The big Swede grabbed hold of the side of the wagon, trying to slow its descent. He grunted and strained with every fibre of his being as his muscles bulged and veins stood out on his face and neck. From the other side of the wagon, two Technicians threw thin nylon loops of rope around the front end of the cannon and tied them to the backs of several 'brids, keeping the cannon from toppling over.

Lang had almost reached Erickson, his hands outstretched to help his fellow freefighter hold up the great weight, when he saw Erickson crumble. Everything moved in his vision in slow motion—Erickson suddenly falling to the ground, his hands ripped and bleeding, unable to support the weight of wood and the black beam weapon. As he fell, the upper half of the broken wagon wheel followed him down like a shark pursuing its prey into the murky waters of the ocean. Erickson hit the dirt flat on his back and had no time to move as the full weight of the load came down on his chest. The jagged half-wheel ripped into his upper body and clean through him, severing the chest and backbone in half like a guillotine. Erickson jerked twice and then was still.

A bunch of Technicians ran over and placed a wooden support rod beneath the wagon and slowly, using the 'brids with ropes attached to their backs, righted it. They brought in a new wheel from their supply wagon and carefully replaced the damaged one. Within minutes the wagon had been repaired and the cannon was out of danger, tied down more securely to the back.

Lang kneeled down and looked at the dead Erickson. His life had vanished in a split second as the wheel had sliced through all his inner organs, his lungs and then the backbone itself, severing the entire nervous system in one swift chop. The freefighter's eyes were still open, staring up at the sky as if trying to get a final glimpse of the beauty of the planet he had died trying to save. Tears welled up in Lang's eyes. He wasn't used to such feelings. Death came too easily on the plains of America 2089 A.D. to feel for those who died. But he and Erickson had grown close on the long trek out. And now—he was dead.

The Technicians secured the last rope around the cannon and the team was ready to move on. They placed Erickson's body by the side of the ancient buffalo migration route they were following, leaning his head against the bottom of a tall sequoia cactus, rising like a dark spear from out of the gray plains. Lang stood over him, his jungle hat, for sheltering his head from the boiling temperatures of the day-time sun, held loosely in his hands while he spoke:

God, whatever or whoever you are,
take this man into your heaven
and know that he was a good and caring Ameri-
can
and a hell of a fighter.

When he finished, Ullman, surrounded by the rest of the Technicians, their faces somber with the reality of the sudden death of this harsh world, stepped forward. The leader of the Technicians stood motion-less beside Lang as he spoke.

"He is subtracted from the reality equation but his formula lives on. His physicality will ascend to the ultimate logic where he will compute in peace." The entire group of humans and mutants stood for several minutes, their heads bowed, in acknowledgment of one man's bravery.

At last they headed back to the teams of still-nervous hybrids and got them moving again. There was not time to dwell on the dead. The living must always move on. The hybrid pack horses slowly picked up their pace, heaving with every step. Lang took one final look back. Erickson's corpse looked strangely peaceful, as if it were just sleeping in the shade of the towering cactus. But as soon as the team of animals and humans was out of sight, the earth around the corpse began moving. Tiny holes opened up in the hard-packed dirt and shapes emerged from them—long and undulating. Nearly five-feet long and a foot thick, they wriggled their blood-red bodies toward the dead human. Their small, curved beaklike jaws snapped into the cooling flesh. Within minutes the body was covered with thirty of the flesh-eating blood worms. They consumed the dead freefighter until there was nothing left.

Chapter Twelve

Rock and Archer could hardly believe it—there in front of them stood the high, cloud-slicing shape of Mt. Carson, beneath which Century City had been built. The truck they had taken from the dead Car Ones had held up for five days, at last sputtering out of fuel. But another four days of fast walking through the northern Rockies, terrain which Rockson knew well, had brought them home. The two men who had been through a lifetime's worth of death and pain in the last two months turned and looked at each other, bursting with the emotions of those who have survived and returned to tell about it. Then they reached forward simultaneously and clasped one another, wearing big shit-eating grins, and headed toward one of the many camouflaged entrances to the hidden ultra-modern fortress city that housed over fifty thousand men, women and children.

"Halt—who goes there?" a voice snapped out in the semi-darkness of the ramp leading down into the constantly guarded security checkpoint that was just inside each of the entrances.

"Rockson," the Doomsday Warrior said softly. "I'm afraid that I don't know what the password is for this week." Two guards cautiously peered around a rock wall, their Liberator automatic rifles clutched in sweaty hands, at the ready.

"God—it is Rockson," Calvin Jones, one of the city's one thousand-plus black population said. "We thought you were d-d-dead," he stuttered.

"Not yet," Rock said with a thin grin.

News spread quickly around the city, by phone and grapevine. Everywhere, the workers of the city, in the Liberator factories, the hydroponics facilities, even Dr. Shecter's science labs, came rushing from their jobs to see the returning hero. For Rockson was more than just a man to them. He was a symbol to the freefighters of the city—and to all America. That a single person *could* make a difference. That even the overwhelming military superiority of the Russian occupying forces was just a paper tiger. For Rockson had stood up to everything they could attack him with—and he had survived. More than survived—he had dealt them a crushing blow on their home ground, the first time since the outbreak of war that the Russian continent had been attacked. Ted Rockson, the man whose face hung on Wanted posters in every military barracks in America, was proof that the Red bear could be cut down to a bleeding bearskin rug on the floor.

By the time Rock and Archer reached the main thoroughfare of the underground city, crowds were already beginning to gather. The smiling and screaming throngs, yelling out his name as he entered, were held back by a struggling crowd of security officers. Reporters from the city's two newspapers, *The Century City Gazette* and *The Freefighter News*, stampeded through the security ring, snapping at the two heroes with cameras, yelling out questions about what had happened to them. Before Rock could speak the crowds surged through and lifted the two freefighters on their shoulders, carrying them in a triumphal procession around the underground square.

Detroit Green appeared from out of the milling thousands, his ebony face beaming.

"Well, look who's here," he shouted up to Rockson perched on the broad shoulders of two machinists. "Get tired of all those Russian girls?"

"The food, pal, the food," Rockson yelled back down, clamping his hands over his mouth like a megaphone to be heard. Suddenly the Doomsday Warrior saw Chen, the Chinese martial arts expert of Century City and one of his closest friends. The master of six fighting arts bowed and then looked up at Rockson with a relieved expression. The last time any of the Rock team had seen their leader was six weeks earlier when they had been attacked by a Red regular army commando force. With the president of the Reunited States of America, Charles Langford, and his daughter, Kim, the woman Rock had fallen in love with, traveling with them, the Doomsday Warrior had decided so create a diversion so the two of them and the Rock team could safely escape. He and Archer had run out of the cave they were hiding in, screaming their heads off. And it had worked—the Reds had followed them and the rest of the freefighters had made their way to cover. And that had been the last they had seen of Rockson—until now.

Rock made a slight bow to Chen, who then walked quickly away, not wishing to partake in such emotional displays. Rockson understood, they would talk later.

McCaughlin pushed his way through the crowd, his wide girth knocking people aside. He came up to Rock and looked up with a big Irish smile.

"Thought you was bear meat," the big man said.

"A few tried, but they spit me out." Rock motioned to be put down and the carriers at last complied.

"Come on, folks," Rock said, feeling a little sheepish at all the attention. "Time to get back to work—I'm sure there's plenty to do around this place." But they paid little heed to his words. His return had given them hope. Rockson was alive.

Suddenly a shape darted out of the masses straining to get a look at him, and threw itself on top of him. Rockson instinctively wrapped his arms around the person and prepared to throw him over his shoulder.

"Hey, you mismatched eyed mutant, it's *me*," Rona Wallender, the statuesque, acrobatic redhead who had been in love with Rockson since their teens, said. She reached over and landed a big kiss on his lips, oblivious to the crowds around them who laughed at the display of affection. She threw her arms around his wide shoulders like a she-cat refusing to let go. She had missed the only man she had ever loved too much to let him stray even an inch now that he was in her grasp. Even though he was in love with Kim,

Rockson had to admit to himself that it was good to see and hold her, pressed to close to him, her firm big breasts crushing against his chest.

"After this is all over—you know where my room is." She pressed the magnetized card key in his palm. "Just come—and plan to spend the night." She let him go only when he nodded yes, and then was lost in the press of people who had come everywhere from the multileveled city that swept Rockson on, in a flood of adulation. Rock and Archer gave up and let the river of humanity release their stored-up feelings. There wasn't a hell of a lot of good news that hit these parts, Rock knew, so he might as well let them have their moment.

Century City had been born out of death. September, 1989—when out of the skies, thousands of needles of flaming death, multiple warhead nuke missiles rained down on America. The attack had taken everyone by surprise. Everyone knew times were tense, but both sides continued to talk peace, even while they prepared for war. Until at last the nightmare of the twentieth century came true in a maelstrom of blood and fire that even the darkest imagination could never have conceived.

On Interstate 70, winding out of Denver and into the mountains toward Utah, thousands of vehicles—cars, trucks, tractor trailers—were moving through the five-mile tunnel bored through the very core of the surrounding mountains. The nukes that hit Colorado Springs, Longmont and Ft. Collins shook the Rockies. The tunnel entrances were lost in an avalanche of rocks and boulders, sealing off the stream of drivers in their Mack trucks and Chevys and VW buses—but saving those trapped inside the eight-lane tunnel from the effects of the blasts going on outside as well as the immediate rain of fallout blotting out the sun for days.

The survivors, men and women and children from all the broad crossections of American culture and races, got together and planned. They divided up the small amount of food and water that some of them had happened to be carrying—fortunately for them, two long diesels filled to the brim with supermarket goods had been trapped inside as well—and tried to figure out just what the hell to do. Five days later they dug small holes through the eastern entrance to the tunnel for air which they filtered through make-shift charcoal filtration systems. But they quickly understood the enormity of what had happened—and, even worse, the first man out spotted giant Soviet airlifters dropping paratroopers over Denver. The Reds weren't content with blowing up half of America, now they wanted to take it over as well.

They sealed themselves off again and worked on survival—that was the name of the game now. All the goals, careers, loves and hates that had meant everything to them just days before were now but dust blown into the stratosphere by atomic destruction. They worked at building some kind of base, a headquarters to live in and from which they could strike out at the Russians. But soon leaders emerged—men like Bonne, Ostrader, Taggart—who elected to do more, they would build an actual underground city, linking up some nearby mining tunnels and the tunnel of Interstate 70. They would construct lighting, ventillation, even hydroponic tanks so they could have their own food supply, for amongst the involuntary inhabitants of the new subterranean world were experts in almost every field: doctors, chemists, mechanics, scientists in almost fifteen different fields. After all they were Americans, a people whose country had been born out of hardship, pain and an eternal struggle for freedom. And they would one day be free again—of that there was no doubt. Even if it took a hundred years—hence the name Century City—a city born out of the ashes into a world of flames and unimaginable ferocity.

Rockson couldn't help but think of those early years as he was rushed along at the head of the swell of people past the brilliantly lit Liberator rifle factory which shipped out nearly one hundred rifles a day to other freefighting cities; past the giant central library; past the Museum of America's Past, filled to overflowing with artifacts of Americana—everything from bicycles to cowboy boots, rock posters to football uniforms, dug up on scouting missions for supplies; past the entrance to Dr. Shecter's science labs where miracles of technology were turned out on a monthly basis, the aging Shecter responsible for the ultra-modern conveniences and weaponry that Century City now possessed, making it the most advanced of all the hidden cities throughout the country. Rockson took it all in as the crowd pushed him forward, and realized for the first time just what a marvel the place was. And how glad he was to be in the only place he called home.

At last the crowd reached the largest open area of Century City—Lincoln Square, with its steel sculpture of the famous president, ten-feet high, sitting in its center. There, it seemed that half the damned city was waiting to greet him. They edged him forward toward the speaker's platform, a big aluminum and wood affair where the politicians of the city loved to exercise their oratory skills. It was nicknamed "the soapbox" as any of the city's inhabitants could get up on it and make a speech on any subject that his heart desired. Free speech was alive and well though living underground, in a world where for most people, under the Red rule, even one wrong word overheard by a Red soldier or the dreaded KGB meant death—violent and instantaneous.

As the throngs pushed him toward the wooden stairs to the twenty-foot-square platform, Rock saw Shannon, the well-endowed blonde who was assistant security chief, and Rath, her moody, dour boss, come from out of a doorway straight toward him. Rath eyed the crowd nervously. He didn't like dramatic displays and this group was getting out of hand.

"Rockson I've got to—" the security chief began to say, but was cut off by the crowd which pushed Rock up the stairs, yelling, "Speech, speech."

The Doomsday Warrior quieted them down after a minute with waves of his hand.

"Well, I really don't know what to say," Rock said, looking out at the parade of faces he knew so well.

"Say anything, Rock, we just want to hear you talk," Betty McCarthy yelled up. "So we know you're actually alive."

Rock looked down for a moment at a loss for words and then began.

"Well, I guess I can tell you a little about what

Archer and I saw out there in the unexplored North. Going through South Dakota, Iowa and God knows whatall, we met a lot of people. A lot of good and evil. But America is as alive out there as it is here. The entire North is growing stronger—if not always nicer." The crowd laughed. "Now I don't want you to think it's a picnic out there—cause it ain't. We came in contact with everything from Amazon women warriors, to car-driving cannibals. But I will say this, on the positive side—we didn't see a damned Red anywhere."

The audience listened with hypnotized eyes. They knew every time they came in contact with the Doomsday Warrior that he was history—a living legend whose name would go down in the schoolbooks of the future as one of America's greatest heroes, alongside such men as Nathan Hale, Paul Revere, and John Paul Jones. This made him almost unreal to them in a way, a man more than mortal whose eyes were fixed on the destiny of the entire planet—not just his own human concerns. To them he was like a living god in their midst, a solid but intangible presence that gave the entire city a feeling of pride and specialness.

"And as for our Moscow trip," Rockson said, glancing over at Archer who had been pushed toward the edge of the platform and sat stubbornly on the stairs, not wanting to get dragged into all the fool talk. "I think we gave a blow to the Reds that they'll never recover from. We—"

Rock's words were cut off in mid-sentence by the head of security, Rath, who jumped up on the platform and grabbed the microphone that stood on its dais.

"I'm sorry, folks, to cut your fun short," Rath said, "but Rockson and Archer here are tired and for security reasons we can't allow any more information out about any military actions taken in Russia. You can hear the unclassified versions of the tapes we'll make when we debrief them—in a few weeks. Now, there's Liberators to be assembled, tunnels to build, game to be gathered. We may sometimes feel like life is getting sweet—but it's not. Don't any of you fool yourselves for one second that things are all OK around here these days—cause they're not."

The crowd slowly dispersed, depressed by Rath's words. The man had a real knack for busting balloons and making even the sunniest of days feel like a thunderstorm was brewing. "Oh come on," they muttered, "the guy's gonna make me cry if I hang around here any longer." They headed back to their work stations at the various levels of the underground world.

"You're sure a cheery fellow," Rockson said as Rath released the microphone and turned toward him.

"Things are bad, Rock, very bad," he whispered, not wanting any of the spectators to hear.

"What?" Rock asked, growing alarmed by the usually confident albeit depressing Rath's look of fear and anxiety.

"Come on, let's get you through decontamination and then we'll talk." The security chief, his long back hunched over as if he were deep in thought, headed back toward his office as Shannon led Rock and Archer to the decon chamber.

They walked inside the glass booths that stood built into the solid rock walls, twenty of them, shaped somewhat like telephone booths, standing several feet apart. Rock began taking off his clothes on the wooden platform outside and glanced over at Shannon who was staring at him hard.

"I'm not into exhibitionism," Rock said with a half smile. Shannon blushed brightly, not having been aware of looking at him like a lovestruck teenager.

"Sorry," she said with the anger of someone caught showing more than they should. Rock undressed and stepped inside the booth, shutting the door behind. The decontamination unit worked in three stages. First, he was sprayed with hot water mixed with a special cleansing agent from nozzles above him, then rinsed free of the suds. The second stage set powerful vacuum pumps in motion on all sides of the chamber sucking off any small particles of radioactive substance that might have adhered to his skin. The third and final stage set a series of ultraviolet and infrared lamps to turn on, bathing him with a relaxing heat that also destroyed any microbes or bacteria on the surface of his body.

"Decontamination procedure over," a soft voice said from a hidden speaker and Rock exited again, a new set of civilian clothes awaiting him outside the booth, deposited through a computerized slot next to the unit. He dressed and quickly headed over to Rath's office to find out just what the hell had been going on while he was away.

"I've been waiting for you," Rath said pleasantly as the Doomsday Warrior walked into the security chief's spartan office. "Sit down, please," he said, motioning for Rock to deposit himself in one of the chairs in front of Rath's small wooden desk.

"How are Kim and her father?" Rock blurted out, unable to contain his anxiety. The entire time he had been away, first in Russia and then in the wilds of North America, the question had sat like a festering wound in his brain. He leaned forward, his eyes showing his desperation.

"Fine, fine," Rath said, waving his hands, as if that were the least of their problems. "It's a long story—but they're safe."

"Well, where are they?" Rock cut him off.

"After you created the diversion, the rest of the squad was able to get away. They accompanied President Langford and his daughter to Omicron City for a conference on developing a unified military council for all the Free Cities—and also a demonstration of some new anti-aircraft missiles, small enough to be fired by a single man. Dr. Shecter has been developing them and plans to begin delivery of hundreds of them within the next several months."

"I know nothing of these missiles," Rock exclaimed, his eyes wide in curiosity.

"Developed while you were away. He's been working on them for a long time and had a recent breakthrough in construction based in part on some of the technology you brought back from the Technicians."

Rock almost sagged in relief. Kim, the woman he loved, the only woman he had ever really loved was safe . . . safe. The words echoed through his mind like a chime of hope. Rath began the arduous, detailed debriefing with Shannon standing nearby taking it all down on tape. At the end of the two-hour monologue by Rockson, Rath at last said, "Well, I think that's enough for now. Though we may want to fill in more details later. Jesus, Rock," he said with a thin smile, one of the few Rockson had ever seen make. "You really busted some Red ass while you were over there."

"I saw an opportunity—and took it. Any freefighter would have done the same."

"Would have tried, Rock, would have tried," Rath said. "You made it happen." He sighed, looked down at the desk as if not wanting to say what he knew he had to and then went on. "But I'm afraid it's one step forward and two back. Your actions in Moscow have apparently infuriated Premier Vassily to have a shit-fit. The Reds are preparing a tremendous assault against us. The likes of which we've never seen in the hundred years of the existence of C.C."

"But I told you I took out their ICBM and Satellite Control Center. They can't launch any big nukes against us from there. And if Shecter's air-defense missiles are being installed here—what can they do?"

"It's grim, Rock," Rath said, pulling at his hair as he was wont to do when nervous. "Vassily has assembled nearly three hundred thousand German troops. Nazi troops I should say. This Nazi army has apparently been in the works for some time, under the firm grip of the Moscow central command. They were just waiting for the right time to use them—and it's here. They're fanatical, well-trained and armed. Already nearly two hundred thousand of them have been airlifted to America and set up in a new fortress city the Reds have built called Dzersch, just eighty miles south of here. They've already sent thousands of advance commandos into the mountains, searching for Century City. And from our reports, the rest are soon to follow."

"All this—just for us?" Rock asked incredulously.

"Just us, Rock. They're not after any of the other free cities. They want to destroy Century City, grind it into dust—and they want you. They've already started northward through the Rockies, blasting everything in their path. And they outnumber our fighting forces at least fifty-to-one. Even if we mobilized every man, woman and child in the city, we haven't got near their fire power. They're moving in with artillery, armored assault vehicles, tanks, and a good hundred attack helicopters."

Rock whistled. "Out of the frying pan and into the fire. It seems to be the story of my life."

"It could be—the end," Rath said in a cracking whisper. "We can probably assemble perhaps ten thousand trained fighters armed with Liberator rifles. Plus perhaps one hundred mortars and an equal number of .55 millimeter machine guns. We've got plenty of grenades, small-scale stuff—and of course the four black beam pistols you brought back."

"Four? I thought there were five," Rock said.

"One just gave out. Shecter has no idea why—could be power loss or inadvertent misuse of the weapon. But he is concerned that the rest might not last much longer."

"What about the second expedition led by Erickson and Lang to bring back more particle weapons?"

"Haven't seen or heard from them for months now," Rath said, discouraged. "They're way overdue.

I hate to say it—but I'm afraid that they may have bought it."

That really hit Rockson. The Swede, always as fast with a joke as he was with his hands. They'd been through a lot together—a hell of a lot. And Lang, the kid who had matured so much of late and who reminded Rock more than any man he had ever met of himself.

"But enough of all this glum talk," Rath said, flashing a phony smile. "We've got to do the best we can—and hope. We have no choice—whether we like it or not, they're coming. And coming fast."

"We'll build a number of defensive perimeters around Century City," Rock said, his mind instantly shifting into overdrive as he searched for some sort of strategy that could hold the Nazi killers off. He realized with a sinking feeling in his guts that as the top military officer of the city, it was going to be up to him to come up with something. Come up with a miracle was more like it. "And let's get Shecter to move up production of those new missiles of his—and none are to be shipped out."

"That's positive thinking, Rock," Rath said, glad that the Doomsday Warrior now held the responsibility for the military defense that had been resting heavily on his own shoulders while Rockson was away.

"Can you assemble all the top military staff and Dr. Shecter to meet with me at 0800? Tell them to bring every goddamned idea they've come up with—no matter how bizarre."

"Sure, Rock, will do," Rath said, his enthusiasm beginning to rise as Rock's energy caught hold of him.

"I've got to get some sleep or I'll pass out at the meeting," Rockson said, rubbing his eyes. "Ring me up at 0700. Also you'd better put the entire city on Security Status Red. No outside excursions unless absolutely necessary. Have all internal radio and telecommunications systems shut down dead. Those Germans will have the most advanced Red technology at their disposal. Even though we're shielded in here—at close range they just might pick up something."

"Yes, sir," Rath said, looking suddenly embarrassed as he realized what he had said. "I'll get on everything right away."

Rockson looked the intel chief square in the eye. "And don't forget, Rath, the Third Reich was supposed to have lived a thousand years. But it died in a hell of blood and fire. Maybe we can send these neo-Nazis down into the same grave where their Führer lies. I'm sure they'd be happy to join him."

Chapter Thirteen

It seemed like he had just closed his eyes when Rock's newly strapped-on sub-sonic intercom watch began buzzing. It was Rona. Rona, the woman he had grown up with since coming to Century City as a teenager, who had shared his bed for years and who, like Rock, was one of the premier fighters of the city.

"Where are you?" she asked petulantly. "I've been waiting all perfumed and ready." Rockson knew that she was aware of Kim and that she didn't like it one bit—but she was a big girl now. She had told him a long time ago that she would be available to him when and if he needed her . . . always. It was a temptation the trail-weary freefighter found hard to ignore.

"Sorry, sugar," Rock said, sitting up in his bed. "Must have passed out. I guess the air is too clean in here."

"Well?"

"I'll be there in ten minutes. Don't let the perfume evaporate." He clicked off. He rose and walked over to the mirror that sat on one wall of the ten-by-ten foot room. Most of the freefighters had fairly draconian living spaces. Except for families with children—where the need for extra rooms was undeniable—the city's populace lived in simple rooms with but a bed, dresser, mirror and washbasin, and whatever decorations they deigned to put up. Space was at a premium here with much of the additional chambers that were painstakingly carved out of the sheer granite bedrock surrounding the city used for science or the military. They were at war, every minute, every day of their lives, and perhaps their plain though comfortable living quarters made it that much easier to never forget it.

Rockson splashed cool water over his face and stared at himself for the first time in ages. His violet and aquamarine eyes stared back as if looking at a stranger. His face had the look of weathered granite, tanned, with thin lines around his eyes and mouth. He could see the life he had led over the last twenty years, years of violence and struggle, of desolation and awesome beauty—could see it all in that face looking back. Every encounter with the enemy, with the wild beasts of the plains and jungles, had left its mark on him, had grooved itself into his very flesh. He was like a walking sculpture, etched in blood, chiseled with knives and bullets. Plus he hadn't shaved for days. A thick stubbly beard had worked itself out over his lower face. He took the magnemicrorazor from his drawer and shaved the whiskers off until he looked at least vaguely presentable. Then he headed over to Level 3 and Rona's room.

She was waiting for him, stretched out on her bed

decked out with multicolored scarves and pillows so that it somehow resembled a sultan's lovemaking chamber. Unlike many of the city's inhabitants, Rona reveled in beautiful objects and around her room were lilies in vases, bright pictures on the walls and an immense gold-gilded mirror that she had somehow finagled from the Century City Museum.

"I know you had to fight your way through grizzlies and sabre-toothed mountain cats—and that's why you're late getting here. Right?" she asked sarcastically, her long red hair flowing like a curtain of flame over her shoulders and onto the pillow behind her.

"How'd you know?" Rock asked with a smile, walking over to the bed and gazing down at her beauty. She was an extraordinary woman, voluptuous, smart, and tough as nails. In the days before the war she most likely would have been a movie star or model, her loveliness was that eye-catching. She was a direct descendant of the famous Flying Wallendas trapeze act, one of the most famous acrobatic and high-wire circus teams that had ever performed. And she had been brought up in their footsteps, touring the country when just a child with her father, who had his own mini-circus. Until the Reds caught up with him and found out he had been performing intelligence services for the hidden cities. He had been taken away and she had never seen him again, somehow finding her way to Century City where she had been welcomed and stayed for the last twenty years. Here, she had studied martial arts under Chen, until she was unquestionably one of the best hand-to-hand fighters in the city. Even Rockson had been thrown a few times by her quick moves. Unlike most of the women of C.C. she had demanded to be part of the combat squads that went out and raided Red convoys, and had joined Rock many times in attacking the enemy. She was as fearless as him—and as passionate.

"Cat got your tongue?" she asked, looking up from the wide soft feather bed. She was wearing a nearly transparent negligee which accented her large perfect breasts, thin waist and soft red triangle in a most complimentary way. "Well, look at that," Rona said with a laugh. "The poor man's been out sleeping with the buffalo and muskrats so long he's forgotten what a woman looks like." She reached her arms up for him, her eyes wide with desire.

Rockson laughed out loud. He was treated with such ultra-respect by most people that it was refreshing to be with someone who didn't give a shit about his "fame." He could let his hair down here, say anything, do anything—and it felt wonderful. He bent down over her, gazing on her white luscious flesh, a feast of sensuality. He could feel his manhood stiffen inside his loose-fitting pants and suddenly he dropped on top of her, like a panther on top of its prey.

"Now that's what I like—a man who knows what he wants," Rona squealed, wrapping her strong arms around his muscled back. He pressed his face to hers and kissed her. Her lips opened for him and her tongue darted out, seeking entrance. Within seconds they were passionately kissing, their hands searching over each other's flesh in wild desire. He bit softly into her neck and she opened her mouth, letting out a deep moan. Her hands searched lower and found his hardness, rubbing against it with desperate urgency.

Suddenly she sat up and pushed him down on the bed. She slowly undid his trousers as if partaking in a sacred ritual and slid them off the steel-hard legs. A shiver coursed through her spine as his stiff rod sprang into full view and in a flash she moved down to it. Her full lips engulfed the spear of flesh and she began moving up and down on it, taking it deep into her throat as little groans of pleasure came from her mouth. Rockson trembled from the incredible sensation until at last his passion became too powerful. He reached up and grabbed her, pulling her down alongside him. He flipped the negligee aside and spread her silky thighs, rubbing his hand over the wet mound of her sex. She lay back, her lips wide apart, eyes closed, making almost imperceptible catlike sounds. He could feel from her velvet wetness that she was ready for him and he slid on top of her, crushing her full breasts beneath his chest. He guided his rigid staff into the luxuriously full bush of red hair, parting the pink lips of her womanhood with his fingers. Then, poised above her, he pushed the living spear in, as the puffed lips opened wide for his entrance. She was so filled with the liquid of a woman's desire that the rod slid all the way in a second, deep into her most hidden parts. She groaned aloud and spread her legs further to give him room.

Rock began pumping, slowly at first, and then as he entered into the realm of total passion where the mind disappears and the body takes over, harder and faster, until he was ramming into her like a piston. Her body quivered in uncontrollable desire as she took his every stroke. At last her back arched up high and she let out a deep guttural groan of climax, jerking around beneath him, as her body released its stored up well of sexual energy. Her hands flew to his chest and stroked them mindlessly over and over. Her groans pushed Rock over the edge and he too released his load, shooting into her like a cannon firing white-hot lava. They twisted and writhed against one another for nearly a minute until every last ounce of passion had been released. Then they tenderly held each other as Rockson drifted into a deep and peaceful sleep.

He awoke early at 0600, still hours before the military council meeting. He felt rested for the first time in weeks, thank God, and knew he was ready to deal with the complex battle plans they would have to formulate. Rona was still sleeping, a wide smile on her creamy face. He rose and dressed silently, not wanting to disturb her, and made his way out of the room, leaving a note on the table that read, "Thanks for reminding me just how beautiful a woman can be. Those buffalo can get pretty ornery sometimes."

He tracked down Archer, who had become sick and tired of all the attention that was being bestowed upon him, finding him in a faraway corner of the city—in the steam-pipe conduit tunnel that led from the geothermal source of Century City's power under Ice Mountain.

"Had a hell of a time finding you," Rock said. Archer was lying atop a pile of flea-bitten hornbear rugs, half asleep, a bottle of C.C. Beer next to him.

His eyes were red and puffy. The near-mute snarled a halfhearted hello and turned over. His world was out there in the wilds, fighting things, surviving. Only then did he feel fully alive. Here in C.C. the formalities, the politics confused and bored him.

"Hey, pal, no time for sleep, your public—and I—need you."

"Noooo, Rooockson. No speeech," the big freefighter growled, pulling one of the torn bear rugs up over his head.

"How about some breakfast then? My treat—in the Skyview Room. Everything you can eat: steak, eggs, anything." Rock laughed as the pile of bear fur moved and the giant's head came into view once more.

"OK," Archer mumbled and within seconds dragged himself out from under the mass of fur, adjusted his clothing, patted down his beard with his hands and said, "Anyyythiiing?"

After the sumptuous meal at the Skyview, an ingeniously designed restaurant located at the uppermost level of Century City which used baffles and mirrors to allow light through from camouflaged gaps and fissures in the mountain peak above, Archer went off to help set up the missile defense system at the top of Carson Mountain, the wall of rock adjacent to Ice Mountain. His great strength would aid greatly in the placing of the launch tubes as they were short of heavy equipment to move the high-tech weaponry around.

Rockson headed down to the Military Operations Room where the general staff was waiting for him around a large three-dimensional map of the Rockies for three hundred miles in every direction. They greeted him warmly—Colonel Fenton, Major Norton, and Generals Wooster and Janet Crawford, the only female general in America's long military history. Rock had put on his full military uniform, razor-creased and bedecked with the medals that had been presented to him on numerous occasions. This was one of the few times he had worn the damned thing, usually feeling it representative of a military mentality and rigidity that he did not wish to display. Today he wore it not out of pride but as a confidence builder. He had to make the military council believe anything was possible—for the hero of the Moscow attack, who had survived all these years with nothing but his skill, strength and brains to guide him.

The entire council stood up straight as poles as the Doomsday Warrior approached the oval operations table, their hands snapping to salutes.

"Please, please," Rock said with a cursory, half-hearted salute, "let's not get into all that. As far as I know, a salute has never stopped one Russian soldier." The group laughed and relaxed a little, sitting back down in their wooden, hard-backed chairs. "All right, let's get right to it," the Doomsday Warrior said, as he lowered himself into the chair at the head of the table.

"Intelligence reports first." He looked over at Rath who appeared somewhat uncomfortable around all these military types. He preferred to run his section his own way.

"Reports are coming in every hour, Rock. The Nazi troops have been dropped over a wide range of territory to our south. Apparently, as far as we can tell our forward observation posts, nearly fifty thousand commandos have already begun search-and-destroy missions through the Rockies. Apparently the bulk of the force is to be landed by transport chopper at Forrester Valley, you know, that fairly flat plain, nearly twenty miles across. It's about thirty miles south of—"

"I know where it is," Rockson said curtly, having spent many nights there while a teenager, watching the stars and the meteors slash across the vast open skies.

"Anyway, it would appear, although I don't want to say it's a surety, that the Germans will link up their forces there, the commando units coming down out of the southernmost mountains and joining with the main army—and, Rock, these guys will be equipped with tanks, the works. I can only guess that they'll continue from there heading north, blasting the damned range to bits until they find us."

"Who's the actual man in charge of the entire operation?" Rock asked, opening the stiff collar of his uniform so he could breathe. Now he knew why he hated the thing.

"Well, the chain of command, as far as we can make it out," Rath said, looking down at a binder full of notes, "is Vassily at the very top—though beyond setting the whole thing in motion we believe he's back in Moscow now, waiting. The commander of the U.S. operations is a pleasant fellow named Von Reisling—from old German stock, eye patch and all. Beyond that—we don't know a thing."

"How the hell did all these goddamned Nazis spring up out of nowhere?" General Wooster asked, his jowled neck puffing up over the top of his collar like a rooster's fleshy throat.

"I don't know," Rath said, looking a little embarrassed, for he prided himself on keeping tabs on all the Red innovations throughout the world. "We'd heard rumors of a neo-Nazi resurgence in Germany over the last few years, but, Jesus Christ, I never knew they'd assembled an actual army. It must have been Vassily's ace in the hole, kept top-secret until he needed them. But from what we can gather, these guys are tough, well-trained, not babes in the woods. And they want to prove themselves. Let's not forget the military history of Germany or the fanatical violence with which the Nazi troops of World War II fought. Every one of these guys is a killer."

"What's our exact military strength, Fenton?" Rock asked, turning to the colonel, who was in charge of battle-ready units. "And I don't mean bullshit strength," the Doomsday Warrior added, wanting to let them all know that this was not the time to play games.

"I'd say ten thousand combat troops and another ten thousand we've been working real hard with, Rock. They haven't been under fire, but I'd swear my life on them. We've been increasing all advanced training tremendously in the last six months, Rockson. And we've come up with what we think is a new concept in attack strategy."

"Shoot," Rock said, leaning forward with interest.

"Well, we'd been feeling for a long time that our attack strategies were outmoded. We started looking for new ideas and I went down to our Military Literature Archive and dug up some books from the

1980s. They were the training and tactical manuals for a special group called the Rapid Deployment Strike Force. Apparently the American government, after a number of terrorist attacks on Americans around the world, decided to create a highly mobile, super-efficient unit, capable of dealing out tremendous fire power and devastation. My entire staff studied them and we came to a decision to implement these types of units."

"The book is mightier than the bullet," General Crawford joked.

"They're fast, they're deadly—and the Reds won't be expecting anything like 'em. We've been fighting a guerrilla war, Rock, for a hundred years now. Hide, run, strike, hide—small units of men attacking convoys, blowing up a few tanks now and then. Times are changing. There's a president now, a military council to oversee all freefighter actions and coordinate them for maximum effectiveness. We need to be bold, now. To attack *them*—make them run and hide. I believe this Rapid Deployment Strike Force is a vital step in that direction." Fenton sat back, breathing out as if he had just delivered a long-thought-about speech.

"Sounds great," Rock said. His eyes narrowed. "But I gather from what you said that their entire mode of operation revolved around attack helicopters. I didn't know we had a fleet."

Fenton smiled. "But we do, Rock, we do. It's not huge but it's deadly. Over the last few years we've stolen nearly twelve attack choppers from the Reds—five of them jet-powered. Every one of those things is armed to the teeth, with .55s hanging out of both doors, missile racks, napalm, phosphorus, anti-personnel bombs, even some air-to-air missiles capable of taking out a MIG. These things can do incredible damage, stun the Reds before they can stun us. We may wind up losing every goddamned one of them but the pilots and crew are trained and raring to go. Begging to go, I should say. They want to show that the freefighting forces have teeth—that can sink deep into the throat of the military giant of the red empire."

"Excellent," Rock said, looking down at the three-dimensional contoured map of the Rocky Mountain range that filled the table. "What else do we have, what's our combat fire power?"

"We're in the best shape we've ever been in right now. Two large munitions convoys were attacked within the last six months carrying heavy stuff. We've got brand-new still-in-the-crate mortars, .55s, recoilless rifles, nearly two dozen stream-lined field cannons, a ton of grenades and magnesium bombs. I needn't go on—we've got more than enough for the number of people we're going to be able to send out to battle."

"Well, we've got the tools," Rock said, looking around at the assembled officers, the men and women who would have to decide on the strategy that would save or destroy Century City—and perhaps the world.

"I've got a few thoughs on that," General Crawford said, her blue eyes gleaming in her deeply wrinkled sixty-year-old face. Crawford had begun her career in the army unwittingly. At Century City University as a young woman she had majored in Russian Studies—reading and absorbing everything she could on the nation that ruled a global empire. Her expertise over the years made her the leading mind on understanding the Red mentality. Gradually her studies headed toward the military machinations of the Red army, its weaponry and strategies. Before long she had become the city's military staff's main consultant, spending her time helping them develop counterstrategies to the Russian brand of war. Somehow over the years, she had become one of them, been given a rank and a uniform and, without anyone really noticing, worked her way up to the rank of general. Her words were highly respected by everyone on the military council, and though just a frail-looking thing, more like somebody's grandmother than the razor-sharp analytic brain that she was, her words brought instant silence.

"Go ahead," Rock said, smiling. Although they had had their run-ins over the years, as Rock had had with all the top army brass, he knew she knew her stuff.

"Well, we have to understand the military mind of the Reds in order to predict what they're going to do. There are basically two things to take into account here. One—the Reds have operated under the same basic strategic guidelines since World War II when they fought the Nazis. That is, large, dare I say gigantic, concentrations of troops and armor sweeping forward as a single unit. They believe in the power of strength, brute strength. There's little subtlety involved in how they operate. Secondly, they need to create an image, a dramatic demonstration not just to us but to the rest of the freefighters in

America—that they can crush us as easily as an ant. Both these factors lead me to believe that Rath's conclusions about their beginning the main thrust from Forrester Valley with virtually everything they've got is true."

"But the Nazis are running the show," Rock protested. "This Von Reisling—surely he'll prefer to use the German tactics developed by the Third Reich."

"I doubt it, Rock," General Crawford went on. "You've got to remember the paranoia of the Russian command. In their own way they're probably quite apprehensive about turning this Nazi army loose. How do they know it won't turn again *them* at some point? The Russians and the Germans have fought more wars than there are teeth in a sabre-bear. They've got a history of confrontation and mistrust between them that goes back for centuries. I'll stake my reputation on the fact that the tactical maneuvers have been drawn up by the Russian high command and that the Germans will have little latitude in carrying them out. They'll be there all right, the entire goddamned army, all quarter million men will no doubt join in the Valley and then begin an advance several miles wide, sweeping north until they find us. In my opinion the time to strike would be there. We know where they'll be, all their forces will be contained in a box in effect twenty miles long by five miles wide. Strike and strike hard," Crawford said, slamming her thin veiny fist down on the table top. "We can't let them begin advancing through the mountains beyond that—or it will be too late."

"I agree with your analysis," Rock said. "I think we must strike—with everything we've got. Flank them, break up the large force into smaller units that we can more readily attack. Our strategy must be to create confusion, break down their communications, destroy their offensive advance before it even has a chance to get going."

The rest of the staff concurred. They spent the next few hours hammering out just how their attack and defensive maneuvers would proceed, at last reaching a general consensus.

1) Construction and demolition crews would construct, in the old gold mine ten miles south of the valley, five fake Century Cities, complete with entrances and makeshift structures inside that created the appearance of a real city. They would be filled to the brim with high explosives. The Nazis might waste precious days, battling their way into each of these—giving the freefighters more time to deploy.

2) Three fallback positions, each the responsibility of different units of the city's army would be set up, in five mile intervals falling back from the Valley.

3) The basic attack force would consist of fifteen thousand troops broken into five basic forces. A) Artillery and heavy machine gun units that would be set up at the northern edge of the Valley on the slopes that rose above them. B) Combat units, armed with Liberators, smaller machine guns and grenades that would take up camouflaged positions on the lower portions of the slopes, holding back whatever troops actually reached the bottom of the mountains there. C) A cavalry riding hybrids that would pour into the Nazi forces from the right and left flank and if possible from their rear. They would be broken down into twenty-man units, all carrying satchel charges

that they would heave into the heaviest concentrations of equipment and troops. D) The Rapid Deployment Strike Force, using the choppers, would sweep the Valley wreaking havoc. Their main target would be the tanks leading the advance. E) Guerrilla attack units under the direct command of Rockson himself would enter the field of combat dressed in the same color uniforms as the Nazis. They would try to infiltrate the ranks—and their main targets would be officers, especially Von Reisling. If they could take out enough of the field command, the battle would collapse out of sheer confusion. F) A special unit of men who had become proficient in the use of the remaining four black beam pistols would be spaced a mile apart with the artillery units. Their main target would be Red helicopters and jet fighters.

4) If all else failed, Century City would be evacuated through tunnels that led out the back, surfacing three miles north of the underground fortress. The city itself would be blown up with booby traps—creating a living hell for the Germans and their Red masters. It all sounded good—on paper.

"Now what about our communications systems?" Major Norton asked. "The Nazis will be able to hear our attack commands—that is, if they don't use jamming equipment to cut off our radio and walkie-talkie systems altogether."

"I think I've got a possible solution," Rock said. "I know it sounds a little crazy—but when I was with the Glowers they taught me how to use certain telepathic abilities that apparently are latent in all mutants. I've experimented with it to some extent and have been able to make contact with other of the star-patterned mutants in the city. There are about twenty of us by now. I suggest we use our electronic communications network—in code—but if the Nazis are able to shut it down, by whatever means, that we have a fallback system of mutant telepaths interspersed among all our forces so we can remain in contact." The officers looked a little skeptical—but there was nothing to lose at this stage of the game.

"One final question," Rock said, "before we get this whole ballgame going. How long do we have?"

"I'd say up to a week, Rock," General Crawford replied from across the table. "This is a major event for the Reds. Jesus, it's one of the largest deployments of men in history. You've already humiliated Premier Vassily. He can't take another of the same magnitude—or his very power base might crumble around him. No, I'm sure the Germans have been ordered to get everything exactly right, every man, every tank working and ready to go before they risk striking. They've got as much to lose as we do. A week—ten days at the most."

"Well, if we can't get it together in that time—we might as well forget about it," Rock said. "Good luck. And God help us all."

The meeting broke up as the military council rushed off to prepare their units for the battle strategy. Rock called all the star-patterned mutants like himself, those with the slightly luminous five-pointed star on their lower backs, together for the training session in ESP. Even he felt quite unsure of its feasibility. But anything was worth a try. He gathered them around him—Parcell, Watkins, Mooney, even Rona—in Chen's martial arts gymnasium. With its white walls and bare furnishings it was the ideal place, without distractions, to see if the rest of the Century City mutants could do a damned thing with their abilities—or whether Rock could teach them. He explained the battle they were all about to face and just how the telepathy could be used for communications. They sat around him on soft tatami mats, listening intently.

"Now I know you're all quite skeptical about this," Rock said, standing in the middle of the seated circle. "Well—so am I. But I know the damned stuff works, because I've experienced it myself. It's subtle, very hard to use—but it does exist. The Glowers communicate only through telepathy—and I'll tell you when you hear all those minds joining, speaking at once, it's something you'll never forget. Scientists have known for centuries that animals, certain species, exhibit communication abilities that cannot be explained except through some sort of telepathic ability. Even ordinary homo sapiens receive dim thoughts from those around them. But we filter it all out—as adults anyway. It would be too frightening to know what the hell is going on in everyone's mind—so the brain sabotages the potential for ESP by inhibiting these abilities. In us, the star-patterned mutants, who Dr. Shecter believes are the next evolutionary stage of mankind, the ESP capability is much greater. This accounts, I believe, for the so-called mutant's luck that I'm sure we've all experienced. That uncanny ability we have to survive where others don't—to somehow just know many times what is going to happen next."

"Now I learned from the Glowers how to increase,

to amplify our special thought-sending and receiving so that we can consciously use it to communicate—theoretically through almost any distance, through rock, steel walls. The telepathic wave, whatever it is, does not seem to be stopped by solid material. I learned from them out of desperation—Kim Langford, the president's daughter, was about to die. The Glowers needed my special connection to her to enter her nervous system and put their own healing powers into use." Rock noticed Rona looking up at him with clenched teeth as he mentioned Kim's name. But this was no time to hold anything back. With the survival of the very city at stake, Rock couldn't spare personal feelings—even Rona's.

"Now the telepathic ability seems to rise in power under situations of extreme desperation, fear, anger, whatever. Hormones are literally pumped into the body that must escalate certain electrical systems within our bodies, so that without even realizing it—we send out calls for help, try to read our attackers' thoughts. It works the same in mutant's luck stories—you've probably all experienced it. How you got a shiver of apprehension, of danger, and stepped back as someone shot, or moved just as a snar-lizard snapped its jaws. Now, in order for you to learn you have to become desperate, anxious, even terrified. And the situation we're about to face is—I'm sad to say—tailor-made for those sorts of emotions. Because the key to this battle is communications—safe, undetectable communications instantly between all our scattered forces. If the Nazis can hear us they'll know our moves—and our positions." He looked around at them with a quizzical smile. Every face stared up with fascination—and not a small amount of fear.

"Well, let's give it a try," the Doomsday Warrior said. "I'll work with you one at a time to try and get you to feel what I'm talking about. Any questions?" No one uttered a word.

They lined up and Rock pressed his widespread fingers against each forehead. He jagged his thoughts of destruction, hellfire, rape and torture into each brain, sending out the most powerful terrifying images he could muster. And they felt them, drawing back in horror as the death visions entered their minds. They felt both elated and disturbed at the process, wanting to help but feeling that perhaps they were opening up a box that would thereafter never close. But there was no choice.

"OK, now you've at least felt the stuff," Rock said, after he'd worked for a few minutes with each one. "Now I want you to break up into groups of twos and try it yourself. Don't worry about sending complex thoughts right now—just fear, anger. The strong emotions. We can work on the more subtle possibilities later. Meanwhile I'll work individually with each of you to help you focus."

He chose Rona first for his one-to-one. They were already connected by many emotions. She would undoubtedly make the quickest link-up with him—and that would give the others confidence in themselves that it was really possible. They sat kneeling, their faces just inches apart. Rock put his hands over her head and closed his eyes.

"You can hear me," he sent out, concentrating all his energy into that single mental burst. "I'm going to send you images and I want you to feel them and try to send back to me what you see. OK?"

Rona smiled at him, and said softly, "Go ahead, Rock."

He began sending out the foulest thoughts he could—images in his memory of death, mutilation, of bodies lying rotting in fields, of the mindbreaker machine drilling into brain cavities sending up funnels of smoking tissue. He sent out thoughts of all the horror and monstrosities he had seen in his life. And he had seen much.

She winced with the pain of the images. At first they were dim, hazy floating circles of death. But within minutes, as she opened her mind in spite of her fear, the images solidified and she felt and saw things she had never imagined in her darkest dreams. Suddenly she screamed out, in spite of herself. The pain was unbearable. Rock stopped for a moment and held her. Without talking, he telepathically spoke to her.

"You've done it, Rona. You feel it. Rise above the pain. Concentrate on the ability. Now tell me something—with your mind, not your lips."

"What should I say?" she sent back.

"You've already said it," he replied telepathically. Their minds suddenly connected like two pieces of a puzzle linking together. They were joined to one another in a way that they had never experienced before even in their most intimate moments of lovemaking.

She could read his mind. His life was before her, unfolding like a film. Images like a whirling, spinning kaleidoscope flashed through her brain.

She spoke to him, without speaking. *"Oh the pain that you live with each, day, my poor warrior."* For the first time ever she suddenly felt she knew him, understood him. And he felt her great courage, her love, her infinite desire for freedom and truth. And he was glad that they would probably die together on the battlefield. For if Kim were his love, then Rona was his faithful heart.

They stopped at last and hugged, exchanging a tender kiss. Then he went on to the next mutant, to try and bring out his ESP abilities. There was no time for the emotions he wished to share with her. And there might never be.

Rona sat on the white tatami mat, weeping. The pain her lover had born. His family being killed, his lonely, starving trek as a mere child across America. She saw all the horrors he had been privy to. She never knew why he was so hard—before. Now she understood.

Chapter Fourteen

The dawn broke like a shell-burst on the morning of November 13, splattering the purple skies with fragments of red and green, slicing through the high cloud cover with tongues of orange sunlight. Ted Rockson sat high on one of the northern peaks overlooking Forrester Valley, a pair of electron binoculars in his veined hands. He raised them to his eyes and stared out over the vast valley floor below. The Nazi troops were pouring in from every direction, filling the flat plain set between two ranges of the Rockies. They came from the mountain opposite Rock, far across the valley, from the woods on each side, streaming out like an army of ants, joining into bigger and bigger concentrations. Huge helicopter transporters filled the skies above, setting down every second and depositing their loads of M-2 Panzer tanks, armored vehicles and field artillery. The flat valley floor was a beehive of activity as Jeeps and the immense sixty-foot tanks screeched around trying to position themselves. But the picture was becoming clear even in the midst of confusion as the Panzers pulled up to the front ranks and combat troops began falling in behind them, bayonets fixed to their Kalashnikov-5 Autofires.

Rock pushed two buttons on the side of the computerized field glasses and his range of vision suddenly shot into super-magnification. He could see the faces of the troops and their officers, sweating, tense as they set up into formation. He could see the churning treads of the super-Panzers as they sent up waves of yellow dust from the loose-packed dirt of the valley floor. He turned the glasses slightly as he caught the motion of a Soyuz transport chopper landing. It was the largest copter he'd ever seen, nearly two hundred feet long and fifty feet high with immense swastikas printed in red on its black body. The Doomsday Warrior whistled between his teeth as he slid up a little on the rock outcropping at the very edge of the peak. Something was coming down the ramp from its bay door—Jesus, what was it? He flicked the auto-focus button and the thing came into view. It was a tank, but unlike any Rock had ever seen before. In the place of treads it had immense stiltlike steel legs on it that rolled ahead, moving the ovular steel shape atop it bristling with cannon and machine guns forward. He suddenly remembered hearing two Red officers talk about it when he had infiltrated one of their fortresses several months earlier. Rock-Walkers they had called them—tanks capable of climbing right up the sides of mountains.

"Shit," the Doomsday Warrior spat out between clenched lips. They hadn't included these in their defensive plans. Well, it was for damned sure too late now. More of the helicopter transports set down on the near side of the valley, releasing tank after tank, mobile cannons, regiments of men, decked out in full battle gear. "It's like Parade Day in the Kremlin," the Doomsday Warrior muttered, as he realized the full strength of the Nazi forces. It was one thing to see it all down on paper—but now that the men and the machine were stretching out for miles in every direction, it was a little overwhelming.

He shifted the glasses up to the far mountain, twenty miles off and pressed the optimum magnification mode of the glasses. The command tents of the German officers sprang into view as if he were right on top of them. Angular-faced blond officers rushed in and out of what was clearly the main headquarters, with a Nazi flag and a Red hammer and sickle snapping in the wind on each side of the entrance. Von Reisling would be in there overseeing the battle, along with all his top staff. And Rock knew that that's where his team was heading right now. Detroit, Archer, Chen, McCaughlin and Rona, who had demanded to be taken—they were after big game: the entire command of the Nazi forces. He wished he could have been with them himself, not up here on this mountain peak. But the military council had strongly requested that he coordinate the entire scope of operations. The five of them had started out before the sun rose, heading far around the valley to come up behind the German lines. He sent out a silent prayer for their safe return, though God only knew how many of them would be left alive at the end of the day. How many faces he would never see again. He steeled his jaw and banished the emotions deep inside his chest.

The Doomsday Warrior stepped down from the observation post and looked back and forth along the ten thousand-foot mountain peak that he and the main artillery units of Century City stood on. Nearly fifty cannons, some ultra-modern, developed by Shecter and capable of firing 122mm shells at the rate of twenty a minute. Others were old, stolen from the Reds, huge green-painted 85mm's on self-propelled chassis and even a few .152mm monsters which fired six-inch shells capable of taking out even one of the super-Panzers with a single hit. The artillery was hidden under netting and spread out along a two-mile width, with two hundred mortar men and heavy machine guns interspersed between them.

It was his decision—and his alone—on when to begin the attack. Rock knew they were all waiting, the machine gunners and small mortars on the lower slopes, the teams of hybrid squads, carrying their sapper charges, hidden in the woods on each side of the valley, the ski units carrying light auto-fire poodle punchers and wearing cut-off, narrow skis capable of maneuvering at lightning speed on the snow-covered slopes, the Rapid Deployment helicopter force—all waiting for the red flare he would fire high over the valley to signal the commencement of fire. Just a few more minutes, he thought to himself, his jaw tight as steel. Until they've landed more equipment—but are not yet totally organized. We'll strike them when they'll be most off balance. Just a few—

"Hey, Rock, thought I'd come up and see the sights," a voice said behind him, startling the Doomsday Warrior so that he turned, reaching for the .45 strapped to his waist. It was Dr. Shecter, grinning and holding a Liberator, the rifle he had designed and sent out to Free Cities all across America, in his hands. His tall, stooped-over body looked slightly absurd in the flak jacket and army fatigues that he wore, but his aging, mottled face was deadly serious.

"Jesus, Doc, you shouldn't be up here. We need your brains back in C.C."

"Rock, if we don't stop these Nazi slime—there won't be a C.C. Besides, I couldn't stay back there while everyone I know and love is out here ready to give their very lives. I couldn't live with myself, Rock. I'm a scientist—but I'm also a man. And that comes first."

"I understand, Dr. Shecter," Rock said softly. "Well, pick a good seat cause the action's about to start. How'd it go with those phony Century Cities on the mountains south of here?"

"From our transmitters inside the three we managed to build we heard the explosions. I can't tell you exactly how many men they lost—but a lot. We've constructed two more just south of C.C. itself, in case we have to fall back. But they're just diversions, Rock—you and I both know that. It's what happens down there," he said, pointing to the vast assembling army below, "that counts."

"OK, well, I'm glad to have you aboard," the Doomsday Warrior said. "Somehow I never thought we'd be fighting together. But just do me one favor—keep your damned head down. I don't want to have to worry about you when I should be overseeing our battle progress and communications. Sorry to be so blunt but—"

"No apologies, Rock, I understand. I'll stay low and only fire when I see the whites of their eyes."

"Well, get down, Doc, 'cause it's about to begin." Shecter found a cover behind several large boulders at the edge of the peak as Rockson looked around a final time. The artillery squads were looking his way, their hands itching to fire. Everything was in suspended animation waiting for the curtain to open, the death-show to begin.

"There's no time like the present," Rock mumbled to no one in particular. He raised the flare gun, pointing it straight out over the valley and fired. The flare arced up into the morning sky like a meteor, leaving a trail of soft white smoke behind it. Suddenly it ignited, about eight hundred feet up, sending out a burning brilliant light as it began falling slowly toward the Nazi hordes below. Their eyes rose up as a deathly silence settled over the entire army for a split second. Then all hell broke loose.

The artillery units all along the northern peak opened up with everything they had, raining down a tornado of steel death on the army below. From his forward position, Rockson could see the puffs of smoke and hear the thunderous explosions roar through the granite peaks. The German troops began scampering in all directions as shell after shell landed in their midst, sending up little eruptions of dirt, smoke and blood. Within seconds the freefighter helicopter force appeared overhead just above him and tore into the midst of the big cargo choppers still descending with their troops and equipment. They were sitting ducks, with but a few .55s to protect themselves. But the Strike Force wouldn't even give them that opportunity. They came in like a swarm of bloodthirsty hawks, twisting and turning through the air armada around them. They flew in groups of two, to cover each other's back, firing their missiles at everything in sight, spitting out streams of red-hot slugs from their side door machine guns.

Within the first thirty seconds they had knocked nearly twenty of the huge choppers from the sky, sending them plummeting into their own forces below in screaming balls of flaming, twisted wreckage. Rock could see German combat soldiers trying to leap from the careening craft even as they fell, bodies dropping like raindrops until they splashed red on the ground below. Thirty swastika-decorated attack copters were mixed in among the transports but at such close range they found it hard to fire without hitting their own aircraft. The element of surprise was working, the attack force ripping through the nearly eighty-copter force like wolves in a chicken coop.

The artillery continued to pound away by pre-arranged command at the forward tank force and the very rear of the army, trapping them in a barrage of exploding steel. Now it was up to the sappers to create havoc in the mid-ranks, to try and panic them into retreat. Rock edged forward onto the outcropping, hugging it like a piece of paper as bullets whistled by from every direction. He zeroed his field glasses in on the eastern flank, just at the edge of the thick woods. The hybrid cavalry should be coming out just about now. . . .

From the vantage point of ground level the battle was a whole different picture. To Rock, far above, it was almost beautiful as the exploding shells and missiles created a vast mosaic of color—reds, oranges, yellows, shooting up like rainbows of death throughout the valley. But to the waiting hybrid units just inside the woods, it was the deafening roar of the erupting shells, the blood of Germans flying through the air like a hurricane of red, the screams of tank crews trying to crawl from their white-hot burning tanks and the shrapnel whizzing by them like bees.

Sergeant Abrams leaned forward in his saddle, patting

the thick back of his hybrid steed that reared nervously below him. The 'brids had had their ears stuffed with cotton—but even so they knew something was going on. And they didn't like it one bit.

"Let's go, men," Abrams screamed out to the rest of the twenty-man squad behind him. All along the perimeter of the forest he could see the other teams preparing to charge straight into the center of the German ranks. Abrams leaned forward in his saddle, held his pump .12-gauge shotgun in his right arm and kicked his steed hard in the side. It shot from the covering trees like a bat out of hell tearing into the middle of the conflagration. Abrams couldn't help but think for a second about the irony of it all. He was a Jew—his people had almost been extinguished from the face of the earth 150 years before, by these same Nazis, these same diseased minds. He was thankful he had the opportunity to destroy them. The Jews of the holocaust had gone willingly into the gas ovens, had stood in front of their own graves as machine guns knocked them backwards into bloody masses of corpses. But not this Jew, Abrams thought as he ducked a German trying to get a bead on him. Not this fucking Jew. He whipped his pump .12-gauger up in a swift arc and let loose with a stream of lead that ripped the Nazi's head off his body in a bloody ball, sending it flying thirty feet backwards to the ground where it rolled into the tread of an oncoming tank.

"Satchels," Abrams screamed out to the galloping squad behind him. He reached down to the saddle and grabbed one of the high explosive satchels strapped to its side. He flicked the detonator with his free hand and ripped the reins to the right with his other as the tank turret swiveled toward him, trying to get a fix. Abrams tore around the back of the Panzer, heaving the charge underneath it and kicked the 'brid to get out of the way. The steed shot forward just as the explosion rocked the tank from beneath. Flames shot out the machine gun slit and seconds later the death machine roared up in a spitting tornado of fire. Abrams smiled as he rode through the German ranks, the troops diving out of the way. A slug tore into his saddle just inches from his thigh but he didn't flinch. On this clear fine day – he was ready to die.

The sapper teams came out of the woods on each side of the wide valley in waves, one minute apart. They rode at full speed among the panic-stricken troops as Nazi officers screamed out angry orders trying to get their units back in battle formation.

It wasn't supposed to happen this way. The Germans were the attackers – the freefighters the victims. The galloping hybrids covered the field of battle, as shells from the artillery rocked the earth to the north and south of them. They heaved their charges under tanks, armored vehicles, machine gun emplacements, squads of Nazis brave or stupid enough to try and stop them. Everywhere they rode they left a trail of twisted burning scrap and corpses spouting pulsing fountains of blood. From time to time one of the 'brids or its rider would get hit, plummeting in a cloud of dust to the ground. But for every freefighter shot down the Germans lost twenty men, and tons of equipment.

Abrams rode into the thick of an infantry battalion, on his own now as the further the cavalry units got into battle, the more separated they became. A huge smile covered his red-bearded face as he blasted away at full speed, sending Nazis flying like bowling pins. Only these pins spat red and they screamed as they fell to the blood-soaked ground. He felt like an avenging angel, the souls of those Jews who had died in the Nazi butcher camps a century-and-a-half before singing out in joyful vengeance in his head. Yes, this is for you—for all of you, Abrams thought as his steed leaped clear over a mobile field cannon and the sergeant dropped his last sapper charge right on top of it. The blast hit his 'brid before it reached the ground, sending them flying as the .122mm howitzer exploded into smoking pieces around them. Abrams was knocked unconscious for a few seconds and came to, to find himself pinned under the 'brid. It was dead—a piece of still-steaming howitzer muzzle lodged deep in its neck, blood pumping out in great gushes every few seconds.

"Damn," he muttered, trying to extricate himself. But a riveting pain shot through his left leg. It was broken. He could see Nazi troops running at him from all sides, their bayoneted Kalashnikovs held forward. "So be it," Abrams whispered under his breath. "On this day, Jacob Abrams found his peace." He raised the pump shotgun and fired at the closest Nazi's smirking face just yards away. The load blasted through the man's chest, making a fist-sized hole. The smile vanished as the corpse fell like a stone. Abrams pumped the gun, ejecting the smoking spent shell and instantly fired again. The .12-gauge shot spread out in an X-shape, catching two more Nazis in the gut. Their stomachs blasted out, revealing pink sucking innards, as the two crumbled to the bloody dust. But there were too many. Shots were slamming into the body of his dead hybrid, rocking the corpse above him with violent jerks, sending bolts of pain down his broken leg. Suddenly a shot tore into his shoulder, knocking him flat on his back. Abrams sighted two more of the Nazi killers and sent them greetings—pump shotgun style. He had reached down to his cartridge belt to reload when he saw a shadow just below him on the slippery ground. He looked up into the face of a leering German who thrust his bayonet into Abram's belly. The knife went clear through, all eighteen inches of it, burying itself in the ground. The Nazi pulled the blade out, screaming, "Die, American bastard."

"*You* die, Nazi pig," Abrams managed to cough back as he whipped his .45 from its holster. He pumped off three shots point-blank into the German's guts. The man's eyes opened wide in horrified surprise and then he sank forward and died.

Abrams felt his mind growing dim as the blood pumped through the wide slit in his abdomen. "I'm ready," he croaked as he slid back onto his back, his arms and legs no longer responding to his commands. "Take this Jew into never-never land." His eyes closed as the voices of his ancestors cried ghostly tears in the deafening air around him.

On the northern ridge, Rockson could see the battle being played out like some vast choreographed dance of death—the shells falling among the advancing Panzer divisions, hundreds of them, which had managed to regroup amidst the flaming carnage. They swept toward the bottom of the mountain on which he stood, raising their .152mm cannons and beginning to rain their own murderous hail of shells back up toward the freefighters. On the valley floor below, the hybrid attack teams were creating trails of death, leaving bodies and wreckage behind their galloping hoofs. But they were only human, flesh and blood creatures. Round after round poured down on them from the German troops who were slowly reorganizing themselves. One, then another of the brave freefighters fell beneath the fusillade.

The skies were filled with their own roaring air battle. The Rapid Strike Force had taken out half of the eighty Red transport choppers and the rest had finally fled at top speed, hightailing it back over the southern ridges to safety. Now it was a battle between the Nazi attack copters and C.C.'s own fleet. The freefighter pilots were amazingly proficient considering how little training they'd had. But then they were fighting for their country, their city, the very core of their souls—and they didn't hold back an inch. They swirled and dove, always two at a time, one blasting its way through the German helios which were filling the skies by the minute, the other riding shotgun twenty yards behind. The attack formations had been taken right out of the century-old manual from America's first attack fleet and the freefighting pilots followed it to the letter. After all, those guys way back when had had years to work it all out. And it was proving highly successful. The Nazi pilots had been well-trained—but in the unimaginative strategies of the Russian manuals. The Reds were used to strafing rebels, shooting at ground targets; they had never faced a foe such as these speedy devils who didn't seem to give a damn about their own lives. Seventy-five of the jet-powered Stulag-5 Nazi squadron now blanketed the sky above the valley, trying to find, to shoot down these mosquitos that buzzed around them. But their own immense armaments and super high speed capability only added to their problems. At speeds of over three hundred mph it took them precious seconds to turn, to climb, to evade the American steel bugs that seemed to appear out of nowhere and then disappear just as quickly. And with so many of their own in the sky, they were unable to fire their heat-seeking missiles for fear of taking out a Nazi craft. Hysterically they tried to figure out some way of dealing with these pest, these gnats, who were shooting them down like clay pigeons.

Rock swept his computer-enhanced field glasses over the battle scene, barely able to keep up with the action that was unfolding throughout the flat valley. The tempo was speeding up as the Germans at last seemed to get a grip on themselves, their officers taking control, shooting fleeing troops if they had to. Slowly, ever so slowly, they managed to get themselves into their battle formations, the big lines of Panzer tanks taking the lead, grinding toward the northern mountains, two rows of one hundred tanks each—every two hundred feet. The Doomsday Warrior could see their hastily implemented defense strategy unfold as columns of tanks that had been the last to arrive by transport chopper moved from the center of the plain out to the sides, straight lines of steel death, their cannons pumping out shell after shell toward the woods and the concentrations of American hybrid squads. They were going to try and create a box—a square of tanks around the entire valley, protect themselves on every flank, and at the same time box in the freefighters down there fighting for their lives.

Damn, he hadn't expected them to be able to respond so quickly to the surprise party the freefighters had laid out. Perhaps he had underestimated the strategic mind of the Germans—after all, they had once been the most brilliant of military nations, with their blitzkrieg, their mechanization of warfare, their Rommels, their ruthlessness and speed. But it was all too late now. There would be no time-outs, no chance to rethink things. And it was all up to him, to Ted Rockson to somehow make the difference. He felt a strange emotion surge through his soul—something he had never felt before. It was fear. Not for himself—but for all those men and women down there on the plain below who had trusted him and the general staff. Who had gone into battle with smiles on their nervous faces, and hope in their hearts. He couldn't let them down. Couldn't stand up here on the safety of the mountain top and watch them all die. Suddenly he wished he had never become the top military officer of Century City—that he was out there with Chen and Detroit and Rona, who were right now, he knew, fighting with fury, deep inside the German lines. It was too fucking complicated being a general, too much responsibility.

He pulled back from the outcropping and slid down behind it, closing his eyes tight. He concentrated as he never had before and sent out frantic telepathic messages to the mutants who were working with the different forces. *"You are being cut off from all sides. Form a single force and head east before tanks form complete trap. East, hook up and head east."* He dimly heard mental messages being flashed back, signaling they had heard him. He waited a few seconds, breathed out and sent out mental commands to the four mutants spaced wide apart on the northern peaks who were armed with the deadly black-beam weapons.

"Black beam squads—fire at tank column moving from center of valley to east. Trying to cut off our forces. Stop them, concentrate all fire power on column heading east." He opened his eyes, gasping from the strenuous

mental effort. He had done what he could. Now it was in the hands of God. The freefighters would find out on this bloody day whether or not he favored America or was in fact "dead," as the manifestos of Marx and Engels and Trotsky and Lenin had all so loudly proclaimed. Rockson turned his eyes skyward as the maelstrom of sound and flame and blood screamed out from the valley behind him. He searched through the clouds, trying to penetrate the very cosmos, searching, searching for a saving sign.

Chapter Fifteen

The Rock team had set out in the dead of night, far before the battle erupted into hellfire. Chen led them through the thick woods on the eastern edge of Forrester Valley, with Detroit, McCaughlin, Archer and Rona close behind him. They moved quickly on narrow shortened skis through the snow-covered fields and hills, wearing white camouflage body suits and loaded down with weapons and plastique. Chen carried the exploding star knives with which he was an expert—five-pointed razor-sharp blades of steel, tipped with explosive charges, a Japanese short sword at his waist and other deadly surprises. Detroit wore twin bandoliers of grenades across his chest and carried a snub-nosed uzi, which he had found on one of C.C.'s supply expeditions—and had grown quite fond of. Rona was armed with a sawed-off Liberator set on full auto and equipped with Teflon-coated bullets, capable of penetrating steel. Archer, taking up the rear—and having some difficulty on the short skis—carried his ever-present steel crossbow around his shoulders and a quiver full of arrows, tipped with everything from exploding charges to gas pellets, and an eighteen-inch twin-bladed hunting knife he had picked up while browsing through the Century City weapons supply. McCaughlin, moving surprisingly well for a man of his size, was equipped with a .357 magnum and magazine firing .12 gauge.

A light snow was falling as they headed through the still-dark woods, but thanks to Dr. Shecter's going-away present, infrared ski goggles, they were able to see clear as day as they made their way along a narrow path, trampled down by migrating mountain elk. They hit a good pace, moving quickly as they adapted to the yardlong skis with which they had had only two days' practice, shooting down slopes and sliding along flat terrain with the cross-country strokes they had been taught by C.C.'s top ski instructor. Miles to the west they could hear the assembling German army, tanks coughing to life, officers screaming, the vast fleet of transport choppers landing their loads of death. Each carried their own personal thoughts burning like hot embers in their brains. Their mission might make the difference between life and death for Century City—to destroy the central command headquarters of the Nazi army, miles off on the peaks of the southern mountain. They knew their fellows would soon face the battle of their lives out there on the valley floor—but if the Rock team could take out enough of the German officer staff, maybe even Von Reisling himself, it might make all the difference. When the queen bee dies, the colony is lost. And Chen and his team were the wasps equipped with enough poison to do the trick. If, if, if.

They took a circuitous route, heading miles around the valley to avoid encounters with the commando teams that had been scouring the surrounding forests and mountains for days, searching—unsuccessfully—for the famed freefighting city. But as luck would have it, they had gone but halfway to their attack point when out of nowhere a German ski patrol was upon them.

Chen, twenty feet ahead of the others, saw them first, twenty white-suited figures, swooping down from a steep hill to their right.

"Attack," he screamed out, turning his head for a split second to warn the others. Without breaking stride he reached for two of his star knives, set four in a pocket, on a wide utility belt around his waist. The Nazi squad came right at them, eerily silent in the snow-covered woods, with just the faint crack of skis breaking the white surface and the mocking hoot of an early-rising owl whispering through the trees. Then it got noisy.

Chen spun the two five-pointed death stars with a flick of each hand as he skidded to a stop, digging his skis into the three-inch-deep snow. The blades whistled through the air, catching the two lead attackers square in the chest. The whirling blades exploded the second they made contact with flesh and sent out a hail of blood in all directions that mottled the picture-postcard-perfect woods scene with a red stew of steaming flesh. The Nazis began firing from their Turgenev-7 subs, cradled under one arm as they shot forward toward their hated enemy.

But every member of the Rock squad had been

through combat before—and lots of it. They went into their defensive alignment in a split second, stopping dead in their tracks and diving to the cold ground. They had barely stopped moving when their weapons were in their hands—speaking a language the Nazis could understand: death. Chen ducked behind a wide black-barked pine tree and began flinging out his birds of death every few seconds; Rona and Detroit opened up with a storm of automatic fire, sweeping across the front ranks of the screaming Nazi attackers. McCaughlin drew his .357 magnum silencer-equipped revolver, as big as a small cannon and, taking careful aim, fired off round after round, each shot catching German flesh.

Within twenty seconds, half the Nazi ski squad was lying in the snow, sending out puddles of brilliant red blood that soaked down into the soft white. The others, realizing that their reckless macho charge was going to quickly make them join their long dead Führer, pulled back behind a row of low boulders and began pouring down their own hailstorm of 9mm slugs. The Nazi bullets zipped into the snow around the freefighters, drawing closer and closer to target acquisition.

"We can't stay here," Chen screamed over the roar of the firefight. "There's no time to play around with these assholes. Rona, Detroit," he yelled from behind cover of the tree to the two freefighters closest to the firing Germans. "I'm going to count to ten. When I reach it, each of you throw one of your plastique packs into our friends over there." He began counting, throwing out two more of the death stars as he reached "nine" to give them cover. The two unhooked one of their load of ten high-explosive packs, not much bigger than a cigarette carton and when they heard "ten," whipped their arms up and heaved the party treats seventy-five feet to the entrenched Germans. They ducked their heads down into the snow as an explosion flung pieces of meat, arms and legs high in the air ahead.

The freefighters slowly raised themselves, their guns ready. But there was no one to shoot at. Just corpses, hardly recognizable as human, strewn across a fifty-foot area.

"Come on, let's get the hell out of here," Chen yelled. "There's going to be more Nazis than you could shake a stick at here in a few minutes." They tore ass through the woods, luckily hitting a downhill stretch so that they made good time. Behind them they heard the roar of choppers and tanks coming to see what all the noise had been about.

By the time the dawn sun raised itself on glowing threads into the carpet of the fading night, the Rock squad had left their woods cover and began climbing the southern peaks several miles to the side of where they hoped the German headquarters would be. It was rough going as they had to go up a steep rocky slope to avoid detection by Nazi troops dug into the front of the mountain in machine gun and mortar emplacements. With their skis dangling from around their shoulders and laden with nearly a hundred pounds of weaponry and explosives, the freefighters hugged the side of the sheer rock wall, dragging themselves up, foot by treacherous foot. Huge mountain vultures kept screaming out at them, flapping their five-foot wings from their nests inside crevices and small caves. But the Americans were strong, among the toughest that C.C. had to offer, and they made good time.

At last they reached the summit, pulling themselves up over the edge and quickly rolling into scraggly thorn bushes that dotted the plateau of the mountain, in case there were any Nazis looking for strike squads. But there weren't. The Germans, in their overconfidence at the immense power of their quarter-million-man army, couldn't even conceive that the freefighters would dare attack them, much less crawl like spiders up a six- thousand-foot granite wall that a mountain goat couldn't traverse. But they had, and the Nazis' stupidity was the freefighters' good luck.

They scanned the long flat peak carefully, Chen checking every tree, every boulder ahead with his binocs. Nearly a mile away he could see the command tents, five of them, side by side, with officers running frantically past the flapping swastika flags outside their entrances. There were troops and artillery batteries all along the front ridge of the mountain—but also no one guarding the back. Mistake number two for the German invaders.

"We'll have to go way around them," Chen said to the others who sat, breathing hard behind him. "Now, you know our plans, we've been over them a thousand times. There's not going to be one second to figure things out once the action gets going—so be on your toes. Rona, Archer, you take the lead with me. We'll have to dump anyone we run across silently—that means non-exploding star knives and Archer's crossbow. Don't use the heavy stuff unless they actually start firing. Surprise is our only chance—let's not fuck up. There's too much at stake. You got me?" They all nodded in ascent and began moving across the plateau in a half crouch, running from tree to tree, bush to bush, like jack rabbits.

They had nearly two miles to go in their circuitous route around the backside of the mountain peak, but after climbing the damned thing, running on a flat surface felt almost effortless. Small mountain rodents, horned field mice, multi-banded armadillos scampered away at their approach, scuttling off to safety in their hidden network of tunnels. But the freefighters were after bigger game—the Nazi beast. The sun was brilliantly clear as it rose higher and higher into the blue sky. Chen wished it was cloudy, as it had been for days—but nature doesn't fit its plans to the needs of men, rather the opposite.

At last they swung all the way around the three-mile-wide plateau and began moving slower as they came up on the rear of the German command center. Far off at the other end of the valley they suddenly heard thunderous explosions and saw smoke rising high in the air in funnels of blackness. The freefighters had opened up. The battle had begun and there was no turning back. Rona pictured Rockson for a second, giving the command to fire. She tried to reach him with her mind—as he had taught her. But couldn't. She prayed he would survive.

"Let's go," Chen said. "We've got to go full speed from now on. Don't stop, don't look back. If one of us gets hit, he gets left. It's bigger than any of us, you understand?" He looked at them with his almond-shaped eyes, his dark curved mustache contrasting against the pure white of his attack uniform. There was sympathy in his eyes—for all of them—for they were among the closest friends he had ever had. They had all trained with him in the martial arts, had gone out on countless missions against the Reds, had stared right in the face of death and survived. There was compassion—but no mercy.

They shot forward from their hiding places behind a row of dark boulders at a full run. The commencement of the firefight would distract the Nazis. German eyes faced forward, their rear was virtually unprotected. The American attack team built up speed, swooping in from behind like a pack of lions on the scent of blood. The tents loomed in the near distance, growing larger by the second as the echoes of the artillery of both sides shattered the calm of the valley. Their eyes and ears were super-sensitive, their every perception in a state of heightened ability, as are all those who are about to kill or be killed.

Suddenly there was a shout just ahead of them. A guard post. Five Germans. One of them had risen to take a piss and spotted the stampeding Americans. The Nazis reached for their Kalashnikovs and Turgenev submachine guns in a flash. But not fast enough. Chen, running with a star knife in each hand, flung them forward without breaking stride. They whistled through the air like missiles, spinning blades searching for hot flesh. First caught was the German who had spotted them, in the right eye, digging deep into brain tissue which spouted into a thick gush. The second found root in a Nazi throat severing the windpipe and larnyx so that the combat soldier fell to his knees gurgling blood instead of words. Everything seemed to move in slow motion—the guards reaching for their weapons, trying to raise them, Rona's own two star blades, with which she had become highly proficient, streaking out like dark comets across the mountaintop, Archer raising his crossbow to his cheek and firing a four-foot-long shaft of death. The Nazi guns came up, desperately trying to get a bead on their zigzagging enemies. But the freefighters were quicker. Rona's star knives hit home, one lodging deep in a Nazi chest, the other in a soldier's groin. Both fell, spurting their lifeblood out onto the cold ground. The fifth trooper had his sub at chest level, his finger about to squeeze the trigger, when Archer's iron shaft found what it was looking for. The hunting tip entered the German's skull leaving an inch-thick path behind it as it exited the other side in a spew of bone and pink. The German stood as motionless as a rock for several seconds and then toppled forward, in death.

"Move, move," Chen spat out as they sped past the still-quivering bodies by the glowing fire. They ran up to a row of Jeeps parked just behind the command tents and stopped for a second, hidden just behind the steel vehicles. The five tents were only twenty yards away, the largest one nearly a hundred feet of light brown canvas, obviously Von Reisling's headquarters, with two on each side for the underlings. They could hear officers screaming out orders over radios inside as they attempted to deal with the American attack deep in the valley, before their own forces organized into battle formations.

"Satchels," Chen said, his eyes whipping back and forth behind the tents, searching for the sudden appearance of a German uniform that might mean their discovery before the mission had been carried out. Two star knives sat on the fender of the Jeep he was hidden behind, ready for instant deployment. The freefighters reached in their backpacks and took out the deadly packets of high explosives that Dr. Shecter's team had made just for them. "Set timers for ten seconds," the Chinese martial arts master said as he laid his out in front of him. "Rona, you and I will hit the main tent. Archer and McCaughlin—you take the two on the right. Detroit yours are the two on the left. Set the timers and then start heaving—aim for the tops, there's no time for subtlety. The first few may be shielded by the canvas but the rest should drop in—and take care of business. Any questions?" He quickly looked in each wide pair of eyes to make sure they understood. Especially Archer's—who he was never quite sure knew just what was being said. But the oversized freefighter stared firmly back and grunted, "Thrroooow booom-booom."

"Now," he screamed, heaving the first of his deadly packages high in the air toward the command tent. They soared end over end, their steel timing devices on the top glistening for a second as the sun's swordlike rays bit into them. Then they hit. Chen's first pack of plastique bounced off the flat springy surface of the tent roof, detonating almost a yard above it. It blasted a ten-foot-wide hole in the material as the second pack dropped in. A thunderous roar shook the entire headquarters as flames shot out the top. From inside they could hear the desperate screams of the maimed and dying. The freefighters hefted two of their death dealers at a time, heaving one then the other and instantly reaching for more without waiting to see the results. But the results didn't have to be seen. The tents shook and flamed inside as if the very fires of hell had been unleashed on their occupants. Packet after packet spun through the air, every one hitting home with a deafening roar. Within seconds all five tents were ablaze, sending up balls of smoke and fire. Still, the Americans threw death at them, wanting to make sure that not one Nazi commander escaped. It was death wholesale—but when you prepare to kill, prepare to die as well. The Nazis had signed their own death warrants.

At last they had nothing more to throw, and stood watching the tents burn wildly, flames shooting in every direction like immense yellow and orange tongues, searching for even more material to incinerate. And there were no more screams.

"Let's go," Chen yelled after a final perusal of the conflagration to make sure their mission was complete. They tore back across the plateau, heading in the opposite direction of the way they had come up. Behind them they could hear a frantic commotion as troops and vehicles descended on the burning tents in hysteria—their entire command wiped out.

They had gone several hundred yards when Chen spotted a chopper, its rotors just slowing to a stop, ahead on a rubble-cleared circle about twenty yards wide.

"There's our ride," the martial arts master said with a grin. They ran, shotguns and rifles at the ready, straight at the helicopter whose crew and new arrival of more Nazi officers was just descending to the ground. But this time the Germans saw them coming and ripped out their revolvers, sending out a hail of slugs toward the advancing wild-eyed and soot-coated Americans.

Chen unleashed a wave of star knives, flinging them out like bullets on automatic fire. The blades tore into the Nazi faces and chests and thighs, as bodies toppled over from their crouched firing positions in front of the chopper. Detroit let loose with his uzi, sweeping it across the line of twenty German officers, cutting jagged lines across crisply uniformed flesh that instantly poured out bright red blood from myriad holes. Rona and McCaughlin drifted to the right, trying to flank the Nazis, firing as they ran with Rona's Liberator and McCaughlin's .12-gauge pump pounding out shell after shell of bone-shattering death. The big Scotsman suddenly felt a German slug slam into his thick thigh and he grimaced for a second but managed to move on, hobbling slightly. Detroit, Archer and Chen advanced on the now-terrified Germans who slowly began falling back. These crazy Americans didn't seem to give a shit about their lives—but the Germans wanted to live. They could fight another day.

Rona reached the back of the chopper and rushed around to the pilot's seat, pulling open the door. A grinning face met her, holding a 7.22mm revolver at her face.

"Die, bitch," the pilot screamed, pulling the trigger. But Rona was faster. She had trained too long and hard to let some assistant Nazi asshole take her out. She whipped her head to the side as the bullet whizzed past and kicked up with her right leg, catching the German on the hand. The pistol flew into the air as the officer's face sank into an expression of pure terror.

"Not yet," Rona said with the barest trace of a grin as she pumped half a magazine of 9mm Liberator rounds into his body. The bullets cut like scissors, from the navel to the throat as the nearly dissected German fell sideways and out the door. Rona jumped in and swung her rifle around into the passengers' section, letting loose with a burst before she even looked to see who was there. And what was there were three cowering Nazis, their pistols half raised. But speed wins in the game of death. And Rona had been a split second faster. She rushed back to the cargo door and snapped it open, kicking the dead meat out on the ground.

The freefighters tumbled in, McCaughlin bleeding badly from the thigh, Detroit holding his hand over one shoulder that leaked red down onto his khaki jacket. Chen was the last one in, heaving two more exploding star knives out the door at a few Germans who had decided to be heroes. They went somewhere—in a spray of blood and veins, but not to a medal-presenting ceremony.

"Let's get the hell out of here," the Chinese martial arts master yelled out. "Rona—you know how to fly this thing?"

"Sure." The statuesque redhead grinned. "Driven 'em a thousand times." She ran back to the control pit and desperately tried to remember watching Rockson fly one of the damned things. She clicked the ignition on and the blades above sputtered to life, quickly reaching flying speed. She pushed the joystick forward and the chopper, lurching wildly, soared almost straight up into the air as bullets followed it from below. "See—there we go. It's easy," she yelled back to the green-faced crew. She eased the stick forward and the German helicopter, for use by Nazi officers only, charged forward at a peculiar angle toward the back of the mountain. Below and behind her, Rona could see the command tents burning like bonfires in the noonday sun. "Not bad for a morning's work," she said to Detroit who painfully seated himself beside her at the controls.

"You actually know how to fly this damned thing? 'Cause I do," the ebony-faced freefighter said, tying a tourniquet around his upper arm.

"We're flying, ain't we?" Rona replied with a sardonic grin.

"Like an eagle," Detroit said. "Like a fucking eagle."

Far below them, Ubenführer Von Reisling stood alongside the burning tents as troops frantically tried to extinguish the flames. But he knew it was too late. There was nothing to save in there but charred bones. His body was coated with a thin sheen of his own blood. But he was alive. His radar-patched eye had seen the first of the satchels as it flew down onto the command tent roof. He knew there was no time to warn the others—besides *he* was what mattered. He had torn out of the back of the tent at a full run, knocking over officers as they stared after him with puzzled expressions. But they had found out—in a most hideous way—why their commander was fleeing. And by then it was too late.

Von Reisling looked up at the helicopter quickly disappearing over the mountain edge with hate in his eyes. He had underestimated these freefighters. They were more than guerrillas—they were tacticians.

Within his hate was twisted respect as well. They had struck quickly and forcefully, as the Führer himself had conducted his military campaigns. And they had dealt a powerful blow against his army. But *he* was alive. And that was all that mattered. They had won a battle—but the war, that was a different matter.

He walked slowly and painfully over to the edge of the plateau, shaking off field doctors attempting to treat his wounds. The commander of all the German forces looked down on his Panzer divisions as they spread out, boxing in the freefighters on the plains below—as he had commanded just minutes before. Soon they would all be cut off. And then, then they would die.

Chapter Sixteen

From his perch on the forward ledge of the northern peak overlooking the valley floor, Rockson could see the freefighters fighting valiantly as hordes of the hybrid-riding sappers continued to sweep in from all sides. They threw their explosive charges into the advancing German ranks, and under the endless stream of Panzer tanks. But bravery is an emotion and overwhelming numbers of men and equipment a reality. The freefighters had been preparing for this day, for an all-out battle with the enemy for years. But not yet—it was too soon. The Americans were not ready. And it would spell their doom.

He looked through the field glasses with a sinking heart as he took in the full picture of the war—the huge tanks forming a square around the valley floor in which every single damned freefighter would soon be trapped. The sappers were taking Nazis out by the dozen but new ones kept streaming out from the center, taking the place of every death machine that was destroyed. He could see the ranks of Nazi troops goose-stepping forward, alongside the metal monsters, firing from the waist. He could see his own brothers and sisters of freedom falling like flies everywhere. Sacrificing their lives to take out as many as they could.

But it was not enough. The most valiant heart can be pierced by a bullet, the most fearless eyes ripped from their sockets by mortars, grenades. "Shit," the Doomsday Warrior screamed out in rage, slamming his hand down in a fist on the rock beneath him. Tears welled up in his eyes for one of the few times in his life. The freefighters had killed twenty, thirty, forty thousand troops. Who the hell knew. And tanks beyond number. But the Germans kept pouring through the far mountain pass in an endless deathly procession.

He tried sending out his telepathic commands again, although in his heart of hearts he knew it was too late. *"Retreat, retreat now. Further confrontation on the valley floor is useless. Head east—rejoin freefighter forces at fallback position 2."* He sent the message out again and again, until his brain throbbed in pain from the effort. Here and there he got back dim mental signals that they would comply—or try to.

"Give them covering fire," Rock yelled over to one of the gunnery posts just twenty yards away. "And pass the word along. Hit those tanks coming to the left—that column of Panzers." The word was sent along the artillery line by flag and the big guns opened up with everything they had, trying to buy a little more escape time for their trapped comrades.

But there was more to worry about—the German

advance ranks were reaching the bottom of the northern mountain and scaling it. Long lines of black-booted troops came charging up the slope. And behind them, the rock-climbing tanks—their huge steel legs whipping end over end, pulling them up over the big boulders that dotted the side of the mountain. Every man, woman and teenager in their defensive positions along the slope fired down with everything they had—machine guns, mortars, Liberators, .45s. They sent down a stream of death, ripping into the forward Nazi flesh like a shooting gallery. But the Nazi charge was relentless. It was like a nightmare in which whatever one does has no effect on the enemy, on the monster that just keeps coming, reaching forward with hands of death.

There was nowhere really to go, Rock knew. The fallback positions would just slow them down—but even then the freefighting forces would be scattered, what little firepower they had broken down into laughable units that the Germans would run right over. And once they reached the top of the northern ridge, the one advantage the Americans had—firing down from a height—would be gone. When the enemy reached the heights, it would all be over. Death—complete, total—for all of them. Deep in his brain he could hear the desperate messages of the mutant telepaths each with their own frantic plea. *"We are being overun. We can't hold, Rockson. Rockson, what can we do?"*

"Jesus," the Doomsday Warrior muttered through teeth locked tight as a crypt. For a moment he wished he was dead. It would be better than seeing the slaughter of his people. Perhaps a stray bullet would rip into him, a mortar shell would—

Suddenly he saw three huge glowing shapes at the far end of the valley. Strange, floating craft, burning with a blinding blue electricity. He lifted the binoculars to his eyes and broke into a lip-splitting smile. The Glowers—riding into the back ranks of the Nazis on their immense sand ships. The plains below were filled end-to-end with German troops, like a million ants coming forward but the Glowers ripped into them like death itself on a rampage.

The ships sped through the ranks, sending men flying in all directions. The electric force that surrounded each of them individually had been extended through mental power to protect the ships themselves, each with a ball of blue lightning twisting around it like the aurora borealis. The Glowers stood on the bows, their hands just inches apart, like stars in full nova, sending their bursts of death into the universe.

Suddenly he felt the voice of the strange race fill his mind like a rainbow of hope. *"We have come, Rockson. We have come as we promised. Only those with evil in their hearts need fear us. The pure shall not be harmed."* The Germans began firing with everything they had at these bizarre new entrants into the battle, but their bullets and shells harmlessly ricocheted off the blue force field that protected the sand ships. The glowing craft sailed back and forth on the valley floor, their energy sails billowing out high above them, collecting energy from the sun and the stars. Oblivious to the intensity of the fire power being leveled on them, the Glowers on board the craft began sending out their mental waves. They joined their thoughts together and created . . . illusion. The waves of illusion flowed into the brains of the Nazis who fought like tigers all around them. The telepathic commands reached deep into the unconscious of the soldiers bringing up their deepest fears, their dark personal hells, the nightmares that they had pushed down into the sewers of their unconscious. Whatever they feared most, they suddenly saw before them—rats, rabid dogs, bottomless pits that they plummeted endlessly down, mutated horned demons chewing their flesh into bloody pieces. Every Nazi soldier in the valley entered a living hell.

Cpl. Wolfgang Schmidt was just at the bottom of the rebels' mountain, training his submachine gun on a pocket of freefighters ahead when he felt something strange. His body quivered with chills as he heard a sound—a sound he hadn't heard for years. A sound he had hoped he would never hear again. *He was six years old. He was in the German Alpines near Düsseldorf. A shape, a furry body coming at him. A wolf. It was the woods' wolf with its foot-long fangs bared, coming at him with eyes like burning embers. He fired at the thing again and again, too terrified to wonder how such a thing could be on this field of battle. He clicked his Turgenev sub on full auto and swung it around him. The bullets streamed out and into the chests and skulls of his fellow troops. He mowed down nearly a dozen of them before another tortured soul's nightmare, firing back, ended his brutal life.* He fell to the bloody ground, two slugs through the back of his skull, his brain tissue slowly leaking out, unable to receive the hallucinations of the Glowers anymore.

Lieutenant Von Dressler was just at the peak of the mountain commanding one of the rock-climbing tanks. He sighted up a group of freefighters firing at his death machine without effect. He went to push the button that would fire the big .122mm cannon of his vehicle. *Suddenly he couldn't believe his eyes. Instead of a button he was holding a snake, wriggling, with its fanged jaws arched wide and snapping at him. The snake seemed to leap from the control panel and wrap around his neck, the forked slimy tongue licking in and out in front of his horrified eyes. He ripped his combat knife from its sheath and began stabbing into the thing, trying to break its deadly grip on his throat. But the blade passed through the illusion and into his neck. He stabbed himself three times, the blade running deep into the jugular, sending out a torrent of blood before he grew too weak to continue. His body began jerking wildly as if he was a marionette at the end of a madman's string, trying to remain upright. The snake was gone. But, but . . . He fell to the steel floor of the tank in terrified confusion as his heart pumped out precious pints of blood through the gaping wounds. Slowly his eyes closed, but the look of sheer horror stayed, even after death.* The mountain-climbing tank, without anyone guiding it, came up against a twenty-foot wall of stone and tried to scale it. The stilt-legs ripped deep holes in the granite as the tank careened over onto its side and tumbled down the mountain onto German troops below, squashing them beneath its three-ton iron body.

Everywhere around the battlefield each Nazi found

his own doom, his own monster. Demons created by the mind and amplified by the Glowers' telepathic commands. They turned on one another, screaming, "Jew! Traitor!" They saw what they thought were their enemies and fought back desperately to destroy them—shooting, knifing, strangling one another in total and complete madness.

The tide of war was changing. The Nazi troops decimated themselves as the freefighters on the valley floor dove for cover, letting the enemy destroy itself. Their minds were not affected by the Glowers' nightmarish waves. Those who fought for freedom were spared; those who fought for evil were consumed.

Far across the valley, Von Reisling and what remained of his general staff watched with growing horror as they saw their troops being laid to waste—by each other. They had no idea what was happening but could see the Glowers' craft soaring just inches above the ground back and forth across the valley, relentless and overwhelming in their destruction. What had seemed a certain victory only minutes before was rapidly turning into the biggest rout in military history. Von Reisling knew that if something wasn't done, all the Nazi forces would be destroyed. It couldn't be. He had spent years, training, building up the roughest fighting force in the world and now—they must retreat. He could not lose the entire army. There would be time for another battle, another assault on the freefighters—without the wretched glowing mutations that cruised below to protect them.

"Withdraw, withdraw," Von Reisling screamed over his radio to the field commanders on the plain below.

"Set up covering fire, but withdraw now." He peered down through his field glasses and within seconds could see that the orders had been received as the units whose minds had not yet been touched by the Glowers' nightmares began pulling backwards.

Rockson stared down, his grim expression changing to one of exultation as he saw the massacre on the floor below. The power of the Glowers was beyond belief. He wasn't sure what the hell they were doing—but obviously some sort of mental signal was being sent out across the battlefield. Something that he couldn't receive—something he was glad he couldn't. The Nazi ranks pulled back, slowly at first and then on the run, leaving tons of equipment behind them as they hightailed it back to the southern slopes at the other end of Forrester Valley.

"Keep firing," Rockson telepathed to the mutants around the plateau. "Send down everything we've got. Every Nazi we take out now, we won't have to fight later." The mood on the peak, of the freefighting forces, was joyful. They threw their arms around one another and whooped out yells of triumph. Tears of thanks ran down their dirty, scratched faces. Whoever these creatures were that were wreaking such havoc on the plains below—they were clearly friends of free men everywhere. Century City was saved.

Suddenly Rock heard a crack and then a painful cry for help behind him. He turned. Dr. Shecter, some ten yards away, was bleeding from a wound in his stomach.

"Rock, I . . ." He pointed with his eyes behind them both. The Doomsday Warrior turned. A grimy squad of Nazi soldiers were just coming up from the back of the southern mountain, firing their Kalashnikovs and subs as they ran.

"Shit," Rock muttered, diving down on the dirt and edging over toward Shecter. He dragged the tall but somewhat frail creator of all of Century City's marvels up over a rock with one single pull of his muscled arm.

"Stay down, damnit, you hear me?" Rock screamed into the pain-stricken face of Shecter.

"Sorry, Rock, I—" But the Doomsday Warrior cut him off. There was no time for discussions right now. He ripped his .12-gauge shotpistol from its holster and poked his head up over the boulder that shielded them. The Germans were coming full speed right toward them. Rockson fired five times, swinging the spewer of steel death around at the chests of the five lead soldiers. They crumbled to the rocky plateau, their guts bursting out like the stuffing of an old pillow. The rest dove for cover and set up a counter-barrage of fire.

Gunter, who was in the lead of all that remained of his Wolfpack force—only thirty men, shouted out orders to the rest of the commando unit to spread out and flank them from both sides.

"You will soon die, freefighter. Come out now and we will make it less painful than it might be," Gunter barked out in a thick German accent as he slammed another magazine into his submachine gun.

"There's been enough dying of freefighters today," Rock yelled back. "Surrender now—and we'll let *you* live. As commander of the free forces, I promise you that." Gunter answered with a burst from his

Turgenev, spraying a line of slugs that ripped into the boulder, cutting out little craters that erupted in a violent cloud of dust.

It was crazy, Rock thought, as he virtually sat atop the wounded Shecter who groaned but lay still beneath him. The goddamned Nazis were beaten—but these fools didn't even know it. The Glowers' mental signals must have a limit that they could reach. That's why they sailed around the valley, so they could hit all the troops. Rock knew his shotpistol, as deadly as it was, was not going to stop this bunch. He turned around to see if he could get any help. The artillery unit closest to him, some fifty feet away were lying draped over the bottom of the big .152mm cannon, nearly fifteen feet long. The Nazis coming up on him must have caught them with their first barrage.

"Stay put," he screamed right into Shecter's face. But the scientist was already unconscious. Just as well. Rock shot straight up and unleashed six more volleys from his pistol, sending four of the Nazis straight to hell. He ducked down again as they returned the fire, breathed deeply and shot out from the back of the boulder toward the cannon. It wasn't that far, but with fifteen crack shots firing with everything they have at him, it seemed like a million miles off. Bullets dug in everywhere around him, knifing into the dirt and rocks at his feet in little explosions of powder. He felt a sharp pain in his right calf, but was able to keep running.

"Get him," Gunter screamed, rising from the ground and spraying his full magazine of 7.2mm slugs. "He is the leader. Kill him and you will be rich forever." The Wolfpack squad rose as a man and let loose with a hurricane of fire power, the air whistling with trails of screaming white-hot bullets.

But Rock was already at the artillery post. He dove through the air as he heard the hail of slugs behind him, landing hard on the metal emplacement atop which the big gun swiveled. The migration of shells tore just inches over his head and out into the sky above the valley where freefighter and Nazi choppers were still battling it out. The Doomsday Warrior kicked two of the dead Americans off the turret and hoisted himself up into the firing seat. The damned thing was loaded—great. He pulled a lever and the immense cannon began slowly turning around from its previous target on the valley floor. As it swiveled, Rock cranked a hand-pushed wheel that lowered the muzzle of the stolen SS120 cannon until it was aiming almost straight down.

Bullets slammed into the metal all around him, pinging off the hard steel with sharp cracks.

"Get him, get that damned mutant bastard," Rock heard Gunter scream out, as the waves of autofire slowly bore down on him. But that was the last thing the Nazi officer ever said. Rock zeroed in through the twin sights down the immense green muzzle and slammed his fist down on the red firing button. The cannon roared out a deafening scream and sent its six-inch shell out in a blast of smoke. The three-foot-long message of death flew only eighty feet before hitting the ground. It erupted in a blinding cloud of fire and smoke, sending limbs and a rain of flesh off in all directions. When the dust cleared seconds later Rock saw instantly that there was nothing left—not a man, not even a piece of a man. They had chosen—and they had died.

The great sand ships of the Glowers at last came to a rest in the center of the valley. The three bows of the two hundred-foot-long crafts pointed at one another, creating, to those who looked down from above, the appearance of a three-pointed star. They stood on the bows and surveyed the damage they had wrought. They felt no guilt, nor pain for the tens of thousands of dead Germans littered around the wide valley, slaughtered—albeit by themselves—like so many cattle.

"We have changed the time/space continuum," they thought as one. *"We have altered the history of the human species."*

"We are the human species," one of the many thought. *"We are human. We are Americans. We are descended from the same womb that our freefighting brothers are. We have done right."* They took in the magnitude of death and devastation around them. Even *they* had never seen the full extent of what their powers could do. And they, in their own way, were awed.

"We must leave now," a reply came. *"We have done what we must do. Now we must pull back from the human destiny of our brothers. They must work out their ultimate evolution. This is our way."*

"This is the way," the other voices joined in chorus. They hoisted the great sails up to their full capacity and turned the ships around, heading back toward the valley entrance where Nazi troops were still flee-

ing in terror for the safety of the far mountains.

"We shall kill no more today," the voices sang out in a soft harmony as the sand ships' sails filled with the invisible energy of the sun and the cosmic rays raining down from space. The ships quickly reached cruising speed and tore past the German troops as they exited the valley. The Glowers stood on the bows, staring straight ahead, mindless of the Nazis who screamed in horror and flung themselves to the dirt and behind rocks. But the Glowers had had enough of death. They mentally charted their course back home and vanished like a shipful of shooting stars into the slowly darkening sun.

Chapter Seventeen

Colonel Killov looked down through his superscope binoculars from a mountain peak some ten miles to the east of Forrester Valley. He could hardly believe his eyes—the Nazi invasion was turning into a defeat of the highest order, because of these strange glowing mutants. And yet, perhaps it was all to his advantage. Premier Vassily had suffered a mortal blow with the destruction of his German force. The Kremlin power-makers would wonder if he was weakening, would begin casting their eyes elsewhere for a new leader—a stronger leader. And Killov was that man. He could turn the debacle around in his favor by being bold, daring—right at the instant of apparent defeat.

The freefighting forces were spread out over a twenty-mile range—within the valley itself and to the north. He knew that. And Century City, that elusive stronghold of Ted Rockson which he had never been able to find, was somewhere within that twenty-mile width—of that he was sure. He lifted the glasses from his pin-sized eyes and hesitated. There would be problems if he went against Vassily's orders—the use of nuclear weapons. But Vassily was in no position to get him now. The commander of the KGB quickly dug out two pills from his pocket and slammed them into his mouth. He waited a minute or two for the chemicals of the Transcednal and the morphine tab to hit his system. Then he felt the familiar, wonderful warmth stream through his veins, giving him courage in this moment of paramount importance.

The colonel reached over to a small radio transmitter next to him and sent out the command to his fleet of waiting jet fighters, each armed with a neutron bomb. "This is Killov. Strike, strike, you understand. Mode Red strike. Immediately."

"Received and carried out," a voice at the other end replied. Killov clicked the radio off and sat back, his dark eyes burning with excitement. All these years—and now. At last he would destroy his most hated enemy—and in the process strenghten his chances tremendously to become premier. Boldness—that is why he would rule, deserved to rule. Because he had the courage to do what others only thought about.

The fleet of six Illyushin-7 jet bombers streaked out of their landing field some thirty miles away. Swept back wings, noses arched forward like a hawk's beak, they were fearsome weapons indeed, capable of reaching Mach 4 if necessary. Although on this trip there would be nothing to stop them. Major Velinsky piloted the lead jet, the other five, flying in his stream, each a hundred feet apart, forming a V-formation behind him.

"This is not a test run," Velinsky said over his throat mike. "From orders of Colonel Killov himself, we are to proceed to vector five, sector three and deploy our weapons." He paused for a moment, straightening the throttle on his roaring fighter as he nosed up into the clouds beginning to gather above the Rockies. "This is a historic moment, men. The day we have been planning and training for for years. Keep calm, carry out your flight patterns just as you have always done—and we will be successful. Tonight each of you will be a hero—will dwell in Paradise. Of this I assure you, for the colonel will reward us beyond our dreams." His speech given, the major hit cruising speed and straightened out his flight path. There were but three minutes to the target zone.

The Technicians, with Lang leading up the twisting trails behind Ice Mountain, had traveled for days. Everything had gone wrong—from blinding sandstorms, to half the 'brids dying from lack of water. But they were here—and that was what mattered.

"These slopes have a ratio of incline-to-hybrid stability that is quite alarming," Ullman said to Lang, as they at last reached the top of the peak that looked down on Century City, some two miles off.

"Sorry about that," Lang said. "I'll speak to the construction teams as soon as we're home about building some superhighways up here."

"I sense an equation of jocularity," Ullman said, trying to smile, though his exhausted body could barely gather the energy to move his lips.

"Halt," a voice screamed out at them from behind

a tree. "Who goes there?" Ullman reached for his black beam pistol but Lang put his hand out and softly pushed the deadly weapon back.

"It's Ok – it's one of the good guys," Lang said, his mismatched blue and violet eyes, like Rockson's, twinkling with excitement at being home. "It's Lang," the young mutant said, holding his hands out to show he had no weapons. A face peered cautiously from around the tree trunk. "Remember me – Lang? I'm back with the expeditionary force sent to bring back the Technicians." He swept his hand around him, to show that the race of mini-men was indeed with him. "Well, here we are. I must say I was expecting a more fitting welcome.'

"Jesus – Lang," the guard said, stepping from behind the tree, as a dozen other faces in branches and concealed behind rocks lowered their weapons. "Where the hell have you been? Don't you know we got a goddammed war going on around here?" He quickly told the returning freefighter and the Technicians who gathered around curiously what had occurred.

"Well, what happened?" Lang asked, his face draining of blood.

"We don't know for sure yet," the guard answered. "There's wounded already coming back from Forrester Valley and – " his voice cracked – "they said it wasn't going too good at all. Could have used your friends here though – I'll tell you that. Too bad you're so damned late."

Lang's eyes flashed with anger, mostly at himself – for not having arrived in time to make the crucial difference. "Fuck off, Parcells," he said. "We did every damned thing we could to—"

His voice was cut off by the sudden screaming roar of six jets far overhead. Jets that were swooping down in a wide circle obviously preparing to strike.

"Holy shit," Lang shouted. "Maybe we're not too late after all. Ullman—deploy your men. There's no time for setting up tripods or any of that shit. Just tell them to pull them out and start firing. Those are Red bombers—and I think I know what kind of cargo they're carrying."

"There is a sudden necessitation of destructive energy," the leader of the Technicians said, addressing the rest of his race who stood around him in a circle. "Without proper mathematical coordinates we are requested to equate particle-beam energies necessary to terminate approaching air vehicles. Compute?"

"Compute," the voices of the Technicians answered at once. They drew their pistols and unslung their black beam rifles, lying down on the rocky trail as the freefighter guards looked on in amazement. They sighted up the six jets, using the three triangular sights that stood on top of the smooth black barrels.

One after another of the small race of super geniuses pulled the triggers on their deadly weapons. Black beams, as dark as the darkest dream, shot out of the narrow muzzles and in a millionth of a second—traveling at the speed of light itself—slammed into the bombers, themselves moving at nearly two thousand five hundred mph. Most of the black funnels of energy missed, but one clipped the tail off the rear jet. It veered wildly out of control, spinning around like a drill and headed straight for the Rocky Mountain peaks below, exploding in a puff of fire.

"Destruction equals velocity of target divided by acceleration capability of attack force time skill of that which sets in motion," Ullman bragged, turning his head to look up at Lang and the rest of the freefighters who watched, their jaws hanging open.

"Shoot, shoot," Lang screamed. "Talk later."

The black beams tore out of nearly thirty-five smooth plastic alloy barrels. They did not seem to fire so much as just suddenly be there—hanging in the air for miles like some sort of dark rainbow. The planes were fast and began taking evasive maneuvers as soon as the rear Illyushin went down. The beams crisscrossed the sky, moving like searchlights as the Technicians, inexperienced in battle situations, tried to home in on the supersonic jets.

Two of the beams suddenly converged on the nose of Illyushin just behind the leader. They sliced through the magnesium frame like knives, cutting the jet bomber cleanly in two. The two pieces flipped wildly, one of them slamming into another Illyushin just behind it. The plane roared into a ball of blue fire, still moving at triple the speed of sound. The comet streaked in a wide arc far off in the snow-capped mountains.

"Three subtracted—three positive," Ullman muttered under his breath. The three jets suddenly broke formation completely, two of them moving to the right and left, in sharp dives, their wings tilted at ninety-degree angles. The third continued straight ahead, coming in toward the Technicians and Ice Mountain.

"Don't let them get away," Lang yelled to the prone Techs. "If any of them drops its load—it could mean the death of thousands of freefighters."

The Techncians—growing both excited at their successes in their very first firefight and terrified that they were going to miss those that were left—didn't even take their fingers off the small triggers of their weapons. They just let the black beams search across the sky, desperately trying to make contact. Thirty-five beams of the most powerful energy ever known to man searching for three hurtling slivers of steel. Three of the black funnels reached the jet that had dropped to the left almost at the same instant. In a millionth of a second, there was nothing left of it—not even a puff of smoke. It was gone into God knew where.

Ullman, who was beginning to believe he and his people could actually shoot down real, living, firing enemies—could contribute to the freefighter's battle for their very existence—was starting to feel pretty good. Why, it was all so absurdly simple. X = X. Unstoppable force against stoppable mass. He closed one eye and set the other looking down the row of sights until he had the jet that had dropped to the right lined up in the violet glow of the atomic-powered system. Then he squeezed the trigger softly. The beam shot out like a shark hungry for dinner and bit into the engine of the bomber. It ignited like a small volcano spewing out its entire loan of super-high-octane fuel in a single fiery burst. The burning hulk dropped slowly, spinning in blazing circles like a leaf on fire to the smashing rocks below.

"One left to compute," Ullman screamed as loud

as his small vocal cords could muster. The entire race of Technicians trained their awesome fire power on the single craft that hurtled toward them like a spear.

But Major Velinsky was piloting the final jet, and he had seen his share of fireflights—though none quite like this. He knew that only every bit of his experience and cunning would get him through. And he also knew that if he came back in defeat, the colonel would see that he died a horrible death. Velinsky had nothing to lose, and these are the most dangerous of men.

He dropped the Illyushin down to tree level in a screaming dive and straightened out, heading toward the source of the black beams and—he assumed—Century City, at nearly three thousand mph. The tips of the wings glowed white-hot as he approached the limits of its structural endurance. He shot forward like a meteor, the after burner charring the tops of firs and pines in a trail of black. Soon, soon . . .

The Technicians saw the last jet drop like a stone and then lost sight of it. Their beams stopped for a moment, leaving the air suddenly bright and weirdly silent.

"Where the hell is he?" Lang muttered anxiously.

"What goes down—must come up," Ullman said with a trace of a mocking smile as the mini-men strained their eyes, their fingers ready on the triggers for the sight of the supersonic jet. Suddenly it reappeared just over the rise of Ice Mountain. It reached the peak, clearing it by not more than twenty yards and immediately climbed straight up in the air.

"Eliminate, eliminate," Ullman stuttered through parched lips. The beams of instant death shot out from every particle gun. They ripped through the air with a thundering roar, imploding the very atoms of oxygen and hydrogen that they passed through. Suddenly a glinting globe of steel dropped out from the vertically climbing Illyushin and plummeted to the earth. It had barely hit the air when the ripping tubes of utter blackness found their target. The jet had had to slow slightly in its climb straight up to the heavens. The beams touched the fifty-foot-long hawklike jet at the same instant, destroying every atom within, as the steel and Fiberglas, the teeth and flesh of Major Velinsky all fused for an instant before evaporating into pure energy exploded out into the atmosphere. He would no longer have to fear the wrath of Killov.

"Six minus six equals zero," Ullman said, holstering his black beam pistol as he rose.

"Down, down, all of you," Lang screamed as he tore his eyes from the dropping globe. He grabbed Ullman under one arm and carried the Technician leader twenty feet where he dove behind a solid rock peak. Some of the Technicians, realizing something was wrong, followed suit, but many didn't.

The air over Ice Mountain, some two miles off, was suddenly lit with the retina-burning, writhing hell of an atomic blast. Gamma rays, alpha and beta rays, shot out in every direction, burning every living thing they came in contact with to a black porridge. The very cell of the trees, animals and humans that the deadly radiation touched were fried to a watery ooze in the space of a millionth of a second. A mushroom cloud reached up toward the clouds as the second waves of heat and then sound followed close behind the deadly radiation. The Technicians who had made it to the rock covering slammed their hands over their ears' thin screams issued forth from their lips. Their brothers, still out in the open, had not been so lucky. They lay curled up—little fetal balls of black sculpture. Around the mountain rise, the Technicians' black beam weapons lay melted, shriveled up in twisted shapes, nothing but dripping plastic.

The neutron bomb went off just a mile-and-a-half from Century City. One minute the people inside were going about their business, treating the first of the wounded coming back from the Battle of Forrester Valley, sending out more ammunition by hybrid team. The next, they were lying on the concrete floors of the subterranean world as the walls, the very mountain above the city, shook and trembled as if in the hands of a giant. Machinery and equipment fell over, crashing into useless pieces, the computers ignited from the electric pulses of the blast, flames shooting out of their screens. Throughout the city, the lights flickered for long seconds before the emergency system cut on. Shells in the Liberator factory ignited from the heat streaming right through the mountain's two hundred feet of rock and set off an explosion that cracked half the walls of the city, setting numerous small fires. Throughout the multi-levels of C.C., horror stories unfolded as thousands met their deaths—crushed by falling equipment, trapped in rooms suddenly blazing with flames. The hydroponics tanks shattered from the initial blast of the bomb, their ten thousand nutrient-grown vegetables and fruits spewing out onto the floors followed by a cascade of water which shot down the lower halls. Everywhere was death, stalking the halls in dark bloody robes, as the city at last ceased shaking and the screaming began.

By dawn's early light, the first of the returning, victorious forces came to the northern entrance to the city and stared in horror. The wide cave entrance was no more. The soil was black, hard on the surface. Whatever went off had sent an avalanche of rock and dust covering the entire base of the mountain beneath which C.C. was built. The American troops went from hidden entrance to hidden entrance, finding each one covered with tons of debris. They felt a ghastly feeling in the pits of their stomachs. They could survive even the heavy losses of the battle back there in the valley—but if C.C. was gone . . .

At last—a small entrance, hardly large enough for a man to fit through. The freefighters frantically clawed away at the rubble in front of the narrow cavern until they had made an opening. They slid through one-by-one and ran down the corridor as it opened inside, dreading what they would find at the other end.

They emerged into the main debriefing chamber and found more devastation—the walls and ceilings had nearly collapsed, bodies lay strewn around the rock floor, decapitated, ripped open by the falling structure.

"Jesus God," Detroit, one of the first inside, said as he tore into the main thoroughfare of the city. Dust and blankets of plastic coating that had covered the high cavern walls were everywhere. But the city still stood. Wounded, badly damaged—it was there. The thick rock walls of the mountain above had saved it. The freefighters made their way from level to level, helping the wounded, assessing damage. The top brass from civilian and military sectors of the city's inhabitants held an emergency meeting as each detailed just what damage had been done in their portions of C.C.

It was bad—but it could have been a lot worse. All main power and life-support systems, including air filtration, were either undamaged or had already been repaired. Hydroponics was totalled. But basic nutrient stock and stockpilings of unassembled tanks were still functional. Shecter's science labs were coated with at least two inches of dust and rock, and filled with overturned lab tables, but most of its equipment was still functioning. The gymnasium, the communal dining area and kitchens, and the library and video rooms were in shambles. In all, nearly a third of the city had been destroyed, a third suffered slight-to-moderate damage, and a third was unaffected. As the casualty figures poured in from messengers at the makeshift hospitals, it became clear that they hadn't suffered losses as bad as it had at first appeared. About six hundred were dead, another thousand wounded, but most expected to live. It could have been worse—a lot worse.

Chapter Eighteen

Rockson waited on the northern peak until every last Nazi had exited Forrester Valley, until Dr. Shecter, who was in great pain—but would survive—and all the other wounded had been carted off to Century City. He was elated. The battle had gone well—try a miracle. The Glowers had kept the promise they had made to him when he had been in their camp months before (SEE BOOK No. 3): "*If you ever need us—really need us—we will be there.*" And they had. Seconds from complete annihilation and then . . . It was a miracle, a fucking miracle.

He stared out over the valley, filled with smoking ruins, tanks lying on their backs like bloated turtles, flames pouring from their cannons. The bodies of the countless dead Germans only visible from his mountain height by the bright blotches of scarlet that sat on each one as if to prove he was dead. The Nazi artillery units continued to send out random volleys of shells from far across the valley—covering their withdrawal and hoping to take a few more freefighter souls with them, on this day of death for Germany.

Suddenly Rock heard a sound behind him and turned, drawing his shotpistol.

"Rock, y-you're alive. Thank God." It was Rona, dirty, her white ski suit ripped to tatters. She threw her arms around him.

"Where the hell did you come fr—"

"We got the command center, Rock, then split in a Hitler chopper. Detroit took the team back to C.C. I got out—to look for you. I-I had to, Rock, I had the most horrible feeling."

"Well I'm alive—and we won." He put his strong arms around her and pressed her tightly against him.

"I know—the Glowers. I saw them when I was tamping through these damned woods looking for you. Had a few problems on the way." She grinned, holding up bruised knuckles.

"*They* had more trouble than you, I'll wager," Rock said, kissing her. She let go of him and walked over to the edge of the peak, where Rock had commanded the battle from, and stared down hard, her eyes sweeping across the already foul-smelling graveyard of nearly seventy-five-thousand men. Flocks of buzzards and vultures flew from the surrounding towering rises, their immense dark wings filling the sky. They soared down in ever tighter circles amid the many fires below and fell onto the dead with a ravenous hunger, tearing at the once-in-a-lifetime feast.

"Rock, it's so hor—" Rona turned to say. But her words were cut off as a battery of German artillery opened up from across the valley with a few more presents. The shells whistled across the great divide, digging into the upper slopes of the peak which Rona and Rock stood on.

"Rona!" Rock screamed as an arm-sized shell dug into the granite just feet below her. The female warrior was tossed into the air like a rag doll, landing hard just inches from the edge—and a hundred-foot drop. Rockson rushed over to her, grabbing her beneath both arms and gently lifting her. He carried her a few yards to a patch of soft moss and laid her carefully down. Her face was deeply gashed along the temple as blood seeped through her white ski suit from numerous small wounds.

"*Rona, Rona*," he called out mentally. There was a weak, oh so weak answer. He lifted her head onto his lap and kissed her pale lips. She was alive but her wounds were bad.

"Rock," she whispered.

"Don't talk," the Doomsday Warrior said, squeezing her closer, and trying to hide the deep fear in his eyes.

"Why not?" She half smiled. "Might as well tell y-you, Rock. You . . . are . . . my . . . love."

"Always have been," Rockson replied, forcing a smile, as emotions tore at his tight throat muscles.

"Tell me . . . that you love me once more."

"I love you. I do love you, Rona," the Doomsday Warrior half cried out.

"You're a good liar." She grimaced as she lifted her head for a final kiss. She opened her lips for his . . . and fell limp. She was still alive—but she needed help.

He held her tightly in his arms, not daring to let go. As if he clutched her tightly enough, somehow death would not be able to take her into the dark beyond.

Suddenly he heard another whistling sound, and still holding her to him, Rock rolled into a mortar-made crater several yards away. A 155mm round tore into the earth just above the crest of the hole, sending up a deafening storm of sand and stone. Rockson was lifted bodily from his shallow foxhole and flung through the air, his arms releasing Rona as he was knocked momentarily unconscious by the force of the blast. He lay motionless, just yards away her, as she breathed slow, straining breaths.

Slowly he came to, the world spinning around him like a top out of control. He tried to rise but found it difficult to move, his muscles like rubber. Then he turned and saw her, so pale, like a dream, like a princess in a dream. Her eyes opened and she looked at him from a few yards away.

"Rock," she asked with her mind. "*Are you—*"

"*Just stunned,*" the Doomsday Warrior telepathed back. "*I'll be all right in a minute. Just have to catch my breath.*" He turned his face so she couldn't see the deep gash on the right side of his head, slowly dripping, like a leaky faucet, bright red blood onto his shoulder and arm.

"*Oh, Rock, I'm afraid,*" Rona thought through the cold air. "*Not of dying—but of being without you.*"

"*No one's dying,*" the Doomsday Warrior sent back. He mindlinked with her, sending out his strength in telepathic streams, shoring her up with the will of his own soul—as she struggled above the waiting waves of death that slapped around her living flesh.

No—Rockson would not let the Grim Reaper claim this woman. Death would have to fight both of them—two sea boulders rising above the dark rushing waters. He reached into the deepest part of his being and sent out all his life energy, forming a protective circle around both of them.

"*Let it come*," he screamed out at the dark night closing in on them."*Let death stalk us*," the Doomsday Warrior challenged the universe as bony, clawed footprints stamped ever closer in the damp earth. "*Come on—Death! I'm ready for you. Come on—I'm waiting*!"

He felt a black energy soar in toward her, reaching, straining to pull her into its world. And Ted Rockson, using every bit of strength that was in him, struck out at the life-taking claws of the Dark Destroyer.